A
PLAY
FOR
REVENGE

ALSO BY CYNTHIA ELLINGSEN

Starlight Cove Novels

The Lighthouse Keeper
The Winemaker's Secret
A Bittersweet Surprise

Women's Fiction

When We Were Sisters
The Choice I Made
Marriage Matters
The Whole Package

Middle Grade

The Girls of Firefly Cabin

A
PLAY
FOR
REVENGE

CYNTHIA ELLINGSEN

LAKE UNION
PUBLISHING

Published by Lake Union Publishing, Seattle

www.apub.com

Amazon, the Amazon logo, and Lake Union Publishing are trademarks of Amazon.com, Inc., or its affiliates.

ISBN-13: 9781662513640 (paperback)
ISBN-13: 9781662513633 (digital)

Cover design by Caroline Teagle Johnson
Cover image: © L.B.Jeffries / plainpicture; © David Sacks / Getty; © inarik / Getty

Printed in the United States of America

For my father, my hero

Chapter One

The Starlight Cove Playhouse graced the bluff like an actress taking the stage. Sun lit the faded white clapboards, and the shade of the wrap-around porch was inviting, as Lake Michigan's shadowy waters churned on the beach below. The theater seemed to promise good cheer and a strong sense of community—such a stark difference from the tragedy that had darkened its stage over twenty years ago.

Gillian G. Smith, Starlight Cove's most seasoned reporter, clipped across the paved driveway, waving me down.

There were several local VIPs, business owners, and reporters mingling over coffee, pastries, and the mini breakfast quiches I'd set out. Making small talk with them had been easy, but Gillian was a different breed, a master at getting people to share secrets.

You've kept quiet this long. You can last a few minutes more.

"Goodness, it's hot." Gillian considered the dry trees. "Lily, I keep trying to bribe our meteorologist to make it rain, but he claims he's not the one in charge."

"Bad work ethic," I teased.

She grinned. "Dismal."

It had been over three weeks since we'd had a good rain, which was not typical for mid-May. The grass and the trees had started to brown, and the rhythmic sound of lawn sprinklers had become as common as the tweeting of the birds.

"It's good to see you back in town." Gillian adjusted her designer sunglasses. "Your family must be delighted."

The comment was a version of the same one I'd heard for the past eight months, an open invitation to share the details of the marriage that had crumbled and brought me back home, but Gillian managed to deliver it in a way that felt genuine.

"It's been an adjustment for Kaia," I said. "I just keep trying to act like it's a big treat for us to live with her grandparents in a drafty old house on a hill."

"That drafty house is a Victorian mansion."

"Tomato, tomah-to," I said, and she laughed.

The house had been in our family forever. It was in the row of old Victorians overlooking Starlight Cove, and yes, it was beautiful, in spite of the creaky floorboards. Kaia seemed to be okay with our lifestyle change for now, but she was twelve, so it was hard to tell how she actually felt about things.

"So, what's the scoop?" Gillian gestured at the Playhouse. "I'm so intrigued."

I looked at my watch. "I'll tell you in five minutes."

"Oh, come on," Gillian pleaded. "The place has been abandoned for twenty years. The lot's finally cleared, so my guess is that someone's about to raze the theater to the ground. Did the developers decide to move the ski resort here or something? That's the only thing I can come up with."

It wasn't a terrible theory, considering the ski resort was all anybody had been talking about. Starlight Cove's winter population was only about 4,500, so the ski resort had the potential to bring in big business at the time we needed it the most. That said, the bluff where the Playhouse sat was much too small for such a big development project.

"Gillian, I am not saying a word." I paused. "Except one thing."

Her face brightened. "Do tell."

I pointed at the town car parked by the stage door of the theater. "Stand by that car if you want the thrill of a lifetime." The windows were tinted, so she wouldn't know a thing until the doors opened.

Gillian's face lit up. "Thank you, doll." She headed across the driveway, signaling her team to follow.

My assistant, Brad, pointed at his watch. He was waiting by the podium we'd set up on the front lawn, looking casual but sharp in a short-sleeved button up and a pair of fitted navy shorts. I wished he could take the stage, but it was my job, and this particular announcement held a special place in my heart.

After signaling one minute, I headed over to check on my grandmother, who lounged in a wicker chair beneath the cool shade of a tree.

"Do you need anything?" I asked. "We're about to get started."

"For you to knock them dead," she said in a voice as rich as the cherry blossoms.

"Love you," I told her.

I headed for the podium, smoothing my jet-black hair. It fell past my shoulders in gentle waves, which softened my sharp cheekbones. My hair was my best feature, and for the rest, as my grandmother had taught me, there was makeup.

"Good morning, everyone." My voice boomed over the portable speaker, and the crowd gathered round. "They say there are no small parts, only small actors. Well, that's not true. My part today is small. Microscopic. Blink and you'll miss me."

It made me happy when the crowd chuckled.

"My name is Lily Kimura, and I'm the director of the Tourism Council. Today, I'd like to talk to you about the Starlight Cove Playhouse, a theater founded by my grandmother in 1965. It served as a summer stock-equity house that attracted actors from Broadway to the silver screen and played to sold-out houses every night. When it caught fire in 1998, in a tragedy that killed one of our beloved local actresses, our town grieved the loss, and the theater went dark. Well, I'm here to announce . . ."

My grandmother had taught me the power of a well-timed pause. The crowd leaned forward, and even the birds seemed to go silent.

"I'm pleased to announce that two years ago, the Starlight Cove Playhouse received an anonymous donation designed to bring the theater back to life. The interior has been quietly remodeled, and in three weeks, the Playhouse will open its summer season, headlined by none other than box office sensation . . ." I felt ridiculous raising my arms, but it was the cue meant to be spotted from the black town car. "Arlo Majors!"

Part of me feared he wouldn't notice. That he'd be on his phone, posting selfies on social media or whatever celebrities spent their time doing. To my great relief, the door of the town car slowly eased open, the actor stepped out, and the crowd burst into applause.

Arlo Majors wore a pair of tortoiseshell sunglasses, and his sandy-brown hair was tousled, as if he'd spent the day at the beach. His khaki linen suit was reminiscent of the one he wore in a popular spy film. Everyone stared as he lifted his sunglasses and surveyed the crowd with the bright-blue eyes that had made him famous.

I wanted to stare right along with them, but instead I read from the press packet: "Arlo Majors has appeared in nine Hollywood blockbusters and has graced magazine covers across the nation. But did you know that he also spent summers in northern Michigan as a child? The original Starlight Cove Playhouse holds a special place in his heart, because it was one of the first places he ever saw live theater." The crowd gave an appreciative murmur. "When the opportunity to headline the newly renovated Playhouse was presented to him, his agent said no, but he said yes. Arlo Majors," I said, looking up, "welcome back to Starlight Cove."

He was right next to the podium. Our eyes met, and I was surprised to feel lost for words.

"Wow," I said. "You really are Arlo Majors."

The crowd laughed, but I wasn't trying to be funny. It was practically an out-of-body experience to see the guy who always saved the world up close. He was a real, live movie star, and his very presence was as bright as the sun.

I turned back to the crowd. "I confess, I'm feeling a bit tongue tied. Which is weird because I always thought I'd be cool if I met a celebrity." I paused. "Is he still standing there?"

"He is," Arlo Majors said, and the crowd chuckled.

What am I doing?

I pressed my hands into the top of the podium. "I am incapable of being cool right now. So, everyone, please help me out and give a big welcome to *Arlo Majors.*"

The crowd burst into applause as he gave my hand a dramatic kiss. Then, he helped guide me down the steps from the podium before taking over the mic.

"Starlight Cove," he crooned, "thanks for having me."

Legs shaking, I took my place next to Brad.

"What was that?" he said, laughing.

"Was it awful?" I said.

"It was amazing."

The artistic director of the Playhouse joined Arlo at the mic to announce the lineup for the summer season. There were six plays total, each running two weeks. The artistic director promised that those invited to the reception could purchase season tickets first, before they went on sale to the general public, and then concluded her speech.

I kept a respectful distance as she and Arlo filed back down the steps. Then, I took my place behind the mic once again.

"So, that's the scoop," I said. "It is an honor to invite the arts back to Starlight Cove. The theater will now be open for a quick tour. I'll see you at the reception tonight, where you will have the opportunity to meet the incredibly gracious Arlo Majors."

Arlo gave a final wave before heading back to his car, amid handshakes and applause. Brad was going to lead the theater tours alongside the artistic director, so I could finish up plans for the reception. I headed straight for my grandmother and flopped on the lawn next to her.

"You stole the show!" Her dark eyes sparkled. "I didn't know you were going to do a bit with him."

"That wasn't a bit." I tugged at the grass, sneaking a look at the town car. "I saw him and lost my mind."

My grandmother chuckled. "I can understand why."

"Lily, that was hilarious." Gillian traipsed across the lawn with her camera crew. "Great job."

I got to my feet. "Have you seen the theater? I hear it's beautiful inside. With all the renovation work going on, I haven't been able to check it out."

Gillian shook her head. "My other guy is getting B-roll. I know the real story when I see it." She extended her hand to my grandmother. "Maxine Candella, I have been a fan of yours since I was a little girl. Would you be willing to talk to me about your time with the Starlight Cove Playhouse?"

My grandmother's face lit up. "Do you have lipstick, my dear?" she asked, turning to me. "Turns out I'm not quite dead after all."

Chapter Two

It was a whirlwind of a day. Once I'd gotten caught up at the Tourism Council, I treated myself with a walk to the reception at the Harbor Resort Hotel. The sun was bright, and the stroll gave me some much-needed quiet time before the big event.

The quaint shops that lined Main Street, always so charming with their pastel storefronts and detailed window displays, were shutting down for the night. I waved at the shopkeepers I'd known since I was a kid. Meanwhile, the tourists made their way to restaurants that scented the air with roasted garlic, fresh fish, and grilled burgers. From a distance, the Harbor Resort Hotel was already lit up, looking festive and ready for a fun night.

The reception was located on the outdoor porch that overlooked Lake Michigan. Security was stationed at the entrance, and they waved me up. I got to work on finishing touches, making certain the gift bags I'd brought over earlier were in place and checking my phone for last-minute RSVPs. The numbers had nearly doubled since the press conference, which I'd anticipated. The event was in high demand now that everyone knew what the party was all about.

Sure enough, the Whittakers, the Weatherlys, and several other well-known couples arrived early, dressed in summer sequins and silk.

"You were wonderful at the press conference," Maeve Weatherly said, giving me an air-kiss. Not one to show up at an event looking plain, seventysomething Maeve was decked out in a pair of sparkling heels and a dramatic cocktail dress decorated with actual peacock feathers. "Are your parents coming?"

"They will be," I promised. "I'm sure they're running late. My parents take forever to do anything now, because they're so busy doing nothing."

The last forty years, they'd worked day and night, selling bait and renting boats at their popular sportfishing shop. Now, they seemed to find it a struggle to fill their spare time.

"It's all so exciting," Mrs. Whittaker chimed in, her blue eyes bright with anticipation. "I love having the theater back in Starlight Cove. It's a wonder someone hasn't already done this."

"I agree," I told her. "The Tourism Council has wanted to promote some form of theater for quite some time."

Starlight Cove was a summer town. It made sense to have a community theater. Even one focused on Shakespeare under the stars, at the very least, but no one had stepped up until now.

"So, who is backing the Playhouse?" Mr. Van de Camp asked, accepting a glass of red wine from a waiter.

"It's a mystery," I said. "For whatever reason, the donor prefers to remain anonymous."

"Well, that's interesting," said his wife. "Maeve, was it you?"

"No." She looked intrigued. "You really don't know who is behind this?"

I shook my head. "No one does."

Her husband raised his glass. "Well, the Weatherlys will happily take credit where credit is not due."

"Unless something goes terribly wrong," Maeve said, adjusting her feathers. "Then we had nothing to do with it."

They laughed, and we all clinked glasses. The group continued to discuss the mystery donor, and I walked away, hiding a smile.

Our little town loved intrigue. The idea that no one knew who had funded the Playhouse would make it even more interesting to this well-heeled crowd and hopefully result in higher attendance. I wished I knew the donor's identity, since the theater had once belonged to my family, but I hadn't been able to find out a thing.

I made the rounds, greeting people and making small talk. The bright scent of summer perfume lingered in the air, along with the delightful aroma of garlic and seafood. My grandmother was the first from my family to arrive, as regal as a queen in gray-and-silver chiffon.

"You look great," I told her, kissing her cheeks.

"Same to you," she said. "That dress is stunning on you."

The vintage Chanel party dress was one of her hand-me-downs. Quick as a spider, she tugged the décolletage much lower than I wanted. "There," she said. "Now it's perfect."

I pulled it right back up the moment she looked away.

We headed over to the bar, and I got us drinks as she settled in at a small table.

"This turned out to be a great party," I said, handing her an old-fashioned.

It was just crowded enough to feel festive, with a perfect view of the sunset and a gentle breeze coming in from the lake. The heat lamps kept the open-air space comfortable, and a sense of anticipation hung in the air. Arlo Majors was scheduled to arrive at some point, and I kept looking toward the door, hoping to catch a glimpse of him.

"This is fun." My grandmother sipped through the small black straw. "Beats watching the old guys snore in front of the television at the old folks' home."

For years, my parents had tried to convince my grandmother to stay in her house with them. They'd offered to hire an around-the-clock caretaker to deal with her heart medication, drive her around, and play cards, but she refused. My grandmother didn't need a caretaker—she needed an audience. The assisted-living facility gave her that. It also gave her plenty of things that she could complain about, and complaining was a pastime that she cherished.

I noticed my parents walk into the party and that they were immediately swept up in conversation. I had no doubt people missed seeing them at the store, and I'd been trying to convince them to get out more. My mother spotted us, and I waved her over, when a low hum of energy passed through the crowd.

"I think our man has arrived," my grandmother said, peering across the room.

Sure enough, Arlo Majors walked in. This time, he wore a dark-navy suit. His hair was tousled, his face bright, and somehow, he seemed even more tempting than before.

"Bruschetta?" One of the waiters held out a tray with a selection of toasted breads. There were several to choose from, including buffalo mozzarella and tomato, olive tapenade, and some sort of pancetta.

My grandmother had started a conversation with Mayor Matty Brown, who had taken over the next table. The mayor was such a character, with his ruddy face and white mustache, and he loved to dress in colorful suits with matching bow ties. Tonight, he sported a striped seersucker suit that made him appear to be more of a gentleman than he actually was.

I'd dealt with Mayor Matty quite a bit through the Tourism Council and didn't understand why so many people adored him. Nonetheless, I gave him a polite smile as I passed my grandmother a small plate full of hors d'oeuvres.

The band started to play jazz with an up-tempo beat, and several couples headed onto the dance floor. My mother tried to get my father out there, and at first he refused, but she finally succeeded. Their number was entertaining but short lived.

From there, the night passed in a blur. I chatted with more people than I could count and finally, took a break next to the balcony. Couples whirled across the dance floor as I held tight to a flute of champagne.

My mother came up to give me a kiss good night. "Do you mind taking Grandma back to Morning Lark?"

"I'd be happy to." My daughter would already be in bed, so it wasn't like I had any reason to rush home. "Did you two have fun?"

"Indeed." My father patted his lapels. "I ate fifteen fried shrimp, three sliders, and two of those chocolate mini cakes. It was a good night."

I walked my parents to the exit. The valet was busy, and once my parents found their ticket, I headed back up, trying to fight a feeling of melancholy. Since the divorce, I'd felt lonely at big events, mainly because I'd been so used to having someone by my side.

It had gotten chilly, and as I pulled my cashmere wrap close, a warm hand helped secure it. Turning, I came face to face with Arlo Majors.

"Hello." He gave me a bright smile. "I asked your grandmother to dance, and she said absolutely not, that I needed to ask you. What do you say?"

"I say watch out," I told him. "Because it starts with a dance, but then she'll ask you to marry me."

Arlo Majors laughed. He held out his hand, and the next thing I knew, we were gliding across the floor. I had taken dance my whole life, and he must have realized I could keep up, because he picked up the pace, whirling me across the space.

Everyone stopped to watch as we moved in tandem across the floor. He smelled like sandalwood and expensive cologne, and I had to remind myself to keep a respectful distance, but the moments when our bodies did brush together made my knees weak. Once the music came to an end, he lowered me in a dip. As he brought me back up, nice and slow, he brushed his lips across my cheek.

Bright lights flashed, making me fear I'd died and gone to heaven, but it was just the local paper, capturing the photo.

Arlo gave me a big smile, kissed my hand, and then sauntered to the bar. Heart pounding, I accepted water from a nearby waiter, then went to find my grandmother.

"I can't believe you told Arlo Majors to ask me to dance," I said, still trying to catch my breath. "That was probably the most fun I've had in my entire life."

My grandmother grinned. "Watching it was the most fun I've had in my entire life."

Arlo Majors was chatting with some people at the bar, less than ten feet away. It was all I could do to not just stand there and stare at him.

"You ready to go?" I asked my grandmother.

"Good idea," she said. "Or I might just ask that man to marry you."

~

The night had been perfect. Back home, I parked in the old carriage house that had been converted into a garage. Walking toward the house, I breathed in the dry, earthy scent of the fresh night air. In spite of all the rotten things that had happened in the past year, this night had been one to remember.

I walked across the paved driveway in my heels, glad my daughter was snuggled up cozy in her bed. Everything about the divorce had been hard on Kaia, like it would be on any twelve-year-old that had loved her father with all her might only to watch him hit the road. The split caused her to need me in a way she hadn't before, and little things like having a babysitter there instead of me made her nervous, as if I might slip away from her too.

I tried to push past the anger I felt about it all, focusing instead on the fireflies and the faded scent of Arlo Majors's cologne. My heels echoed on the wood of the steps as I headed for the front door, oblivious to the man sitting in the shadows until it was too late.

Chapter Three

I shrieked as a hand shot out and grabbed my arm.

"You need to put a stop to that theater." His breath reeked of alcohol. "Or someone is going to die—I can promise you that."

With a jerk, I wrenched my arm away before racing down the front steps. My heel nearly caught in the wood. The man followed close behind, his breath hot on the back of my neck.

"Hold on," he growled. "You're going to talk to me." He tried to grab me again, but his grip slipped. I dodged to the side, my breath coming in quick gasps.

The house was dark, but Kaia slept with the window open. I could only imagine her rushing outside to see what all the commotion was about. Or worse, thinking she could help.

The thought filled me with a fear so strong that I crashed into the man's rib cage with the sharp corner of my elbow. Then, I drew back my gold clutch and swung it at his head.

He reeled back, probably more surprised than anything, and I kicked him as hard as I could. He sprawled across the ground. After ripping off my heels, I ran toward the forest, the dry grass clawing at my feet.

The man let out gulping, drunken sobs that echoed across the lawn. "Come back," he wailed. "I need to talk to you. Please."

Kaia's room was still dark, but if this guy continued his performance, she would wake up. I wanted to scream for my parents to keep her from coming outside, but they slept with their windows closed.

I waved my phone at him. "I'll call the police!"

He held up his hands. "My little girl died at the Playhouse. You can't let it happen again."

I was completely confused. "Your little girl?"

"Belinda Hamilton," he said. "I'm her father."

~

The mosquitoes circled as I sat on my parents' front porch with Benjamin Hamilton. I'd insisted he take the deep porch swing because its chair was hard to manage. This guy was so drunk, the challenge would buy me a minute to get safely inside if he started to lose it again.

In the meantime, I sat guard in the wicker chair outside the front door. The mosquitoes were strong, and my hands shook as I lit the citronella candle on the patio table.

I didn't want to talk to him but realized the best bet to get rid of him was to listen to what he had to say. He could still go on the attack, but now that I knew who he was, it seemed less likely.

"You have five minutes," I told him.

Mr. Hamilton leaned forward, his elbows on his knees. In the muted light, he appeared a little older than my father. He had pockmarked skin, heavy jowls, and a round face that would have seemed cheerful if not so weighed down with despair.

"I dozed off after lunch." He rubbed his bloodshot eyes. "The Playhouse was on the television when I woke up. I thought it was a nightmare."

It hit me that someone from the Playhouse should have talked to Belinda's family, but maybe they chose not to since so much time had passed. To a grieving father, though, I could see how that amount of time might feel like nothing at all.

Belinda had been the big star in most of the shows the season that the theater burned down. She had stood out to me back then, not because she was twentysomething and incredibly cool but because she seemed to shine. Even my grandmother thought she had star potential.

"I remember your daughter," I told him. "The audience was entranced by every word she said. Even the ones she didn't say."

"Well, I didn't listen." Her father cracked his knuckles. "I didn't listen when she said she was in danger. I have to live with that every day."

The skin on my arms prickled. "What do you mean, danger?"

"Someone wanted her dead." He took another drink. "They got their wish."

That couldn't be true. There had never been whispers about the cause of Belinda's death, not once, and Starlight Cove was quick to share a scandal.

"Mr. Hamilton, the police would have—"

"She didn't tell the police. She told me. I have to live with that every day." Sweat trickled down his cheek, and the smell of whiskey was strong on his breath. "The theater can't reopen. I can't let anyone else get hurt."

The trees scraped against one another in the wind. The sound had always given me chills, but even more so now. Belinda's father had a set expression, like he genuinely believed that the tragedy could continue to play out decades later.

"Mr. Hamilton." I picked up a match from the candle and fiddled with it. Then, remembering how Belinda died, I quickly set it down. "Your daughter's death was an accident. Putting a stop to the theater twenty years later can't change that."

"The theater shut down for a reason," he insisted. "Your family needs to leave it well enough alone."

Finally, I understood the confusion.

"My family is not involved in the revival of the Playhouse." I was careful to keep my voice gentle. "My grandmother sold the building to a development group years ago. Now, it's been rented by a theater company, which we are also not affiliated with, for the purpose of the revival."

"Liar," he said.

"It's the truth." I wanted him to hear what I was saying so he'd get off my front porch. "I'm the head of the Tourism Council, which is why I spoke at the press conference. That's where my involvement ends. You're talking to the wrong person."

Mr. Hamilton launched himself out of the swing faster than I would have expected. He shook his fist in my face.

"Your grandmother started it; you can end it," he shouted. "Put a stop to it, Lily. Or you'll have blood on your hands."

He trudged across the porch and down the steps, muttering something at the sky. I sat, stricken, as he disappeared down the drive. He must have walked from the bars all the way up the bluff to my parents' house, which was impressive and terrifying all at the same time.

Inside, I double-checked each and every lock on the doors. Then, I headed straight for Kaia's room and climbed into bed with her. There were so many nights when she'd climbed in with me, so I knew she wouldn't mind. Tonight I wanted to keep her close.

Pulling the quilt up to my chin, I listened to the quiet rhythm of her breath. Images of Belinda and her father clicked through my mind as I finally calmed down enough to drift off to sleep. The cozy scent of a campfire helped shape my dreams.

Kaia coughed, and my eyes fluttered open. Outside, a hypnotic light crackled in the trees along the horizon. Suddenly, I shot straight up.

It wasn't a cozy campfire at all. The trees outside our house were on fire.

Chapter Four

I couldn't believe I'd fallen asleep thinking about the Playhouse only to awaken to something like this.

"Dad," I screamed, leaping to my feet. "Mom, wake up!"

Kaia was coughing into the sheets. Quickly, I pulled the bedroom window shut and grabbed her a drink of water from the bathroom.

"Here," I said, rubbing her back. "It's okay."

Her pretty face was confused and sleepy. She sipped at the water as my parents raced into the room.

My father grabbed for my cell. "I'll call the fire department."

I looked at my mom. "How long will it take for them to get to the house?"

Two of our largest pines burned bright against the sky, the sparks lighting the night like a swarm of fireflies.

My mother hesitated. "It's so dry. If the wind catches any of those trees—"

I didn't wait for her to finish the thought. "You get what you and Dad need. Kaia and I will get Grandma's things. Let's meet at the car in five minutes."

Kaia and I rushed down the hallway to my grandmother's old room, just as the landline in the house started to ring. The neighbors, no doubt, calling to warn us. The homes along the bluff were far apart, but the families were close.

My grandmother's frilly bedroom lit up when I flipped the light switch. The dainty bed lamps with the ruffled pink shades and the makeup mirror surrounded by light bulbs were relics from another time.

"How do we know what to take?" Kaia asked, hesitating at the door.

"Pictures," I decided, my mind cataloging my grandmother's closet, full of gowns, cases of costume jewelry, and her beloved collection of music boxes. "Those are the one thing we can't replace."

There were two albums that meant the world to my grandmother, in addition to the pictures lining the wall that showed her as a young actress. I pulled one down, charmed by the young girl in the black cocktail dress and the sparkling diamond necklace. She was midlaugh, surrounded by a polished group that hung on her every word.

The wail of a siren cut through the air, and quickly, I set the photograph in the box. From there, I worked fast, gathering pictures, Playbills, and framed awards. Once the box was full, Kaia grabbed one side, and we took the steep staircase together, holding the box tight. My mother stood in the entryway, barely able to see over her stack of photo albums.

"Don't go out unless we have to," my father called. "The smoke will ruin everything."

Through the sidelights by the front door, Kaia and I watched as three fire trucks roared up the drive. I stood so close to the windowpane that I could smell the cleaner that had been used to shine up the glass.

The firefighters leapt out and dragged a long hose to the woods. They turned on the water, and a smooth arc hissed against the orange flames. Branches broke off and fell, as gray smoke billowed toward the sky.

"Whoa." Kaia pressed her face against the window. "That guy's all the way up on the ladder."

Sure enough, one of the men had been lifted above the trees. He held a hose from sixty feet up, the water raining down like a storm.

"That's really cool," she murmured.

It was hard to reconcile the idea that we were witnessing something remarkable in the midst of such chaos.

"It's almost out," my father said.

Kaia chewed on her thumbnail. "I think it is out."

The smoke had lessened into a small trickle, and the big ladder had started to lower back down. The firefighters moved at a much less frenetic pace, and I nodded at my parents. "Yeah. It's out."

My father gave a stoic nod, but I could tell by the set of his jaw that he was shaken. It would have been unspeakable to lose my grandmother's home. There was so much history within these walls, so many memories.

"Let's go see if we can do anything to help," he said, heading for the door.

My mother smoothed her hair. "I need to change first. Maybe we should . . . hold it right there."

My mother stalked over to my father and opened the lapels of his bathrobe.

"Are you kidding me right now?" she said, and he started laughing.

My father had put on his favorite Detroit Lions T-shirt, the one my mother had been trying to throw away for years. It had a big hole in the shoulder and several tiny rips around the hem, and it was so worn that it was practically translucent.

"So, while the rest of us saved the sentimental items that mattered the most, you were busy rescuing your T-shirt?" my mother demanded.

"Grandpa," Kaia said, giggling.

My father scooped up my mother in a hug. "This T-shirt is part of the family. And when it comes to family, like it or not, you're in it for life."

~

Kaia and I headed back up to bed, while my parents went out to check in with the firefighters and look at the damage to the trees. The windows were still closed up tight, the old air-conditioning system whirring away, but the room smelled like smoke.

I smoothed back Kaia's hair. "Try and get some rest, okay? It's been a long night."

She settled into the pillow. "Why did that happen?"

I'd wondered the same thing. I couldn't help but think of Benjamin Hamilton.

When he and I had talked on the porch, I'd felt like we'd reached some sort of a resolution, but now, I wondered if he'd had anything to do with the fire. Maybe it was a careless act, tossing a cigarette into the brush as he stumbled back down the hill. Or perhaps it was something more sinister.

"The fire department will let us know," I said, with less fear than I felt. "We can make sure it doesn't happen again."

The answer seemed to satisfy her. Within a few minutes, Kaia's breathing slowed into a steady rhythm. The gravity of it all made it impossible to sleep, and finally, I headed down to the kitchen. My parents were there, lights low, talking quietly.

"Is Kaia asleep?" my father asked, and I nodded.

My mother pulled me into a tight hug. Her short, dark hair was damp and smelled like shampoo. "Let me make you some tea." She headed to the stove. "I don't know about you, but this gave us the scare of our life."

"It was terrifying," I admitted, settling in at the table. "I keep trying to imagine what it would be like to tell Grandma that we lost the house."

"That's what we were talking about." The kettle whistled, and she poured water into my cup. "If the wind had shifted, this place would have gone up like a bale of hay."

The three of us sat in silence, as the grandfather clock ticked in the hallway.

"Let's talk about something good," my father said. "How was the rest of the party?"

The fundraiser for the theater felt like a hundred years ago, but the reminder did bring back the happier portion of the night.

"Well, Arlo Majors swept me off my feet."

I told my parents about the dance, and my mother put her hand to her heart. "I am mentally putting myself in your dancing shoes."

"You should have stayed," I said. "He asked Grandma first, but she said no, so you would have been next in line."

My mother gave a delighted smile. "Oh, goodness. I could have been face to face with a movie star."

Cheerfully, my father smoothed his terry cloth robe. "Why would you need that? You get to look at perfection every day."

My mother and I laughed.

"It was such a great night but . . ." I took a sip of tea, debating how to bring up Belinda's father. "So, Benjamin Hamilton was on our front stoop when I got home. Turns out, he's against the reopening of the theater."

I recapped the encounter for them, leaving out the part where he grabbed my arm. Still, my parents seemed more shocked with every word.

"He came up here?" My mother was baffled. "To confront you, of all people? That doesn't make sense."

"It was scary," I admitted.

My father shook his head. "He's never been right since the accident that killed his first daughter."

"Losing one child is bad enough," my mother agreed. "I can't imagine losing two."

"What are you talking about?" I said.

My parents exchanged looks.

"Tell me," I said. "I'm a grown-up."

My parents had seemed to forget that fact once I moved in. It was like the last twenty years of my life, the ones where I was a fully functioning, independent adult, had disappeared.

My father sighed. "Benjamin Hamilton's wife left him when his girls were young. He was a good father, and they were great kids. Then, Lucia died, followed by Belinda."

"It was heartbreaking," my mother said. "Such a terrible thing for anyone to go through."

"He used to come to the shop a lot," my father continued. "Spent his days fishing. Usually drunk. It's hard to remember the time when he wasn't suffering."

"That's sad." I turned my teacup in the saucer, breathing in the scent of warm spice. I winced as it all hit me. "Really? Both of his daughters?"

"Lucia died in the bridge collapse," my mother said. "It was about three years before the fire."

"I remember the accident," I said, "but I don't know anything about it. I was too young."

"She'd just learned how to drive," my mother said. "The bridge had opened the day before, and as she reached the middle—I think a bearing in the middle broke—the whole thing went down. She died instantly."

"Bridges don't just collapse," I said. "That's not what happens."

"Of course not," my mother said. "There was a design flaw, something with the structure. I can't remember, exactly. It was a tragedy."

My father shook his head. "It seems some people have an easy time of it in this world, and others get an unlimited bucket of sorrow. I'll never understand it."

"It sounds suspicious," I said. "Both girls died so close together. He might have had something to do with it."

My father drew back. "Lily."

"Look," I said. "If someone gets struck by lightning once, that's bad luck. If someone gets struck by lightning *twice*, that person is standing on a metal roof."

My father wadded up his napkin. "Benjamin Hamilton didn't have a thing to do with it. I don't want to hear you talking like that again."

"Dad, it's—"

"Stop." My father's eyes flashed. "It's beyond disrespectful to speak that way about him."

"He attacked me on our front porch." Pulling up the sleeve of my sweatshirt, I pointed at the red marks where he'd grabbed my arm. "I'm going to have bruises tomorrow."

"He did *what*? That warrants a call to the police," my father said. "First thing tomorrow."

"No." I pulled my sleeve back down. "The revival is supposed to be a happy thing, good for tourism. It won't be if word gets around about this."

"Then I'll pay Mr. Hamilton a visit myself," my father said.

"It's over," I said. "But don't tell me what to think about him. I agree with you that he's been through it, but we don't know the full story. You should have heard some of the things that he was saying. That there were people out to get Belinda, that if the revival took place, the same type of thing would happen . . . he didn't sound like he was in his right mind."

Silence fell over the table. The hands on the clock above the sink pointed at one, so I gathered up my teacup and saucer.

"I should get to bed. Ironically enough, the Tourism Council is meeting with the theater manager and some of the crew at the Playhouse in the morning to discuss how we can help them out. Benjamin Hamilton might be waiting on the front steps."

My mother frowned. "Should your father go with you?"

"To work?" I almost laughed out loud. "Mom, I'll be just fine."

My father checked all the doors and set the alarm, and we headed upstairs. The three of us lingered in the hallway.

"If you need anything, don't hesitate to wake us up," my mother said, and I hugged them.

The wooden floor creaked as I headed back to the room where Kaia slept, and I climbed into my side of the bed, trying to ignore the smell of smoke still in my hair.

The house groaned in the wind.

I never want to hear you say anything like that again.

The disappointment in my father's voice rang through my head.

Benjamin Hamilton had experienced more than his share of grief, but my father was right—it didn't mean he was a criminal. Still, the man was out for revenge, and I had been his target. I'd said it was over, but was it? I didn't want to have to spend the rest of the summer looking over my shoulder.

Pulling the quilt close, I drifted off into a fitful sleep, the encounter as dark in my memory as the shadows that darted against the wall.

Chapter Five

Kaia had her headphones in her ears and video game in hand by the time I woke up. It was only eight in the morning, which gave me plenty of time before I had to leave.

"Morning," I called to my daughter. She didn't hear me under the headphones, so I took a moment to study her.

Kaia was a beauty. She'd gotten my shiny black hair and dimples and Jin's dark eyes. Her smile had captivated me since the day she was born. Now, seeing her folded up in the chair with perfect posture, her long hair pinned up in a messy bun, I wanted to pull her into a tight hug. I settled for dropping a kiss on the top of her head because at twelve, Kaia was the one who decided when she needed me, and that included hugs and conversation.

"Want to come down for breakfast?" I asked. "It smells like Grandma's making French toast and bacon."

Kaia paused her game and pulled out one side of her headphones, and I repeated the question. It was a form of communication I'd gotten used to—working around technology in order to connect with my daughter.

"I already had some yogurt. I'm good."

The idea of skipping bacon never would have occurred to me back when I was a child.

"Well . . ." I lingered for a moment, but she'd already put her headphones back in.

Downstairs, my mother bustled around the kitchen. She used a pair of tongs to transfer bacon from a pan onto a plate with a paper towel and then poured coffee into porcelain mugs. A stack of luscious-looking French toast was the centerpiece of the breakfast table.

"This looks fancy," I said.

"Well, I woke up wanting bacon," my mother said. "Maybe it was smelling that smoke all night." She bustled to the table and gestured for me to join her. "Your father's still asleep. Is Kaia?"

"No, she's up in her room." I poured some cream into my coffee, then took a seat.

"Doing what?" my mother asked. "Can't be more important than a good breakfast."

"Trust me, I know. I was informed that she's already had yogurt." I took two pieces of French toast, its cinnamon scent warming me. "She was playing a video game."

My mother handed me the butter, followed by syrup. "Kaia's been on that video game a lot. I didn't know that she was into all that."

"Yeah." Kaia's time on the video game had bothered me some, but I hadn't realized it was enough that my mother noticed it too. "One of her friends back home got her interested."

I'd been fine with it at the time because, originally, it had been something she did to unwind after a full day of school, activities, and friends. But now, it seemed like it was all that she did. I'd let her keep up with it because it was the thing that kept her connected to our old life, but in some ways, it was because I didn't know how to handle the situation.

Lately, Kaia kept getting mad at me about the little things, which made it harder to communicate about bigger issues. The last time I tried to ask her to pick up her room, she'd slammed the door in my face. She'd lost the video game and her phone for two days, but her rage had lasted for twice that long.

I hated the idea that she would get mad at me again. We barely had enough time together as it was. Not to mention that once school let out, she would leave to spend her first summer away from me, with her father in Japan.

The idea that he chose to move across the world made my stomach turn. It had been hard to manage the idea of her being so far away, and I was terrified she would feel so glad to see him that she wouldn't want to come home. So, too much time on the video game seemed small in comparison.

"I'm not too worried about it right now," I said. "She might be doing it because she's bored."

Nodding, my mother took a bite of French toast. "I understand being bored. Ever since the shop closed up, I haven't quite known what to do with myself either."

I was surprised to hear her admit it, but it made perfect sense. The sportfishing shop that my parents had owned had been their life. They'd been there, rain or shine, every day but Christmas, and there was not one person in Starlight Cove who hadn't passed through those doors.

"I thought you were enjoying all this free time."

My mother took a sip of orange juice. "The days feel long, that's all. I don't quite know how to fill them."

We sat in silence. The window by the table overlooked the lake, and the sun reflected off the water. It was so beautiful out, and I didn't understand why my mother wasn't planning a hike or a bike ride or something to enjoy the day now that she no longer had to go to work.

"What do you want to be doing?" I asked. "This is your time, Mom. You've been working at that shop for the past forty years. I'm sure that you have a few things you'd like to get to."

Her hands fretted with her fork. "So many of them are with your father, though, and he's not interested."

"Interested in what?" I asked.

My mother took a bite of bacon. Then, sounding embarrassed, she murmured, "Dance lessons."

I thought of my dance session with Arlo Majors. "That could be so much fun."

"Your father promised he would learn to dance when and if we ever had time. Well, we have the time, and I've hinted at it a few times but—"

"I'll sign you up at Starlight and Twinkle Toes. Retirement present."

"Your father won't do it."

"He said he would, though."

She considered the French toast still on her plate but didn't answer.

"Mom, he'll do it," I assured her. "He promised."

"Yes, maybe." She added some more syrup and took a bite.

"What else?" I said. "What else could we add to your to-do list?"

"Oh, I don't know . . ."

"Dawn's going to start doing tours of the lighthouse. You could volunteer to help. I've heard it's beautiful inside."

Kip Whittaker, a friend of mine since grade school, had married a woman who purchased the local lighthouse at government auction and remodeled it. She and Kip had been living in it, but they'd spent the winter getting it ready to open up to the public. They'd created a small visitors' museum on the bottom floor, including all sorts of maritime memorabilia.

"I should have asked Kip's mother about it at the party last night," I said. "I think Kip said they're starting tours in June. That's only a month away. It would be so much fun to spend time in a lighthouse. Plus, you'd probably bump into a lot of the people who used to come to the fishing shop."

My mother nodded but didn't seem as enthusiastic as I'd hoped. Moving on, I pulled up a local website focused on senior activities.

Handing her my phone, I said, "You could needlepoint, garden, join a book club, learn stained glass, cook pastries, tutor kids . . ." She handed the phone back to me and gathered up our dishes. "Mom," I said, surprised. "You're not interested in any of that?"

"Those groups have all the same women in them who have been friends forever." She took the dishes to the sink. "You know how it is around here."

"You're friendly with all of those women."

"Yes, but I'd feel embarrassed to waltz into those meetings alone." She wiped down the table with a washcloth. "Without your father."

Huh. I hadn't realized she relied on him so much.

My parents hadn't socialized much because they were too busy working, but when they did, it was often with my father's group of lake buddies. They'd take out Jet Skis, go sailing, and, of course, go sportfishing. Come to think of it, my mother didn't have many friends of her own.

She sat back down and sipped her coffee. "You're disappointed in me."

"No." My answer was too quick. "I'm just surprised. I didn't realize how important it was to you to have a partner in things."

I could relate to that feeling. Once Jin and I had divorced, it was hard for me to set foot back into the places where we'd spent so much time together. It was especially hard when the annual events circled back around because our group of friends had no idea whether to invite me, him, or both of us.

He moved to Japan a few months after the divorce, which solved some of those issues, but I never found a comfortable way to settle into the life we'd built without him by my side. It was a relief when I finally admitted to myself that it was time to start somewhere fresh.

"It appears that I might be codependent." My mother gave a little laugh. "Or whatever the kids call it nowadays."

"You're social, which is why you shouldn't be so isolated," I said.

Moving back here had been great for me because I was no longer alone. I had my family, my childhood friends, and my daughter, not to mention a town that I'd always loved. Things finally felt good for me again, so it was hard to see my mother feeling bad.

"I think it would help you to keep busy," I said. "So, what are you going to do today?"

My mother added some cream to her coffee. "Well, if I can get Kaia off that video game, I'll get her back outside to pull weeds, and she can help cook lunch."

Hardly riveting. Surely, her retirement dreams had little to do with this drafty old house. If she didn't know how to take the steps to find some creative ways to spend her extra time, I'd be happy to help, but she was acting like she didn't want me to do that.

"Keep me posted," I said. "This should be the best time of your life. Don't waste time waiting for excitement to come find you."

"Yeah." She drummed her nails on the table. "So far, it seems to have the wrong address."

~

Thanks to Benjamin Hamilton, I felt like I had to look over my shoulder before driving past our newly blackened trees, along the winding road that led down the bluff, and back up to the theater. I didn't know whether his threats about the theater were empty or not, but I didn't want to make things worse. If he followed me, it would hardly be convincing that I didn't have a part in the revival.

At the same time, it felt like unnecessary stress to have to think that way at all. I shouldn't have to explain myself to some man who'd ambushed me on the front porch of my home. After glancing in my rearview mirror, I pulled out a stick of spearmint gum from my glove box, hoping the mint would help calm my nervous stomach.

I pulled up ten minutes before I was supposed to arrive. I didn't know whether Arlo Majors had flown back to LA, but there wasn't a town car present. His absence was a relief, since I didn't have the first clue about what to say to him after last night.

Odds were good he wouldn't even remember that I'd danced with him, even though it was one of the most exciting moments of my life.

I walked across the driveway, still half expecting Benjamin Hamilton to leap out from behind a bush. It was dark inside the lobby of the theater. Once my eyes adjusted, it was as if the lights went up to reveal a place hidden somewhere within my memory.

The lush red carpet, the gilt on the walls, and the baroque lamps brought me straight back to my childhood. I'd always loved the high arches of the ceiling and the curving staircase that led up to the balcony seating. The sense of history there was so strong that I could practically hear the voices of the actors calling from the stage.

"Hello, Lily." The theater manager, Renee, walked across the thick carpet toward me. "Thanks for coming."

Her shoulder-length blonde hair swished side to side with each step. She'd been at the press conference and the party last night, working hard to build buzz for the theater. Now, she gave me a firm handshake.

"Follow me, we're all back in the conference room."

I followed Renee through the lobby, the rich smell of wood oil emanating from the walls.

"Doesn't it look magnificent in here?" she asked. "The portion of the theater that was damaged in the fire was rebuilt, of course, but the smoke damage was everywhere. The building had sat for so long that it had all of the typical problems, like electrical and plumbing. It was quite a job to remodel it."

Renee pushed open the door to the meeting room, which was just as beautiful as the rest of the theater.

It had shining hardwood floors that matched the wooden walls and large windows that overlooked the water. Gulls soared out over the lake, hunting for breakfast. The view reminded me how high up on the bluff the theater actually was, much higher than my grandmother's house. My mind jumped to the fire so long ago and the reality of how difficult it must have been for the fire department to make it to the scene in time.

"Grab a coffee and a chair." Renee gestured at a display of snacks set out on a side table.

There was a small group chatting by the silver carafe, and the others were already seated at a small conference table. I headed over. The coffee smelled great—rich and intense. Given the night I'd had, I was happy to grab another cup, but I ignored the impressive display of doughnuts. I didn't want to risk having my mouth full the moment someone asked me a question.

"Hey, team," Renee called, once I'd found a place to sit. The room quieted down, and everyone took their seats. "I'd like to introduce Lily. She spoke yesterday at the press conference."

A twentysomething girl, heavyset with a stern cut in her sandy-blonde hair, eagerly stood up to shake my hand. She wore horn-rimmed glasses, a plain white T-shirt, and a pair of baggy overalls. "Hey, I'm Piper, the stage manager."

Quick introductions were made all around, including the director, box office manager, and development manager. The production manager was bundled up in an argyle sweater and held his coffee close.

"Lily, you're from here?" he asked.

"Originally, yes," I said.

"Then I have a question." He leaned his elbows on the table. "When does it get warm?"

I laughed. "It will, I promise. The summers are actually hot, but the weather can seem like it changes full seasons from minute to minute."

He shivered. "I should invest in a fur coat."

"Oh, come on now." A clear voice rang out like bells. "Don't make the Los Angeles people look bad."

A woman swept into the room, a plum silk sundress billowing around her, and took a seat. She was about my mother's age, with glowing skin and bright-green eyes. Quickly, Renee got to her feet and brought her a cup of coffee with a splash of cream.

"You are a doll," the woman said. "But you do not have to wait on me."

"It's my pleasure," Renee said. Turning to me, she said, "This is Jade Noor, the lead costume designer on *Dance with Me*, and I swear, she does not sleep. She's been here since four o'clock this morning, sewing away. We are so lucky to have her."

Dance with Me was a popular dancing show that had been on network television for years. Kaia was obsessed with it.

"What brought you to Starlight Cove?" I asked. Then, realizing that I'd probably spoken out of turn, I said, "I'm Lily Kimura, with the Tourism Council."

Jade's green eyes studied me. "Yes, you look just like your grandmother. I worked with her here years ago, when I was just starting out. It's so nice to be back."

"I hope you brought your Emmys," the production manager said, adjusting the sleeves of his argyle sweater. "I've always wanted to see one."

"Why would I do that?" Jade asked. "My Tony would get lonely."

Everyone laughed, and she winked at me. "Listen, Lily's the one who deserves the spotlight today. She's put the theater front and center in the paper this morning. Well done."

With a flick of her thin wrist, Jade sent the *Town Crier* to the center of the table.

My heart nearly stopped. There I was, on the front cover. My eyes were closed, and Arlo Majors's lips were on my cheek. The caption read *Lily Kimura and Arlo Majors, celebrating the Starlight Cove Playhouse.*

Everyone clamored around the photograph, trilling with excitement. "What a great shot!"

"That is wonderful." The marketing manager squeezed my shoulder. "We knew Arlo would be on the cover, but this is brilliant. Well done!"

"I don't deserve credit," I said, embarrassed. "I was just trying to keep from passing out."

The stage manager nodded. "Low blood sugar?"

"No, starstruck," I said.

Everyone laughed, and Jade waved her hand. "Oh, don't be scared of Arlo. He's the sweetest soul."

"Indeed, and it's going to be an exciting summer with him," Renee said. "It's our job to make sure we can do everything possible to bring in an audience. Things like this will do it. Let's discuss some of the ideas the Tourism Council had to help build awareness . . ."

The meeting continued on, and I spoke in depth about the different plans and programs the Council had put together. The lake shone outside the window, and the energy in the room was bright.

Once the meeting was over, I headed out to the parking lot, feeling excited for the season and the chance to have such a vibrant resource to offer the community. The feeling was night and day from my encounter with Benjamin Hamilton. I was just about to hop into my car when a white Range Rover drove into the lot.

Arlo Majors was behind the wheel, and he pulled into a spot right up front. He wore a pair of dark sunglasses and some sort of a soft-looking white pullover. Noticing me, he lifted his hand in a friendly wave.

"What a day," he called.

"Beautiful." Then, embarrassed, I said, "I was talking about the weather. Nothing else."

To my absolute shock, he walked over with a curious smile. "You are funny. What's your name?"

My mouth went dry. "Lily."

"Arlo." He held out his hand. "You're with the theater?"

"No, the Tourism Council." Part of me felt nervous, like I was about to get in trouble for talking to the talent. "Are you enjoying your time in Starlight Cove?"

Arlo smiled. "Is that really what you want to ask me? You seem like the type of person who says what they really think."

"I guess life would be easier if we did that," I said. "Or harder, maybe."

"Harder, for sure." His blue eyes were so bright, I practically needed sunglasses. "It would be chaos if we blurted out what we were really thinking."

"Chaos?" I said. "Goodness. What on earth are you thinking about?"

"Well . . ." The wind blew, and I smelled that same spicy cologne from our dance the night before. "I fly out of here in one hour. I'm scared to fly, and I'm not supposed to eat carbs. So, I'm thinking I'm going to steal a doughnut from the theater because I don't have an assistant to go to the doughnut shop for me, which also makes me wonder if I can do summer here without an assistant. That thought alone makes me feel completely inadequate as a human. The chaos comes from admitting all that to another person, to a complete stranger, and leaving that person to form an opinion of me based on truth."

"Would it help if I asked you to get me a doughnut too?"

He grinned. "Be right back."

Arlo Majors headed back toward the theater, reciting, "Be not afraid of greatness. Some are born great, some achieve greatness, and others have greatness thrust upon them . . ."

Twelfth Night.

I was surprised that I knew, but of course I did. My grandmother had been in that show a hundred times.

Standing in the morning sun, it hit me that I'd talked to Arlo Majors, the movie star, again. It felt like we had a connection, but he was charismatic. No doubt he connected with everybody. Still, I appreciated the fact that he'd made me feel special.

Of course, as the minutes passed, I felt foolish—he probably wasn't coming back at all. I was about to leave when the theater door flew open, and he burst out like an explosion.

"Run," he cried, clutching an entire box of doughnuts. "I think they're on to me!"

He raced over and dove down behind my car. We crouched and listened for footsteps, but all was quiet. Satisfied, he sat crisscross-style right there in the parking lot. Holding out the doughnuts, he said, "Here you go."

"Thank you." I selected the shiniest one. It was soft and sweet, and it instantly melted in my mouth.

Arlo ate three and offered me another, but I shook my head.

"I can't believe you took the whole box," I said. "You don't need an assistant. You're excelling all on your own."

He gave me a fist bump and then glanced at his watch. It was some brand I'd never heard of and was probably the cost of a small country.

"Yikes." He hopped to his feet. "I gotta go." He handed me the box. "See you soon, Lily. Don't play small."

"Sorry?" I said, scrambling to my feet.

"My mother used to say that to me."

He pulled a baseball cap from his back pocket and pulled it on low, somehow managing to look even more attractive than he had moments before. Then, he took the box back and with a wave, sped off in his Range Rover.

I watched him go, the sugar from the doughnut still sweet on my lips.

Arlo Majors, ladies and gentlemen.

Definitely a performer. He came in hot, took what he wanted, and left me feeling . . . I don't know. Inspired?

Something.

The whole experience with the theater that morning had left me feeling that way. It had been such a joy to be there, if only for a brief period. Whoever had decided to bring the Playhouse back to life had given such a gift to Starlight Cove.

In fact, I had to wonder at the identity of the mystery donor. There were a lot of people who cared about our town, but I didn't know anyone who cared about the theater more than my grandmother. Part of me suspected that she could be behind it all.

It would make sense. After all, she'd founded the theater, and now, toward the end of her life, she'd want to leave a legacy. Like Benjamin Hamilton, I'd been a little confused that no one from the theater had contacted our family. That oversight would make sense, though, if she was running the whole thing.

Doing it anonymously would give her the permission to make all the decisions without having to explain herself to anyone, in particular, my father. He'd have concerns about my grandmother giving away her fortune at this stage in her life—the cost of this venture had to be astronomical.

Time, along with a couple of careful questions, would tell if she was running things. For now, I just wanted to sit in those beautiful red velvet seats and watch the hidden stories of the Starlight Cove Playhouse unfold.

Chapter Six

Once the news got out that I was on the front page of the *Town Crier*, my phone did not stop buzzing. Texts, calls . . . everyone wanted to ask about dancing with Arlo Majors. The only person who didn't seem interested was Kaia, and that was because she didn't know about it.

"Don't let Kaia see the paper," I told my mother when I got back home.

"Why?" She set down the design magazine she'd been flipping through. "What's in it?"

I pulled the article up on my phone and showed it to her. She put her hand to her chest. "I can't wait to see him onstage this summer."

"We need to buy season tickets."

"Oh, we have them," my mother said. "Your grandmother was first in line."

"Mom, do you think Grandma's involved with all of this?" I asked, settling into the couch. "Bringing the theater back?"

My mother shook her head. "She told me to enjoy the season because 'whoever was dumb enough to sink that much money into reviving the theater would be too stupid to create a plan of sustainability.' So, no. Not her. Your grandmother never had illusions of stupidity."

"I guess time will tell," I said. "Where is Kaia?"

My mother gestured at the stairs. "She helped in the garden but went back up to her room after lunch."

Upstairs, I found Kaia back on the video game, in the exact same position as that morning. Earbuds in, glued to the screen. The room smelled like chocolate-mint ice cream.

"Hey." I nudged her knee. When she didn't look up, I put my hand in front of the screen and waved it. *"Hey."*

"Mom!" Kaia shot to her feet, taking the game to the bathroom and slamming the door.

Even though I hadn't planned on addressing the video game at all, I couldn't let her be so rude.

"Honey." I rapped gently on the door. "You've had enough screen time today."

No sound. Frustration building, I knocked again.

Nothing.

I kept knocking until she opened it, her face full of rage. *"What?"*

"Listen, it's time to put down the game. Let's go do something. Do you want to ride bikes?"

She crossed her arms. "It's cold out."

"We could go get hot chocolate at the Sweetery."

"No."

"A walk on the beach?" I suggested. "Shopping? We could do an art project?"

Lately, it felt so difficult to find something she wanted to do with me, but we were running out of time. School was out in a few weeks, and then she'd be gone for nearly three months. It was so hard to think about, and I couldn't help but feel angry that it had come to this, that Jin and I hadn't been strong enough to keep our marriage together for her.

"I would really love to do something with you," I told her.

Kaia sat down on the edge of the bathtub. "I just want to be alone and rest. I'm tired today."

"That makes sense—we were up late. I could get a book or something," I said. "We could sit up here and read."

The sigh she gave was so deep, I felt it in my bones.

"Never mind," I said. "You rest, honey. Love you."

I headed out of the room like I didn't have a care in the world, but once in the hallway, I leaned against the door and shut my eyes.

There were times my daughter wanted to spend every second with me and others where she wanted nothing to do with me. Typical for the age, I kept telling myself, but that didn't make it easier. It also didn't help that I had major mom guilt for having to spend so much time at work.

It already felt like I'd blinked, and she'd changed from a child into a little grown-up. Who was she going to be when she got back from Japan? Time was moving too fast. It felt like before I knew it, she'd be completely grown, and I would have missed out on it all.

"What's wrong with you?" a voice boomed.

My father stood in the hallway, peering at me. He looked like he'd just woken up from a nap, his hair askew.

"It just feels like she's growing up too fast," I admitted. "She'll move out, get married, and I'll never see her again."

"Nah," he said. "You're still hanging around, aren't you?"

He grunted and stomped down the stairs, probably headed for the kitchen.

~

That night, Kaia had plans to go to a classmate's house for pizza and a movie, so I met my friends for dinner at Maddie's, a cute little bar on the water. From the outside, it pretended to be an old shack, but inside, it was always packed. I was the first one to arrive and got lucky enough to grab one of the tables by the sand.

The patio heaters were on, so I undid the buttons on my summer cardigan and draped it over the back of the wooden chair. Fairy lights twinkled overhead, and the lake air made the night crisp and cool.

For a split second, I allowed myself to think about what it would be like if I was still married and Jin was here with me. He and I could lie in the sand, looking at the stars, while I listened to him talk about the constellations. He knew a little about a lot, which made him fun to be around. Of course, his passions were as fleeting as his knowledge, which was part of the reason we fell apart.

"How are ya?" The waitress set a basket of soft-baked pretzels on the table, along with a side of beer cheese. "I'm happy to bring more, so eat it while it's hot. They're the best that way."

The pretzels were, in fact, nice and warm, with large pieces of salt, but it was the beer cheese that made them extraordinary. Maddie, the owner, only served a little taste and then sent the waiters back around to upsell the cheese, which never took much convincing.

"Thank you," I said, smiling at her. "You may as well bring out the beer cheese now because we're going to need it. We'll also need three waters, please, and a bottle of whatever white you have from Harrington's."

My friend Abby was the operations manager of her family's winery, and it would make her happy to see her wine on the table.

The waitress was about to head off when she turned back, snapping her fingers. "Wait! You were in the paper today."

My cheeks flushed. I'd studied the newspaper clipping at least a hundred times already. It was hard to believe that it was really me, laughing in the arms of one of the most famous men in the world.

I gave her a guilty smile. "I work for the Tourism Council, so we were just trying to build some buzz."

People didn't need to think that I operated under any illusion that Arlo Majors was actually interested in me.

She let out a dreamy sigh. "What does he smell like? Is his hair like, so soft?"

"I didn't touch his hair so I don't know, but he did smell amazing."

"Wait, what did he smell like?" Emma squealed. She and Abby rushed up to the table, pulling out their chairs in a flurry of hugs and handbags.

"Yes, I've been waiting all day to ask you that question," Abby said. "Saying he smelled amazing doesn't count. Give details."

"Oh, I don't know." The dance with Arlo Majors seemed like years ago. The moment with the doughnuts was just a few hours ago, but I was not about to get into all that. "He smelled like spice and laundry soap. But a really expensive kind, if that makes sense."

Abby gave a vigorous nod. "That's what I would expect. Or like, leather and sunshine."

I laughed. "I don't even know what that means."

The waitress bit her pen. "You are seriously the luckiest person on the planet." She headed off to get the wine, and my two friends beamed at me like I'd done something great.

"I feel like I should make a candy in his honor," Emma said. She was the owner of the Sweetery, the chocolate shop on Main Street, and was always coming up with new concoctions. "The Arlo-Lily. No, the Arly."

"Oh, stop," I said, laughing. "This has been good timing. It's taking my mind off the divorce. It was two years ago today, so it's been a nice distraction."

Abby was reaching for a pretzel but stopped. "Today?"

"Yeah." I squeezed lemon into my water. "That's why I wanted to get together tonight. I don't expect to have 'feelings,' but I want to be prepared. Last year was hard."

"I can only imagine." Emma scooped from the sample of beer cheese, added a pretzel, then set it in front of me. "Forever meant forever to you. He's the one who missed the memo."

True. I'd done what I could to salvage things, but there had been problems between Jin and me long before we split up. It started back when Kaia was in the second grade. Jin's work travel was endless, and he started to spend time with other women, which I'd never predicted. Still, I pushed for marriage counseling, a trial separation, anything other than divorce. But he fell in love with someone else and married her a few weeks after ending it with me.

It had been hard, of course. These days, though, it was more that I had to get up and get on with it, for the sake of my daughter.

"I'm sad about it," I said. "Mostly, I'm angry. I hate knowing that my failed marriage is the reason my daughter won't be with me this summer. It doesn't seem right."

The wine arrived then, and Abby held out her hand. "Thanks. I'll open it." She got right to work using the corkscrew on her keychain. She poured and passed us our glasses. I smelled the bright citrus of the pinot grigio before taking a sip.

"It's such a long time to be away," Emma said. "You're going to miss her."

"Like crazy," I said. "Plus, she won't get to have a summer here. Days at the lake, bonfires, and secrets with you guys—those moments are my memories. I wanted her to have something like that."

"It's frustrating," Abby said. "Not to mention the lack of stability. That's going to be hard on her, and I know you would never choose that. Are you worried about her being around Jin's new wife? I can't even stand saying that sentence."

I fiddled with my napkin. "Yes, but the biggest thing is that she's flying there alone. It's too expensive for me to go and then turn right back around, so I'm not going with her."

"Why couldn't you stay?" Abby said. "Make a vacation out of it?"

"Jin thought it might be confusing for Kaia to see us together."

Abby made a face. "In other words, his new wife said no?"

Emma frowned. "You know, I only met him at the wedding, but if we ever meet again, he's going to get a piece of my mind."

Abby ripped off a piece of pretzel. "Same."

"I don't know how I'm supposed to let her go for three months." I rolled a piece of pretzel in my hand like a worry ball. "That's too long, especially at her age. I don't want to be away from her."

"I'm sure she feels the same." Emma took a sip of water. "Have you asked her?"

I looked out at the lake to hide my emotion. The deep blues churned with gentle waves.

"No," I admitted. "I mean . . . what if she's excited about it? I want her to be happy, but . . ."

The three of us were silent. The waiter came and dropped off the round of beer cheese. She must have picked up on the vibe because instead of asking for our order, she headed for another table.

Abby toyed with the stem of her wineglass. "You know, there were so many things I was dealing with emotionally at such a young age. So much fear. If someone had talked to me about how I was feeling, it would have helped me feel less alone."

"I need to talk to her," I said. "Before she goes."

Emma nodded. "One of the hardest things about dating Cody is that he's always asking me the tough questions, ones that I would rather avoid. Eventually, I'll talk. It might be like that with Kaia. Don't expect a response the first time around, and if she says something too hard to hear, you don't have to respond. Just listen."

"And let her know that you love her," Abby agreed.

Such good advice. Exactly the reason I'd planned this dinner, because these were things that I could only talk about with friends that had seen me at my best and my worst.

The waitress returned. "You ready to order?"

"I think so," I said, and they nodded. "Chicken tenders all around."

"The best in town," the waitress agreed.

"The best anywhere," I told her.

There had been many benefits to moving back here. Family and friends, for sure. But the food had definitely made the list.

"Bring Arlo Majors next time," the waitress told me. "We could get his opinion."

The girls squealed at the prospect. I passed around the pretzels and beer cheese, and Abby refilled our wine. Lifting her glass, she said, "To new beginnings."

The three of us clinked glasses, the sound as bright as laughter.

~

My mother texted me around nine that Kaia was back from her friend's house, so I got a ride home, hoping that I'd get a chance to spend a few minutes with her before bed. I was on high alert walking to the front door, but this time, my parents had the porch lights on, and no one was there to surprise me. I dropped my keys on the table by the door and headed upstairs.

The television was on in my parents' bedroom, but when I peeked into Kaia's room, I was disappointed to see she was curled up in bed. Quietly, I shut her door and went to my room.

There, I flipped on the lights and stopped short at the sight of a crumpled piece of paper on my pillow. It was the front page of the paper with the picture of me and Arlo Majors. The floorboard creaked, and I turned to find Kaia glaring at me.

"Really, Mom?" she said. "You couldn't warn me?"

For a split second, I considered lying and telling her that I didn't know about it. The most important thing, though, was helping her to work through whatever feelings this had caused.

I took a seat on the bed and slid off my flats. They still had sand in them, but my fun evening suddenly felt incredibly far away. "I didn't know whether or not I should say anything about it," I told her. "Either way, I wanted to wait until we were together and could talk."

"Talk about you kissing another man on the front page of the newspaper?" she cried. "Do you know how humiliating that is?"

Even though I wanted to argue that technically, I was not kissing anybody but was being kissed, it didn't matter. Her words made it clear she was upset to see me with someone other than her father. Completely unfair, considering Jin had already remarried, but it wasn't the time to dive into double standards.

"I'm sorry that you feel embarrassed," I said. "I was at the celebration for the Playhouse, Arlo Majors asked me to dance, and at the end, he did this fancy dip. He was giving a performance for the crowd, Kaia. It wasn't like he was really kissing me. I certainly didn't know it would end up on the front page of the paper. I'm sorry."

She balled up her hands into fists. "Are you dating him?"

The question should have made me laugh, but none of this was funny. "No, honey. I'm not dating anyone." I thought about her father and wondered if maybe Kaia was worried that I'd get married and leave her too. "Honey, I want to make it clear that even if I did date someone, I would never leave you. You're stuck with me. Not just until college, but for life. I know you're worried about that."

"No, I'm not." Kaia glared at me. "Why would you even say that?"

The idea that I had just added to her anxiety made my shoulders tense. "I wanted to make sure you knew, though," I said. "Because I love you more than anything and—"

Kaia stormed out of the room. I silently counted to five, long enough for her to get to her room. Sure enough, the door slammed.

My mother came out into the hallway, her hair in rollers. "What was that?"

I held up the crumpled paper. "Kaia saw the picture."

My mother looked down the hallway, then back at me. "Oh."

"Yeah."

She pulled me into a hug. "It's okay. Things will look better in the morning."

"Sure," I said.

I didn't believe it, though.

This wasn't about the picture. It was about the insecurity of everything that had happened in the past few years. It was my job to keep things stable for my daughter, and it felt like I was failing every step of the way.

Chapter Seven

It had taken nearly the full day on Sunday, but Kaia was at least speaking to me again by dinner. Then, I made the mistake of saying, "Do you feel ready for the end of the school year?"

Kaia's eyes filled with tears. She knocked over her milk as she left the table and stomped up to her room, but my mother waved me off. "I've got the milk. Find out what's going on."

I found Kaia face down in my bed, her thin shoulders shaking. I laid a hand on her back. Finally, her sobs turned into sniffles, and then she was quiet.

"Do you want to talk about it?" I asked.

"No." Then, she flipped over and stared up at the ceiling.

I handed her a tissue from the bedside table, and she blew her nose.

"I'm supposed to do this big interview for English class," she said. "I forgot all about it. It's thirty-five percent of our grade."

My stomach dropped. "When's it due?"

"This Friday."

"That's plenty of time," I said, relieved. "Interviews are the best assignments ever. Making up the questions is the hardest part. The rest is simple."

"Finding the person to interview is the hardest part." She sat up. "The kids in my class sent emails to all of these people like, months ago. I thought I'd interview Norah, so I wasn't even worried about it, but she's too busy."

It took a moment to make the connection. Jin's wife. Technically, my daughter's . . . I couldn't even think the word. I could think of lots of other words, though, the ones that described my absolute rage that Norah had said no to something so simple.

"Why did you choose her?" I said, careful to keep my voice light.

"Because it has to be someone who's won an award," Kaia said. "Something real, not like Grandpa's fishing trophies."

Norah was a decorated scientist. It had been the only thing about her that I respected.

Calm down. Take a breath.

I picked up one of the pillows from the bed and hugged it close. It smelled clean, like fabric softener.

"What if you interviewed Gigi?" I suggested. "She's won several awards. It would give you an opportunity to learn about her career and how she got there."

Kaia made a face. "I don't want to show off."

"Show off?" I echoed.

"Yeah. It would be me being like, 'Look at my famous great-grand-mother. Did I mention she's famous?' Right after you were making out with a movie star."

I sighed. "Look, it wouldn't have to be like that. You could focus on the fact that she was a woman, making her way in a business that caters to men and excelling at it."

Kaia wound a strand of hair around her finger. "Do you think she'd talk to me?"

"Of *course* she'll talk to you," I said. "She'll probably talk so much that you'll have a hard time writing it all down."

Kaia made a face. "Mom, I don't have to write it down."

"It's English class."

"Right. I just have to write down the questions and then record it. Like a podcast."

"I see," I said, feeling about as old as a mountain.

Kaia made me call then and there. Of course, Gigi agreed to the interview. In fact, she sounded absolutely delighted that Kaia had thought of her.

"I think you just made her day," I said once we'd hung up.

Kaia gave a shy smile. "Do you think so?"

"Well, she gets to talk to a kid who she thinks is great about a time in her life that was pretty great. So yeah, I think that's a win."

"It is a huge win," Kaia agreed. She hesitated, then fell into my arms and hugged me. I squeezed her tight, grateful the crisis had been averted and fully aware that the biggest win of all was right there in my arms.

~

Once Kaia was asleep, I sat in my bed, catching up on a few last-minute emails. The phone rang, and I didn't recognize the number, but it was local.

"Hello?" I said, picking up.

"Hi, Lily. This is Grayson Waymark, from Waymark and Williams. I apologize for calling so late, but it's a matter of some urgency. How are you this evening?"

I vaguely knew Mr. Waymark. He was a partner in one of the most influential law offices in town, and he'd been in touch with the Tourism Council a few times over the years about this issue or that. I was surprised he was calling me on a Sunday night.

"Hi," I said. "Is everything okay?"

"Well, I hope so," he said. "I'm contacting you on behalf of the Starlight Cove Playhouse. The donor would like to offer you a permanent role this summer."

"I'm not an actress," I said, confused.

He chuckled. "The role of running the theater."

I took off my reading glasses. "Wait, what?"

"Renee Rogers, the theater manager, has made an abrupt exit due to a family emergency," he explained. "It's been a scramble, trying to figure out who in town could serve as a figurehead. The donor took into account the press conference you did, the fact that you are on the front page of the paper with Arlo Majors, and your role as director at the Tourism Council. Of course, they also acknowledged your family's former affiliation with the theater. In a town this small, it's clear that you're the person ideal for the job."

"This is probably the last thing I would have expected you to call me about," I said, worrying the quilt with my thumb.

The entire proposal threw me. Getting out of bed, I began pacing the floor.

"I'm sorry," I said, "but I don't see how I could. I'm already committed to the Tourism Council."

"Yes, and it's probably the one place that would truly understand the importance of this theater to Starlight Cove. I'd imagine they'd be more than willing to fill your role for the summer and welcome you back in the fall."

I tried to wrap my mind around the idea of being the head of the Playhouse, but I couldn't do it. My brain couldn't process it—I already had my whole workweek planned out at the Tourism Council. In fact, I already had the next six months planned out.

"I'll email you the contract for review," Mr. Waymark told me. "However, we'll have to move on to the next option if you do not respond by midnight tomorrow."

"That's a little quick for such a big decision."

"The Playhouse opens to the public in just a few weeks. Talent flies in from New York, Chicago, and Los Angeles the beginning of next weekend. The people in place can handle the majority of the work, but it would be complicated to get someone else. I'll wait for your call."

My parents were still awake when I knocked on their bedroom door. My mother was reading in the small living area by the fireplace, and my father was up on a step stool, messing with the base of a curtain rod.

"Do you have a minute?" I asked.

"We're 'retired.'" My father somehow made it sound like a bad word. "We have all the time in the world."

The curtain rod chose that moment to dislodge from the wall, practically knocking him off the step stool.

"Dad." I rushed over, but he steadied himself, holding the rod and panels up like an umbrella.

"I've got it," he said, voice muffled.

My mother rolled her eyes. "He's had it for about two hours, now."

"These curtains are too heavy for the wall," he said. "Forget it. They're coming down."

With that, my father pulled out the entire thing, hardware and all. Green-and-gold drapes practically swallowed him up as tiny pieces of plaster floated through the air like flurries.

"I think you probably needed a little patience," I said, peering up at the gaping hole in the wall. "Now you need the Henderson brothers."

My mother's face brightened, her mind perhaps going to the same place mine had, straight to the guys who owned the local hardware store.

"We just need curtains that don't weigh a hundred pounds," he complained. "Would you hang an elephant up on the wall?"

"Why? Is that your next project?" my mother asked.

I snorted, and my father glared at us both.

"So, what's your question?" He shut his toolbox and sat in his chair, brushing the plaster off his hands. That, coupled with the dust from the curtains, made me sneeze.

Wiping my nose, I said, "Well, it's kind of wild." I took a seat on a footstool and explained the phone call from the lawyer. "I looked at the contract, and it's like, a year's salary for four months. I really think Grandma's the donor."

My father gave a slow nod. "I've been thinking the same thing. I don't know why she wouldn't tell us, though."

"Because we'd have opinions," my mother said. "I think at that age, you probably don't care much for opinions."

"I don't care much for opinions now. Must be in the blood." Turning to me, my father said, "Do you want to run the theater?"

Pulling a white shag pillow close, I said, "I loved being back there. I'm committed to the Tourism Council, though, and I don't know that I'm qualified."

"Sure, you are," my father said. "You've run huge businesses."

Before moving back, I'd managed several hospitality companies out of Indianapolis. The Tourism Council ran at a much slower pace, one that I'd enjoyed. But there was something about the theater that drew me in.

"I have to admit, I'm thinking about it," I said. "This is such an important project for the community, and I don't see how they're going to find someone else so quickly."

"Don't base it on that," my mother said. "Think about what you'd like to do."

One thing that was holding me back was what Benjamin Hamilton had said. I didn't want to let someone like him influence my decision, but he'd said that someone would get hurt if the theater continued. It was vague, he was drunk, but was there any truth to it? The theater was an important thing for our town, but I had a daughter. I couldn't put her at risk.

"I think the Tourism Council would be able to last a few months without you," my mother said. "You're doing such good work there, but I've heard you say before that there's not much to do, now that you have everything under control."

"Yeah." I thought for a minute. "The Tourism Council runs itself because I've got everything planned out months in advance. It wouldn't be hard for them to bring someone on to pick up the slack. This would be a big job. The contract said there will be times that I'll be needed seven days a week, but the hours are somewhat fluid. I think being a part of the theater would be an exciting thing but . . ."

"Sounds like you want to do it," my dad said.

The problem with it was that it would be starting over again. I needed stability, and I needed to give that to Kaia too. That said, she would be on the other side of the world this summer, so it wasn't as if stability was even a possibility at this point.

"The Starlight Cove Playhouse is important," I said slowly. "To the town and to our family. I want to help out, but the whole thing makes me nervous. There's a lot of heartache and history there. I don't want to mess it up."

"You couldn't mess anything up," my father said.

"Tell that to my marriage," I mumbled.

My parents exchanged glances.

My mother spoke first. "I don't want to speak unkindly of Jin—"

"I do," my father said.

"*But,*" my mother continued, "you seem to be putting a lot of the blame on yourself. It takes two, Lily."

"That's exactly my point," I said.

Even though I hadn't been the one to step outside of our marriage, something about me drove Jin to find someone else. We went from being the couple who bought matching pajamas to people who barely spoke at dinner. We'd waited to address our problems until it was much too late.

"It's in the past now," my mother said. "Don't let it play into your future."

We were quiet for a moment; then my father stretched and got to his feet.

"Sleep on it," he suggested. "Then, why don't you go pay a visit to your grandmother tomorrow. If she's the one behind all of this, maybe she can give you a piece of advice."

～

I arrived at Morning Lark shortly after the sun was up and found my grandmother out back near the garden, doing group yoga led by Cody Henderson. Spotting me, he beckoned me to join them. I shook my head and stood off to the side to watch.

My grandmother was at the very front of the crowd, decked out in a hot-pink leotard over a pair of sparkling black leggings. Her body was not lithe anymore, but she seemed to relish trying every move.

It was pretty clear that the older men in the back were not interested in yoga at all but in watching my grandmother. It was also clear that most of the older women were there to watch Cody. His bodybuilder's physique was made flexible, he'd once explained to me, through the study of yoga.

I settled in under a shaded tree to watch the show. The grass was still dry and scratched the backs of my legs. The news had reported another big fire the night before at an old shack in the woods. It happened near the area where the ski resort was going to be built, but nothing had been damaged.

"Let's finish with a bang," Cody called, and the group launched into sun salutations. He led them into the final pose and then a bow. "Drink water. Namaste."

My grandmother gave a pert bow to Cody and draped a towel over her shoulders like he did. Then, she strolled over to a table where the assisted-living facility had already set up a tray of water and beet juice.

Lifting the bug protector covering the tray, she selected two cups of beet juice and walked them over to me.

"The fountain of youth," she said, handing me a glass.

I wrinkled my nose. My grandmother could put back a bag of barbecue chips with the best of them, but she had a thing for beet juice. For years, she'd claimed it was the magical elixir that kept her young and beautiful.

"Cheers," I said, lifting my glass. She downed hers in one drink, and I dumped mine in the grass when she wasn't looking.

"Do you have a few minutes to talk?" I asked her.

"Well, hold on," she said. "If you don't make some small talk with this group, I'll hear about it for days."

Sure enough, the other yoga participants had swarmed the drink table, ready to chat. With the smell of freshly squeezed beets in the air, I worked through several different conversations: Arlo Majors, oatmeal cookies, and oddly, the evolution of modern art. My grandmother was talking and laughing with one man in particular, and when we finally headed back to her room, I asked about him.

"Oh, that's just William," she said, waving her hand. "He wants me to speak at his funeral because he knows I'll be really dramatic. He keeps trying to lock in a commitment."

"Speaking of dramatic," I said, "I dropped by because I need to know whether or not you are responsible for the revival of the theater."

My grandmother's face fell. "I thought you were bringing me some good gossip. What a letdown." She opened the door to her room, and we settled onto her couch. "Lily, I gave that theater up years ago, and in life, I never look back. Well, I do if there's an attractive man walking by, but that's the only exception. Why do you ask?"

I explained about the job offer. "I figured it was you heading it up because otherwise, I don't understand why they'd pick me."

My grandmother sniffed. "Truly, Lily, I try to keep my mouth shut but—"

"No, you don't," I said, laughing.

"Fine. That man you married really did a number on you. I don't think you understand what a striking, commanding woman you are. It's a shame because the one person who doesn't see it is you."

Apparently, I couldn't express a reasonable amount of hesitation or mindfulness about a major life change without my family turning it into a therapy session.

"I'm just saying that I've never run a theater before," I told her. "I'm not qualified in that field."

"Perhaps, but the interview process for a theater manager takes time. Sounds like they don't have that time." My grandmother pulled her hair out of its ponytail and shook it out like a teenager. "Darling, you're gifted at bringing people together. Organization. Motivation. The Tourism Council was a hot mess before you swept into town and cleaned it up. Choose the life you want, but I think you'd be wonderful at this."

The words touched me. "Thank you," I said. "I . . . I guess I have a lot to think about."

"I have a lot to think about too," she said. "Like, is it a.m. or p.m.? These things get confusing when you're old."

"Well, you're clearly young and in demand," I said. "Kaia is so excited to interview you for school."

My grandmother grinned. "How long do I get to talk about myself?"

I kissed the top of her head. Her hair smelled like roses. "You're wonderful. I'll get her over here tomorrow."

On my walk back out to the car, I thought about how people often talked about being born into something. Most of the time, people talked about being born into money or status, but I felt like I'd been born into a sense of possibility. My grandmother had taught me the importance of seeing the world as there for the taking. It was the one thing that kept me moving forward, the belief that I had it in me to do something great.

~

My father was out watering the grass when I got back home.

"Hey," he called, dropping the hose. "Come here, I want to show you something."

He led me to the garage. "What do you think?"

The garage smelled like sawdust and the faded scent of gasoline. I blinked in the dim light, unsure what I was looking at. Then, I noticed the small workstation he'd crafted for himself in the back. He'd hung up a tackboard complete with tools and had a power saw set up and ready for action, as well as a perfectly organized bin of every size screw, nail, or bolt you could imagine.

"It's a retired man's dream," I said. "Dad, this looks great."

"It's something I've always planned to do." He straightened the hammer and wiped some dust off the saw. "In my mind, it was bigger—a full woodworking shop—but when you get older, you realize things don't have to be perfect. You just have to do your best."

"So, what are you going to work on first?" I asked.

My father considered his collection like a tea reader studying loose leaves. "Crown molding."

"Nice." The living room could use it, but I wasn't aware my father knew how to install it. "Which room?"

"The whole house." He scoffed at my expression. "How hard can it be? I always told your mother I'd have the time to gild up the ole palace, and now's my chance. Rome wasn't built in a day."

"Excellent." It pained me to imagine my father installing small boards that could fall on top of our heads, but I didn't want to discourage him. "Sounds like it will keep you busy."

"What about you?" He rubbed his hands together. "I've been looking forward to hearing your decision about the theater all day."

I hesitated. "I'm going to do it."

His hand shot out for a high five. "Good for you! The show will go on. No matter what."

"Because I've got a great family by my side."

"Yeah, well." He pulled on a pair of safety goggles. "That and three dollars might buy you a can of worms."

Chapter Eight

It was easier to transition into the job at the Playhouse than I would have ever imagined. My colleagues at the Tourism Council echoed the sentiment that I was the only person in town that would be a good fit for the job.

"It will almost be like you're still working with us," Brad said, "because the Playhouse is going to be the most important part of tourism this summer."

I knew he was right, and I signed off on the paperwork that night. I had everything wrapped up by Wednesday and headed over to the theater Thursday morning, a little surprised at how simple it had been to make the change.

On the way there, I dropped a note in the mailbox:

> *Dear Mr. Hamilton,*
>
> *Over the weekend, I was offered a position as the theater manager. Ironic, considering I just told you I literally had nothing to do with the Playhouse. Well, now I do, and I wanted you to hear that from me first.*
>
> *I completely understand that the revival might bring up memories you'd rather not revisit, but I do wish you*

peace and comfort. If you'd ever like to see a show, please
do not hesitate to contact me.
  Sincerely,
  Lily Kimura

I sent the letter by mail, hesitating only an instant before dropping it in the box. I wanted to be up front with Benjamin Hamilton because I didn't want any trouble from him. At the same time, I wondered if I should leave well enough alone.

If he'd heard secondhand that I was heading up the theater, he would think that I'd lied to him. He'd scared me that night, and I didn't want to risk setting him off again. I still half wondered if he was responsible for the fire in the woods.

Either way, the letter was sent. Hopefully, it would have the desired effect, and I wouldn't hear from him again.

The lobby of the Playhouse smelled like new carpet and fresh-brewed coffee when I walked in. The sconces were low lit, the space was quiet, and I stood in silence for a moment, taking it all in. The stage manager and production manager rounded the corner. Spotting me, they broke into bright smiles.

"I'm so excited it's you!" Piper, the stage manager, bounded over and gave me a big hug. "You're going to be perfect for this."

Piper looked about twenty-two and fresh out of college, but I already appreciated her enthusiasm and confidence.

"I'm delighted you decided to join us," the production manager said. He was decked out in another argyle sweater and sipping on coffee. "You'll be great because you have no idea what you're getting into, and by the time you figure it out, the season will be over. Voilà!"

I laughed. "Thanks a lot."

"Do you have any questions?" Piper asked. "I mean, you must have a hundred, but anything we can help with?"

I thought for a moment. The night before, the former manager and I had spent two hours on a Zoom meeting. She walked me through every aspect of the job and gave her perspective on things that never would have occurred to me. The first show was only three weeks away, so things had to move fast.

"Nothing at the moment," I said. "Actually, yes. Which one is my office?"

Piper brightened. "I'll show you. Come with me."

The production manager headed back to work, and Piper led me through the main lobby and around the corner of the hall. There, she pushed open a heavy carved wooden door. The office was large and formal, with decorative rugs, expensive-looking leather furniture, and bookshelves painted a deep navy blue. Sweeping curtains were drawn back from large windows that overlooked the front lawn.

"I remember this room," I said, delighted. "It was my grandmother's office. She barely spent time in here, but I used to love it."

"Things really have come full circle," Piper said. Her mood turned somber, and she shut the door. "Listen, I have to talk to you. Can we sit?"

My shoulders tensed as I wondered if she planned to leave too. Renee had told me that Piper, although young, knew everything backward and forward, and could easily serve as second-in-command.

I took a seat in the chair across from the leather couch. "How can I help?"

Piper pulled out a folded piece of paper from her pocket. "We recently received an email that's disturbing. I thought you should know."

She slid the printout across the table, and I opened it up. Two lines, typed.

Belinda Hamilton is dead. Who's next?

The room suddenly felt a little too cold.

It had to be from Benjamin Hamilton. But at the same time . . . maybe not. It seemed like a pretty big risk to use his daughter's name. On the other hand, there was no proof the man was all that bright.

"What do you think?" she said.

"I don't know," I said slowly. "It could be someone expressing concern, or it could be a threat. Either way, it's weird."

"Yeah." She chewed on her lip. "The first one was worse."

"Can I see it?" I asked quickly, trying to keep my mind from skipping too far ahead.

"Renee deleted it from the junk folder without making a copy, so it's completely gone." Piper held up her hands, her bracelets shifting down her arms. "I know. But she didn't want to say anything because this theater is such a big deal to the town, and Arlo Majors is coming, so I think she wanted to wait and see if anything else happened."

"What did it say?" I asked.

"It was a photo of the front page of the paper when the theater first burned down. Here's the thing, though." Her cheeks flushed. "The date had been changed. To the date of our opening night."

My stomach dropped. "You're kidding."

The idea that the former manager of the Playhouse had almost swept this under the rug was unnerving.

"Piper, thank you for telling me this," I said. "It's incredibly important that you did. I'll set up a meeting with the police, and we'll let them decide the next steps. Can you please forward me all of the information connected with the account it was sent to? The police might be able to trace it."

"Absolutely." Piper adjusted the strap of her overalls and got to her feet. "I don't want anything to ruin this summer, you know? This is my first big job, and it means a lot to me."

"Everything will be fine," I told her.

Piper gave a brisk nod. "Let me know if you need anything."

I waited for the door to click shut and then took another look at the note. The words were stark, simple, and direct.

Who's next?

A chill ran through me.

Picking up my phone, I set my first official meeting of the day—with the police.

~

Dispatch sent one car, without its lights on. I spotted it out my office window and headed to the front door to meet the officer. There, I was surprised to see that it was Dean, Abby's older brother.

Back in high school, I'd had a huge crush on him—we all did. Of course, he never thought of me as anything other than his little sister's friend.

"Hey, Lily," he said, his dark eyes locking onto mine.

"Dean." I indicated his gear. "Did you come here to audition, or are you actually a cop?"

"Hard to tell. The police chief lets me drive the car with the little flashing lights, but it might be a trick. I keep waiting for him to take me in." Dean's voice had a richness to it that I remembered from so many years back. "How are you? Abby said you were in town now."

"Good." Then, because it was Dean, I said, "Well, I'm okay. I'm actually living with my parents at my grandmother's house. I can't decide if it's embarrassing or super family oriented."

Dean studied me for a moment. "If it makes you feel better, I still live out at the vineyard with that whole bossy crew."

"You mean, your family?" I said.

He shrugged. "Tomato, tomah-to."

"Did you really just say that?" I said, surprised. "I'm the only person I know who says that."

"I've always said that."

"Huh." I studied him. "Maybe it came from you."

Dean opened the front door and indicated I should go first.

"Thanks," I said as we headed inside.

If Dean was impressed or interested in the remodel, he didn't say anything. He'd always been a rebel in high school, rolling around on his motorcycle in a black leather jacket, so I doubted he was into the arts, but anything was possible.

In my office, I showed him the printout. Then, I described the other message, including the details about the date change. "I didn't see it—it was deleted from a junk mail folder, apparently, but its specificity is a little unnerving."

Dean frowned, studying the first one I'd given him. "We can get our technology guy on these. It's either going to be a quick answer, where the person involved didn't consider that their email could be traced. Or it's going to be a longer process, if the person who sent the email is more than aware of that reality and has covered their tracks."

"Do you think it's a real threat?" I asked.

Dean hesitated. "Hard to say." His dark eyes studied me; then he returned to the printout.

I would bet he could see a lot about a person in a quick look, and I wondered what he'd guessed about me.

"Regardless of what I think, I have a duty to treat this as something real," he said. "I won't recommend closing down the show or the theater at this point, but—"

I let out a sharp breath. "That's a possibility?"

"It's a fine line to walk, Lily. Some threats are credible, some aren't, but we can't ignore this. You know?"

"Yeah. But—"

The radio on his belt crackled, and he turned it down. "But what?"

It was so frustrating to step into the excitement of running the theater and, hours later, consider the idea that the whole thing could get canceled.

"Nothing," I said. "Safety comes first. That said, I'd also like to put all the necessary precautions into place so that shutting down is the last resort."

"You got it." Dean got to his feet. He seemed taller than I remembered, with broad shoulders that filled out his uniform. "I wouldn't suggest sharing this with anyone new. Instead, create a culture of caution. People can't enter the building without their key card. The doors can't be left open for any reason. If you see something, say something. Et cetera, et cetera."

I nodded. There had been a handful of people that had worked here for a few weeks, but it would make sense to put security measures into place since the cast was about to arrive. Arlo Majors was a movie star, after all, and several of the cast members were known on Broadway. It wouldn't set off alarm bells, and it would control who was in the building.

"You don't have cameras here, right?" Dean asked.

"No," I said.

"Order some," he said. "Get them set up at each entrance and exit. As long as the theater is secure, it won't seem so simple to someone like our email friend here to cause problems." He studied me again. "Good?"

"Yeah," I said. "I'm impressed, actually. I still remember the days you put frogs in Abby's bed."

"Toads." He thought for a minute. "A snake or two, but only for special occasions." With a grin, he headed for the door. "I'll be in touch. Let's start by trying to figure out who sent this."

"Wait," I said, pressing my hand against the back of the couch. "I need to tell you something, but I don't know the etiquette behind it all."

Dean squinted at me. "Etiquette?"

"Well, I mean, I don't want to accuse someone who might be innocent."

Quickly, I explained what had happened with Benjamin Hamilton.

Dean frowned. "Well, using my best etiquette, I think I know who to have a chat with first."

～

Once he'd left, I shut the door to my office so I could take a moment with my thoughts. I was relieved that he hadn't seemed too alarmed but still planned to investigate the threats. Hopefully, it was just someone causing trouble and nothing serious.

I would definitely put the security measures into place, but I refused to waste time worrying about it. There were countless pieces to pick up and rehearsals to run. On top of that, I had to make sure all the details were in place for the performers that were coming in, including flights, lodging, and any last-minute changes. Not to mention getting up to speed on publicity, ticket sales, set construction, costumes, and payroll, and the list went on. There were so many moving parts that there was little point in focusing on the things that didn't matter, like the fact that someone out there didn't want the Starlight Cove Playhouse back in business.

～

That night, my parents went to a fish fry together, so Kaia and I made a spaghetti dinner and sat out on the back porch.

It was the perfect evening, with a perfect blue sky. The water in the distance was beautiful. I stared out at the lake, determined to talk with Kaia about her upcoming trip.

"Are you excited about Japan?" I asked. "It's not too far off."

Kaia had her tongue between her lips, fully concentrating on sprinkling parmesan cheese over every inch of her spaghetti and salad. She didn't look up until she was finished. "Yes."

I waited for her to say more, and when she didn't, I took a bite. The spaghetti had smelled delicious, full of roasted garlic, but I could barely taste it.

"Listen, you are not obligated to stay there," I said. "If it's not fun, or you feel uncomfortable, or . . ."

"Mom." Kaia gave a little laugh. Reaching for the garlic bread, she said, "It's definitely going to be fun. Dad keeps emailing me all these things that we're going to do, links to different parks and activities and restaurants."

"Really?" I said.

I don't know why it surprised me that he'd made the effort.

"Yes." Kaia twirled some spaghetti on her fork. "I'm excited to finally eat some real Japanese food."

"You've had it before," I said, thinking of some of the small restaurants we'd found with Jin. There had been a few that he had declared even more authentic than the ones in Japan.

I'd always wanted to visit Japan together as a family. We didn't do it at first because Kaia was too young, then his mother was too sick, and then it was too hard to travel . . . the list went on. I couldn't believe the first time Kaia and Jin would be together in his home country would be without me. There were a million reasons that this trip had me upset, but that was definitely one of them.

"What's wrong?" Kaia asked, studying me. "You're not eating."

"I was thinking." I picked up the fork and took another bite. "I'll miss you. There's no secret about that."

"Mom." She rolled her eyes. "I'm not leaving anytime soon."

"Time flies," I said. "You'll be a grown-up before we even know it."

"What's it like?" she asked, taking a drink of milk.

"Japan?" I asked. "I don't know, I've never been."

"Being a grown-up."

The question made me laugh only because I knew what she was thinking. That it was something exciting, where you got to make your own choices instead of letting someone make them for you. That wasn't always the reality, though. There were times that life made choices for you, and you had to make the best of it.

"Being a grown-up is fine," I said. "You can stay up late if you want, eat as much ice cream as you want, but . . ."

Kaia nodded. "But what?"

"Trust me, being a kid is the better deal."

"How come?" she asked.

What was I supposed to say, that being a grown-up was hard because you had to take care of yourself? Clean the house, do the laundry, make money? Those things were true, but really, it came down to the fact that every choice came with a consequence, and the wrong choice could set you back years.

Not that marrying Jin had been that bad of a choice, considering I'd ended up with Kaia. But the fact that we'd fallen apart made it harder for me to move forward with an open heart. To trust that the decisions I made would lead to good things.

"Being a kid is more fun because there's always time," I finally said. "To learn, grow, and to make mistakes."

"Grown-ups do those things too," she said, finishing the last piece of garlic bread. "Look at Grandpa. He's made like, fifty thousand mistakes trying to fix up the house, and he keeps going for it."

"Then, maybe that's the secret," I said, smiling at her. "We just have to keep going for it, no matter what age we are." Kaia had finished her dinner, so I said, "Ready for a cannoli?"

"Yes!" Kaia hopped up, gathering up the plates, and took everything inside to the dishwasher.

I set the cannoli onto the fancy dessert plates Kaia liked, then made hot cocoa for her and a decaf coffee for me. Since it had started to get chilly out, we snuggled up on the couch together to watch a quick show before bed.

I looked over at my daughter, her eyes intent on the screen while she laughed with a mouth full of chocolate. I was so grateful I had this time. The heartbreak of the past two years had been hard to handle, but in moments like these, it didn't seem to matter at all.

Chapter Nine

The next morning, I arrived at the theater eager to start the day but feeling a little nervous about whether or not another threatening email would be waiting. There was nothing in my email or in the main inbox, but that didn't mean one wouldn't show up. I wanted to know if Dean had talked to Benjamin Hamilton, or if he had any news about who'd sent it, but he probably wouldn't reach out until he knew something.

I got to work and didn't look up until my first meeting of the day, which was with Piper. She walked in carrying two steaming mugs of mint tea and set one on my desk.

"Those are pretty," she said, pointing at a bouquet of lilacs.

My grandmother had sent them late yesterday afternoon with a card that read *Lily, I have never been more proud.* Her words had stayed with me, the sentiment as sweet as the flower's perfume.

"Thank you," I said. "No emails today, so we're in good shape with that for now. I wanted to talk with you about the ensemble members. They're coming next weekend, right?"

Piper nodded, settling into the chair across my desk. She wore another pair of overalls, this time stonewashed, with her white T-shirt.

"Yes. They're all part of the Equity Membership Candidate Program, working to earn credit to join Equity. You know what that is, right?"

"The union for stage actors," I said.

"You got it." Piper gave a vigorous nod. "So, once that whole crew gets here, they'll be at the theater every single day, to help out both onstage and backstage. There are tons of rules, so familiarize yourself with them, but production will manage that group. Then, there's the shows to consider. We're only a few weeks away from putting up *Chicago*, but right when we get ready to open, we'll start rehearsing the next one. Each show will run two weeks."

It sounded like a grind to me, but my grandmother had always relished the back-to-back feel of summer stock.

"Arlo is perfect for *Chicago*," I said, thinking about his general charm as well as how striking he looked in a suit. "People will love seeing him play that role."

Piper nodded. "The most complicated part is the dance numbers, but the choreographer's pretty brilliant."

She ran me through the rest of the details, and I shook my head, impressed.

"Did you go to school for this?" I asked. "You're so on top of it."

Jade, the costume designer, appeared in my office door. "Piper is one of the most talented stage managers I've ever seen," she said, striding into the room. "Her future will be paved with gold."

"I literally just died." Piper put her hand over her heart and rushed out of the room.

Jade laughed. "Welcome to the theater," she told me. "Where absolutely everything is a performance." She settled into the couch and drew a knee up to her chest. Her skin seemed to shimmer in the afternoon light, but she didn't seem to have on a touch of makeup, in spite of the laugh lines around her eyes.

"How's your first week going?" she asked.

"Honestly, I feel like *I'm* in a performance," I said, gesturing at my new office. "I feel like I'm on set, playing the role of someone who's just trying to keep up."

"Yes." She gave a little stretch. "I know that feeling."

"How are you doing with all of this?" I asked her. "I know that you came here expecting things to be a certain way, and now, here I am. I do want to make it clear that I have no intention of trying to run the show. We have directors for that."

Jade waved a finger at me. "Be careful talking to theater people like that. Every single one of us secretly wants to run the show. If you say that you don't plan to, we'll trip each other trying to take over. Except for me. I have no plans to do much of anything this summer, other than enjoy the freedom to make costumes with no pressure, however I please."

"That's exactly what I want you to do."

She smiled at me. "You know, I used to work with your grandmother here. Things ended in a pretty awful way. One day we were having the summer of our lives, and the next . . ." A shadow crossed her face. "So, there's nowhere to go but up."

I nodded, wondering if Jade had been close with Belinda Hamilton. Probably not, since Belinda had been in her early twenties, and Jade had been nearly my age back then. Still, it would have been a hard thing to go through.

"I'm here to help in any way possible," I said. "It's an honor to have you here."

"You're too kind." Jade got to her feet. "We've met," she said suddenly. "Did you know that? You used to sit in that little windowsill by the stairs all the time, reading. You were what, fifteen or so that summer, right?"

My heart caught as I thought back. Reading in the windowsill had been one of my favorite pastimes.

"Yes," I said. "I can't believe you remember that, but it was me."

"It's still you," she said, resting her hand on the door. "The past is a part of who we are. Ghosts are everywhere. It seems like they're always coming back around, doesn't it?"

Her words came back to me later that evening, when I was wrapping up the day. The window was cracked, and the earthy smell of the woods drifted in on the lake breeze. It hit me, where I was and what I was doing. Even though I'd left Starlight Cove to build an entirely new life, somehow, I'd ended up right back where I'd started.

Like the production manager had said my first day, I had no idea what I was getting into, but I did know this: if someone had told the young woman sitting in the windowsill that one day she'd be in this office, running the theater, she would have been so shocked she would have dropped her book.

~

I'd managed to push the incident with the threatening emails to the back of my mind until the following Monday, when I received a phone call from Dean.

"Hey." He didn't bother to say who was calling, just launched right into it all. "The emails are untraceable. So, that means we're dealing with someone intelligent, which is not ideal."

I'd been about to pull out of the driveway but instead idled at the edge of the road. "Not ideal because . . ."

"They bothered to cover their tracks." His tone was dark. "Which means this could be serious. Do you have the cameras set up yet?"

"Yes," I said, grateful to our tech guy. He'd managed to hang them up and sync them to the network without a problem. "They're obvious to anyone looking, and they record movement."

"Keep me posted on anyone who tries to enter the theater without a key card," he said. "For now, we'll just wait for the next email and go from there."

The fact that he was so certain there would be another note was discouraging, but I nodded. Then, realizing he couldn't see me, I said, "Sounds good. Thanks, Dean."

He hung up.

The forest across the street seemed darker than usual, and I stared out at the trees for a moment. My skin prickled with the sudden thought that someone was watching me, but quickly, I pushed the fear aside. The sun was shining, the vanilla creamer in my coffee lingered on my tongue, and there was no reason to be paranoid. Still, I glanced in the mirror as I pulled out, half convinced I'd seen a dark figure standing somewhere in the shadows.

Chapter Ten

"Arlo will get here tomorrow," Piper mused, studying her schedule sheet.

We were at the morning meeting, discussing the arrival of the per-formers, as well as their lodging and rehearsal schedules. My first full week had gone by fast, and it was hard to believe that everything was about to kick into high gear.

"I can't wait to work with Arlo Majors." Sebastian, the director, flipped through his binder with gusto. It was filled with detailed notes about each production. "He's going to be an exceptional Billy Flynn."

"I think so too," Piper agreed, pulling out some paperwork. She studied it for a moment. "It says here that he's flying private. We'll have a car there, per his agent's request, but someone should greet him at the airport. Lily?"

My palms started to sweat, but I nodded. "Yes, sounds good."

"Great." She crossed it off her list and passed me the paper with his flight information and the details about the car service. "The driver can meet you here at the theater, or you can drive separately to the airport, but you'll have to ride back with him."

Even though the idea of making small talk with Arlo Majors in the back of a town car sent me into a mini panic attack, I gave a game nod. "Sounds good."

The last item on the agenda was also for me.

"We need to run open auditions for a few of the smaller parts," Piper said. "Let's put something in the paper and online for about . . . five ensemble parts?"

Sebastian nodded. "Yes."

"I can do that." I chewed on the eraser of my pencil. "Should they prepare something to read?"

"I'll put two short speeches up on the website," Piper said, adding it to her list. "Comedy and/or drama. We'll also have everyone sing a line from 'Happy Birthday.'"

Sebastian smoothed his neck scarf. "Lily, you're from here. Do you think anyone will show up?"

I laughed. "This is a pretty small town, and everyone knows that Arlo Majors is in the show." I could already imagine some of the people who might come, like the young pharmacist who secretly read gossip magazines in between filling prescriptions. "You're going to have a line out the door."

Sebastian gave a world-weary sigh. "I'll be sure to drown my coffee in vodka that day."

"How is that different from any other day?" the set designer asked, and everyone laughed.

I'd just made it back to my office when my cell rang. The call was international, so it had to be Jin.

"How are you?" I said.

It was hard to be cordial when I spoke to the man who had destroyed my family, but I did my best.

"Hi, Lily," he said. "Do you have a minute to talk?"

The sound of his voice—the deepness, the vague shortening of certain letters, and the cadence—was like stumbling across a song I'd once loved but hadn't heard in a while.

"Sure." I kept my voice bright. "Give me a second."

I shut the office door. Then, because I'd already learned that someone was always popping by with a question or anecdote, I locked it. The theater people were like little kids. If they knew I was on the phone, they'd demand attention, which at the moment, I was not equipped to give.

Sliding down against the door, I breathed in the sweet scent of the lilacs from the bouquet my grandmother had sent. "What's up?"

No doubt he wanted to go over details about Kaia's flight, as well as their plans while she was there.

His voice was tight. "Are you alone?"

If the lock held, yes.

"I am," I said.

"Good. I'm calling about Norah." The name of the woman who'd broken up our marriage felt as sour and dissonant as always. "She's received a substantial research grant to study the underwater caves. It's captivating work that she's doing, centered around limestone and—"

"I'm at work," I said. "Can we get to the purpose of your call?"

I didn't want to be rude, but I also didn't want to hear that Norah was great. One of the things I couldn't stand was how she continued to impress Jin in a way that I never had and probably never could. Not even being the mother to his daughter had made a difference.

"Well," he said, "it turns out the timing of this opportunity is all wrong. It's a six-month grant."

There was a knock at the door. "Lily?" It sounded like the production manager. The handle rattled, and I felt grateful I'd locked it. I got up as quietly as possible and moved next to the window.

"You still there?" Jin asked.

"Yes. Like I said, I'm at work." I kept my voice low. "So, what were you saying?"

"It's an impressive grant," Jin said. "Huge. She begins gathering data in two weeks. We're headed to the site tomorrow to search for lodging."

Realization began to dawn. "Two weeks?"

That's when Kaia was leaving.

"What are you asking me, Jin? To sign off on sending Kaia to who knows where? I don't know if I can do that."

Silence.

"Wait." Ice settled in my stomach. "You don't want her to come at all, do you?"

More knocking at the door. "Lily?" It was Piper this time. "You in there?"

"It's not that I don't want her to come," Jin said, in that same tone he'd used to convince me that Norah was just a friend. "The timing is terrible, though. I was thinking we could reschedule for—"

"Why do you have to be there at all?" I said. "Norah can go, and you can be with your daughter."

"Lily, look." Jin sounded tired. "It's just not going to work out. I've looked at it fifteen different ways, and I can't take Lily for the summer."

"Jin, that's going to crush her."

He hesitated. "Do you think so? I don't want to upset her but—"

"But what? You're her father. She hasn't seen you in six months."

There was a pause. Then, quietly, he said, "Do you know what I was thinking about the other day? That time she got into your makeup. It was all over her face. She looked like a mural."

In spite of myself, I laughed. "I loved that you told her she looked beautiful."

"You did too," Jin said.

For a split second, I thought he was saying I'd looked beautiful, but then I understood what he meant. The exchange made my heart hurt.

"We're good parents, Lily," he said. "In the end, I think she'll realize that."

"Well, there's quite a long time until the end."

"This grant is such a big deal. There are only a few times in life where the opportunity comes up to be a part of something important. How often do we get to fly close to the sun?"

In the beginning of our relationship, I had fallen in love with Jin's passion. Time had taught me that his outlook was not actually passion but immaturity. He didn't dwell too much on who he hurt, as long as he got what he wanted.

"Do your thing," I said. "I'll let Kaia know."

"You don't want me to tell her?" he asked.

"I think she'd take it better coming from me," I said.

"Thank you." He hesitated. "It feels like she's growing so fast. Do you ever feel like that?"

"Yes," I said quietly. "I was thinking about that the other day."

Our silence brought to mind the way he and I used to stay in bed on Sunday afternoons, reading. Often, Jin would take my hand, and we'd hold tight until one of us had to turn the page.

"Well," he said, now. "We'll figure out a time—maybe Christmas?—when she can fly over."

The audacity made me laugh out loud.

"I won't give you Christmas," I told him. "So, you'll have to figure something else out."

"Why? You'll have her all summer."

"Because it's Christmas," I said. "Before you leave on your trip, please send Kaia a handwritten note telling her how badly you'll miss her this summer, and how you are counting the seconds until next year or the next time you can get over here. This is the only time I'm going to let you cancel on her. If you do it again, I'll file for full custody, because I can't let you hurt her like this again."

"That's fair." His voice was somber. "Thanks for watching out for her, Lily. You're a trooper."

I pressed my lips together and hung up.

Seconds later, there was another knock at the door.

"Lily? Why is this locked?" It was definitely the production manager, and he sounded panicked. "I really need to talk to you!"

My beautiful daughter.

My eyes filled with tears, but quickly, I blinked them away.

Striding across the room, I threw open the door. "Yes. How can I help?"

He gave a petulant glance around the office, as though expecting to find someone there. Satisfied, he said, "You really need to talk to Jade. She is completely hogging the fridge."

I stared at him. "That's why you've been banging on my door?"

"You didn't answer. I didn't know where you were."

I sighed. "Let's go figure it out."

Kaia will be with me all summer. She won't fly to Japan alone.

The realization wrapped around me like a warm blanket. Maybe I was just as bad as Jin, because as much as this would hurt her, I couldn't fight the relief I felt that I would have my daughter home.

Chapter Eleven

I decided to take my lunch break and gather my thoughts in the part of the theater few people knew about, the bar off the lobby. It was slated to be stocked and deep cleaned two days before opening night, so it was still an untouched space, one where I could get my emotions under control.

It was also one of the most striking rooms we had. Deep-burgundy leather booths circled smooth metallic tables, each holding a small lamp in the center. At one time, cigar smoke had lingered overhead like clouds.

As the heavy wooden door shut behind me, I let out a deep breath and sank against the wall.

"Can't a person get a moment of peace around here?" a voice drawled.

The yellow light of a lamp flickered on, and my heart nearly leapt out of my body. Arlo Majors sat in the back corner, a cup of coffee in hand. He wore a soft-looking navy sweatshirt and had a script in front of him and a pencil behind his ear.

"You're . . . you're not supposed to be here." I was embarrassed to stumble over my words. "The paperwork said you weren't coming until tomorrow."

His blue eyes studied me over a pair of tortoiseshell reading glasses. "It will always be wrong. It's easier that way."

"Easier?" I echoed.

My mind kept wondering if his sweatshirt was as cozy as it looked, which was something I did not need to be thinking about.

"The wrong information keeps people confused," he said. "They don't need to know where to find me. I don't always want to be found."

Giving an awkward thumbs-up, I backed toward the door.

"I don't mean right now." He gave me that playful grin. "Grab some coffee. Have a seat."

I glanced at the bar where he'd set up a coffeepot. I rinsed out an old glass mug I found on one of the shelves and poured a cup, hesitating at the protein shake nearby.

"That's the creamer," he said. "Take it or leave it."

I took it, mainly because I was curious about what a movie star would put in his body. Other than doughnuts, of course. It made the coffee surprisingly smooth, while adding a hint of chocolate and vanilla.

Being so close to Arlo Majors made me nervous. I'd come here to plan my conversation with Kaia, but now, I found it hard to think at all. He was so good looking that it was nearly impossible to figure out what about him made him that way.

His eyes.

They had a hooded, dreamy quality and seemed to work in tandem with the slight upturn of his lips.

"How did you get in?" I said suddenly. "You can't get into the building without a key fob."

He grinned. "They probably thought I looked like Arlo Majors."

I took a sip of coffee, not sure what to say next.

"So, I'm struggling with this scene," he said, shuffling the papers on the table in front of him.

I looked at them. The pages were from the third play of the season. The majority of the shows we were doing were big, splashy musicals, but Arlo had insisted on having at least one drama on the books.

"Why are you struggling with it?" I asked, finally feeling brave enough to take a seat at the table.

Arlo ran his hands through his hair, and his subtle curls somehow remained perfect. "Every scene in good art is supposed to be played out of love, right? But I can't find the love here. The rage, yeah. It's his chance to tell his sister every rotten thing she's ever done that's stopped him from meeting his potential. He destroys her here, breaks her heart." He made a face. "Where's the love in that?"

"No clue," I said. "I'm not an actor."

"You're a human being, though. You've laughed, cried, loved, and been hurt. The people on these pages are you." He tapped the words with fury. "They're *me*."

"Can I see?" I asked.

Arlo handed over the script.

"It seems like . . ."

He leaned forward. "Say it."

My nerves got the best of me. "I don't know."

I'd read the play. I'd skimmed all six productions the day I accepted the job. But even though my grandmother had talked motivation at the dinner table since the day I was born, I had no idea how to help him.

"Tell me what you thought," he pressed. "It doesn't have to be complicated. What's he trying to do?"

"It seems like he's trying to apologize."

"How?" Arlo demanded. "He's shouting at her."

"Right, but . . ." I took a sip of coffee, the protein shake sweet on my tongue. "I think he's mad at himself, not her. He's blaming his sister because he hasn't met his potential, but you can't blame another person for that. That's the lie he's told his whole life—that it's her fault—and I think he's sorry. He says the most awful things to her, but I think they come from a place of regret."

"It kills him they can't get along."

"Yes," I said.

"He's too weak to push past their problems . . ."

"He wishes so badly that he could . . ."

"So he's thinking, *I'm sorry, but I have to take this all the way. I have to make you hate me to exonerate you, so that you can let me go.*" Arlo took off his glasses. "That's it. That. Is. It." Then, he scrambled out of the booth, grabbed me by the hand, and scooped me up into a spinning hug. "Do you know how long I've been trying to crack open that scene?"

His exuberance was so genuine that it made me laugh.

"Put me down," I said, swatting at him, even though that was the last thing I wanted. The scent of that incredible cologne made it hard to think of anything but staying in his arms.

"I have been trying to pull that scene apart for days," he said, letting me slide to the ground. "Sometimes, you just need a fresh perspective."

He flopped back down in the booth, beaming at me.

I took my seat again, the leather seats firm. If sense memory was real, then I remembered sitting in these booths as a teenager, watching my grandmother hold court in her jewels and sparkling dresses.

Arlo read the scene again. "That makes perfect sense. I can't believe I didn't see it." He sat for a moment, studying me. "Have you ever felt that way? Like you're lying to make someone feel better?"

I hesitated. "I don't know."

He took a sip of coffee. "Sure you do."

The room was dim other than the lamp. It felt strange sitting across from someone I barely knew but whose face was so familiar. It felt even stranger to think that he wanted to deep dive into this type of conversation.

"Yes," I admitted. "I have to lie to my daughter later today. I actually came in here so I could plan what to say."

"Why do you have to lie to her?" he asked.

"Her father backed out of their summer together," I said. "She was supposed to leave in two weeks."

Arlo winced. "Ouch."

"Yeah." I fiddled with the coffee cup, thinking about how relieved Jin sounded when I agreed to keep her home. "I'm the one who is going to have to tell her because I'll be careful with her heart. If I cover for him too much, though, I'm afraid she'll believe that he's something great and that I'm . . ."

"The problem." Arlo nodded. "My mother did the same song and dance for me. My dad got to be this mysterious, absent, heroic figure while my mother, who raised me, got blamed for every problem because she was there. It was only when I was older that I realized the sacrifices she made. Emotionally, you know?"

I rested my chin on my hand. "Would you have wanted to hear the truth? Instead of the song and dance?"

"No." Arlo chewed on his lip. "I could handle the truth in my twenties. I could look at different sides of it and try to understand my father. But back then? It would have devastated me. My mother let me feel loved and important during the time it mattered most. You're doing the right thing."

The words hovered overhead, just out of reach of my heart.

"I don't know how this turned so heavy," I said, getting to my feet. "Sorry. I—"

"Life is heavy." Arlo shrugged. "We can carry each other."

I blinked, at a complete loss for words. Heading for the door, I fought back the emotion that threatened to pull me under.

Outside, I leaned against the wall in the lobby. Piper rounded the corner. Spotting me, she raced over. "Hi! We need you to take a look at the dimensions of the set for the townspeople's chorus."

"Sounds good." Quickly, I wiped my nose. "Lead the way."

Linking her arm in mine, Piper led me to the back of the Playhouse where the sets were built. On the way, she updated me on some issues the lighting crew had with a particular brand of colored gels.

I did my best to listen, but in truth, my mind was on my daughter and what I would need to do to help carry her through.

Chapter Twelve

My mother was plugging in the air fryer when I walked into the kitchen, still mentally rehearsing what to say to Kaia. There was a cutting board full of sliced zucchini, mushrooms, and onions.

"You've been busy," I said.

I tried my best to sound normal. I couldn't tell her a thing about what had happened with Jin before I discussed it with Kaia. "This all looks really good."

"Thanks." She tucked a loose piece of hair behind her ear, then got to work dicing a red pepper.

"Is Kaia upstairs?" I asked, and she nodded.

I headed up, hoping Kaia wasn't in the middle of her video game. Of course, she was, looking cute as ever with her dark hair pulled back in two braids. It dawned on me that I would actually have to set screen time limits, since she would be home for the summer after all. The thought that she would be here filled me with a sense of relief, especially after spending the last two months worrying about her leaving.

"Wrap up the game," I said. "I need to talk to you."

Kaia didn't look up, but by the set of her mouth, I knew she'd heard.

"Five minutes," I said, and she waved me away.

This was not off to a great start. I spent the time folding and rehanging the jeans and colorful striped sweaters she'd tossed around the room, and then indicated that it was time.

"Come sit up here on the bed with me," I said.

Kaia pushed back her braids and joined me with a questioning look. I decided to get right to it.

"Honey, there's a problem with the trip to Japan," I said. "We have to postpone it."

Her expression froze. "Why?"

"Because Norah got this big grant that will put them in a remote area during the time you're supposed to be there," I said. "You'd be bored, uncomfortable, and we all decided it was not a good fit for your first trip there."

It made me cringe to include myself in the decision, but I could have fought it—insisted that he take her. I didn't do that for my own selfish reasons.

"When am I going to see Dad?" she asked, pulling her knees to her chest.

"He's going to figure out a time," I said. "He was really upset. I think he started to cry on the phone."

"He did?" She gave a little laugh. "He cried?"

"It sure sounded like it." I shifted on the bed, tucking my legs under me. "Kaia, your father loves you and misses you so much. This has been really hard on him, to be away from you. I imagine it's been hard on you too."

She gave a vigorous nod and hugged a pillow close. Her legs were longer, and her arms all elbows. She must have had another growth spurt that I'd somehow missed.

"It's okay to be disappointed," I said. "I'm really sorry."

"Yeah." She fidgeted, moving her collection of silver rings up and down.

I reached out and smoothed her hair. "The one thing I'm not sorry about, though, is that I get to spend the summer with you."

Her face brightened. "You're not going to work?"

"I . . ." I swallowed hard. "I have to go to work, but we'll still see each other all the time. You won't be on the other side of the world."

Kaia nodded. Then, she gave a pointed look at the chair where she liked to play her video game.

"Do you need to talk more?" I asked.

"No." She considered me, her dark eyes clear. "I didn't really want to go to Japan."

"You didn't?" The news surprised me. "You wanted to see your father, though, right?"

Even though I was furious at Jin for so many things, I wanted Kaia to have a good relationship with him.

"Of course."

"Good." I nodded. "We'll figure out another time. Speaking of, do you want to do anything special with me tomorrow?"

It would be Saturday. I had to get some work done at the theater for a few hours, but then, I'd be free.

"I'm going to that track meet," she said. "Downstate."

"Oh, that's right." I hesitated. "Should I be there?"

She shook her head. "Parents can't go on the bus."

"I could drive down," I suggested.

"You don't really need to be there," she said. "I'll be with my friends."

I would have liked to watch her meet—I'd always loved watching her run—but it gave me a sense of relief that she'd started to develop a group of friends that she wanted to spend time with.

Kaia's game lit up, and she practically leapt off the bed to get to it. She held it up, and I nodded.

"Thirty minutes," I said, setting the timer on my phone. "Then you really need to go find something to do."

I walked out of the room feeling unsure that I'd handled the conversation correctly, but life didn't come with a script. I didn't know if Kaia was hiding her true feelings, but a trip across the world would have been a lot to take on at that age. I hoped that she felt relieved.

I knew that I did.

~

The next morning, I was about to head into work for a few hours when I noticed that my mother was awake but still in bed.

Rapping on her door, I said, "Hey, are you sick?"

She rolled over and peered at me. "Just resting."

We looked at each other for a minute. The room smelled stale, like it needed some fresh air.

"So, what's on the schedule for today?" I asked. "More adventures with the air fryer?"

My mother draped her wrist across her forehead, as if the idea of planning the day was too much to take on. "Oh, I don't know. I'm just going to take it slow."

It would have been fine if this was the first morning that my mother had stayed in bed. Or even the second. But this was the third time in two weeks that I'd seen her plan to lie around all day, doing nothing.

"That's it, get up." I switched on the lights and opened the window, letting in the fresh air and the bright light of the morning. "Go take a shower."

"What on earth are you doing?" My mother pulled the bedsheets close, looking horrified.

"I'm not going to let you sit around this house feeling bored every day," I insisted. "You need to get up and do something."

My mother grabbed her brush from the bedside table and began furiously brushing her hair. "I think I deserve a rest after so many years of working hard!"

"I agree," I said, softening my tone. "You worked incredibly hard. It's also a very real thing that when people stop working, if they don't have a plan, they can start to feel depressed."

"I was just laughing at dinner with your father last night."

"Feeling depressed doesn't always mean that you don't laugh, Mom," I said. "It might feel like a lack of motivation, a lack of desire to do anything. Without a schedule, it might feel harder to get things done. Do you feel like that?"

"Sometimes." Her voice was small. "I do question where the day went, and I haven't done much of anything other than read a little bit of a book and maybe heat up a piece of cherry pie." Her face fell. "That does sound rather pathetic, doesn't it?"

"No," I said quickly. "It just sounds like you need to take action. At the shop, there were certain things you had to do every single day—you even had a schedule on Sunday."

My mother brightened. "We still do. Tomorrow, we'll go to church, have a family meal, and get some reading done. Then, we catch up on our shows."

"See?" I said. "Sunday's a fun day because you've planned it out. You just need to manage the other six days. If you want to take naps and eat pie, fine. Put it on the schedule. But I also want you to get moving on those interests you were talking about. Plan an activity every day."

She settled back down into her pillow. "Lily, I understand everything that you're saying, but really, I'm fine with how things are."

My mother was far from fine. She'd always enjoyed being on the go. Now, she was holding back, waiting on my father, but he was already off doing his own thing.

"I'm sorry if I'm overstepping," I said. "I'll give you one week to relax and enjoy your vacation. Then, I expect to see you have a plan in place because you aren't just going to loaf around this house for the rest of your life."

My mother's mouth dropped open. "That's not your decision."

"Mom, your happiness is something I'm willing to fight for," I told her. "You have one week."

The wind was blowing when I left the house, and I pulled my cardigan close. I really hoped I wasn't pushing her too hard.

Maybe my mother did just want to lie around for the rest of her life, but based on the woman I'd always known, I doubted that was the case.

Chapter Thirteen

The morning flew by. There were production meetings, onboarding for the actors that had just arrived in town, and debates about whether to add a matinee to the schedule, as the majority of the shows were sold out. It was in the contract that two performances may be required on Sunday, but I knew we shouldn't schedule that without talking to Arlo first.

"He's on the schedule this morning at ten," the production manager said. "Piper, can you send him to Lily when he arrives?"

She noted it on her clipboard. "Sure thing."

Piper linked her arm in mine when we walked out of the meeting. "Don't be nervous when you talk to him. Just remember, he's a human being too."

"Thanks," I said, wondering what she'd say if I told her I'd actually had a real conversation with him the day before, and that he'd picked me up and spun me around.

"Do you also mind giving a visit to Jade to talk about the costumes for the third show?" Piper asked. "She had some questions."

"Sure," I said.

I had meant to set up a meeting again to touch base with Jade, but things had been so busy that I hadn't gotten to it yet. I wanted to get to know her, though. She seemed a little guarded, and whenever I tried to talk about anything other than surface topics, she made an excuse to go get coffee, look for a new piece of fabric, or simply exit the conversation.

Arlo Majors, on the other hand, seemed to live for deep conversation. I was curious to see if our discussion from the day before would carry over or if it would pass by, like it had never happened at all.

I headed into my office with that on my mind and instantly came to a stop. A yellow Post-it Note that I'd attached to the phone on my desk was in the process of gliding to the ground, and I could have sworn someone had darted across the room. Quickly, I flipped on the lights, but no one was there.

What in the world?

"Hello?" I said cautiously.

My eyes flew to the window. It was closed, and the vent for the air-conditioning was on the opposite side of the room, so I couldn't figure out what had made the paper move.

Taking a step backward, I kept my eyes on my office and called Piper. She worked from the meeting room, which was right around the corner.

"Come here for a sec," I said, sounding much braver than I felt.

Piper rounded the corner and came to a stop. "You look like you just saw a ghost."

"I think I—"

Piper gave me an expectant look. "You did see a ghost?"

Even though I had intended to share my skin-prickling moment of panic, I came to my senses. Piper seemed like a kind, responsible person, but the odds were good she had expectations that her boss would act like a grown-up. Telling her that I thought I saw someone who wasn't there wouldn't exactly give her that vote of confidence.

"No, I forgot to show you the casting call I put in the paper," I said, pulling back my drapes and then looking behind the couches.

It was a relief that no one was there, but also, it was odd, given the Post-it Note on the ground. Timing was everything, though. Maybe it had just stopped sticking, right on time to freak me out.

"Yes, it looked great," she said, adjusting her glasses. "We should have a nice turnout."

"Perfect," I said, taking a seat at my desk. "Well, sorry to bother you. I just wanted to check in before I got into a bunch of meetings."

"No worries," she said. "Let me know if you need anything else."

The moment she was gone, I did one last sweep of my office to be sure. Nothing. Shaking my head, I picked up the rogue Post-it Note, wadded it up, and threw it in the garbage.

❦

Arlo Majors sauntered in for his meeting with me twenty minutes later. I had just run the ticket sales and had coffee brewing.

"It's real creamer," I said, standing up to greet him. "I didn't have a protein shake."

"Smells great."

Today, Arlo wore a button-up black shirt that made him look more formal and his hair darker, almost brown. His movements were deliberate, like a panther scoping out a new space. It was as if he took in the whole room before making a decision where he wanted to go. Straight to the couch, no coffee.

"Would you like a cup?" I asked, wondering if he expected me to serve him.

"What?" he glanced at me. "No, thank you."

I sat down in one of the leather chairs. Even though I wanted to claim that connection we'd made the day before, his mind seemed elsewhere, so I got right to it.

"So, production wanted me to talk to you about—"

"Can I say one thing?" Arlo interrupted.

His hands were clasped, and he leaned forward, watching me.

"Sure," I said.

"I was thinking about what you said about your daughter yesterday," he said. "Now, to see you here, running things, it's impressive. You're this mother with a huge heart, but you're also keeping this whole place in line. It's impressive. I hope you know that."

I wanted to run down the list of all the reasons I was not impressive. Like the fact that I'd forgotten to floss, that I lived with my parents, and that I'd probably hurt my mother's feelings right before I walked out the door.

Instead, I managed to say, "Thanks. That's kind."

His gaze was frank. "Kind?"

I shifted in my seat. "Was it meant to be unkind?"

"How do you think it was meant?" he asked.

Our eyes met. Electricity passed through me, and quickly, I pushed the feeling away.

"Sorry," I said. "It's hard to take you seriously because you're so . . ."

He gave me that slightly dismayed look. "Handsome?"

I burst out laughing. "No! Famous."

He kicked his Gucci loafers up onto the coffee table. The luxurious leather fit right in with my ornate office.

"I absolve you from all liability," he said cheerfully. "I get it that you're my boss, and we're in this intense, very well-decorated office—"

"I was just thinking that," I said, laughing. "It's very well decorated."

"You need to quit being a chicken, though," he told me, "and say what you want to say."

"Do you really think you're going to trick me into acting unprofessional by calling me chicken?"

The playful gleam in his eye got me.

"Fine," I said, leaning forward. "I did want to say handsome, but I can't. I also can't say that when you walk into a room it's like there's this beautiful sunset, and everyone's thinking it, but it would

96

be inappropriate to be like, 'Oh, look at that beautiful sunset.' Instead, everyone has to pretend that we don't notice that the sky is pink and red and orange because to acknowledge it would be rude or *illegal*, actually . . ."

Arlo started laughing.

"See?" I demanded. "It's so easy for you because you're just this huge sunset!"

Now he was laughing so hard that it was contagious. The moment one of us would stop, we'd make eye contact again and start all over. Finally, there was a loud knock at the door, and the production manager walked in.

"Am I interrupting rehearsal?" He looked back and forth between us both, his face baffled. "I knocked a few times, but it didn't seem like you could hear me, so—"

"No, no." Arlo wiped his eyes on his shirt, which sent a breath of that incredible, spicy cologne my way. "We were just discussing the importance of a good sunset."

I choked, which made us both start laughing again.

"Well, I won't interrupt." The production manager slid on a pair of reading glasses, looking down at his iPad. "Lily, when you get a chance, come find me. I need to go over a couple of budget issues so . . ."

"You go ahead." Arlo got to his feet. "I'll head out."

"Hold on," I protested. "I still have something to talk to you about."

I hadn't even touched on the idea of a matinee.

"Find me later." Then, he squeezed my shoulder and murmured, "You're hilarious."

The door clicked shut behind him, and the production manager's mouth dropped open. "Did he just touch your shoulder?"

I stared at the door. "I don't even know what just happened."

Chapter Fourteen

The day was packed, and even though I'd only planned to be there a few hours, I was still at the theater at six o'clock, with tons left to do. Kaia's track meet had gone well, but she wouldn't be back until late and then had to study for her chemistry final. There wasn't any point in me rushing home, so I settled in for the night.

I cracked open my window to let in the soothing sounds of the forest and bring in the breeze. It was so dry out, though, that the evening smelled thick and almost dusty. Outside my window, the flame of the gas lamp danced prettily. When the clock hit nine thirty, I called Kaia.

"Everything good?" I asked. "It's about time for bed."

"Mom, I'm not a baby," she said, but there was a smile in her voice. "I have one more chapter to review, then I'll go to bed. Grandpa's been tearing apart the living room ceiling—I'm pretty confident my bed is going to fall through the floor."

"I'll text him and tell him to stop working," I said.

"When are you home?" she asked.

I considered the pile of work on my desk. "There's a ton to do, so not anytime soon."

"You're working the graveyard shift," she said.

I laughed. "I guess so. Love you. I'll be there as soon as I can."

The graveyard shift.

I pushed it out of my mind, but about thirty minutes later, the walls creaked, and my hands paused over the keyboard. It had to be the wind. It happened a lot on the bluffs, but it did make a spooky sound.

I considered the stack of work that remained. It probably wasn't a great idea to stay so late at night, especially since I was the only one here. There was still a ton to do, but I could take it home. I was packing up when I noticed the sudden flickering of light in the hallway.

I hesitated, thinking about the moment in my office. "Hello?" I called. "Is someone there?"

It went dark. Then . . . there it was again. The light.

A flashlight?

It took two seconds to shut and bolt my office door. Then, I considered what to do. The front door was locked after six, but the perimeter of the theater had so many doors. There had already been moments when they'd been propped open in spite of the rules, which meant anyone could have walked in, including Benjamin Hamilton. Maybe he was still a problem after all and had come to pay me a visit.

Beneath the gap in the door, the light glowed. I braced myself for someone to lunge at it with a sudden bang. Nothing happened. The light flashed off again, and it hit me.

The lighthouse.

I stared at the gap in the door, waiting. Sure enough, the same stretch of light flashed on moments later. The sigh of relief that swept through me was louder than the wind, and I opened the door.

The arched window in the hallway overlooked the lake, and the beam had begun its nightly stretch. It circled back around to cast a spooky aura into the windows. I had just headed for the front door with my bag slung over my shoulder when the unmistakable sound of singing cut through the night. High pitched, almost ethereal.

I stopped short.

It couldn't be one of the actors. On the computer, I'd watched every single one of them clock out with their key card. On top of that, we'd made it more than clear that they couldn't hang out at the theater at night.

I rested my hand on the rail of the swooping staircase that led up to the balcony, breathing in the scent of the cleaning polish used on the brass accents, and listened. It was definitely someone singing.

"Hello?" I called again.

The singing seemed to be coming from the stage area. It was odd—disjointed and eerie, not at all like someone rehearsing a number.

It gave me chills, especially since my daughter had so kindly used the word *graveyard*. Plus, the theater was dark, it was late at night, and I was scared to walk into something that I shouldn't.

I fumbled for my phone and switched on the flashlight. Gripping it tight, I aimed it at the entryway to the orchestra seating. The red light of the exit sign and the dim light of the flashlight did little to illuminate the stage. I squinted but couldn't see a thing. The silence and deep cavern blackness made me take a few steps back. There, I bumped into a solid and silent mass of flesh.

With a scream, I whipped around, aiming my flashlight like a can of Mace. The last person I expected to see was Arlo Majors putting up his hands, looking gorgeous but incredibly irritated.

Pulling out earbuds, he rubbed his eyes. "Paparazzi have never succeeded in blinding me, but I think you just did."

"What are you *doing* here?" I demanded. "Was that you singing? Please tell me that was you singing."

"Was it brilliant or painful?" he asked.

I let out a sigh of relief. "The truth?"

"Yep."

"Brilliant," I lied.

He beamed. "You working?"

He said it as if it was a perfectly normal thing to work at ten o'clock at night, but on the other hand, his life probably ran on its own schedule.

"Heading out," I said. "What are you doing here?"

There was no point in telling him talent wasn't allowed if there wasn't a rehearsal because obviously, he was the exception to the rule. He was also the only one who didn't use his badge, which is why I had no idea he was in the building.

"The truth?" His expressive face went boyish. "Tatiana Marise flew in to surprise me. I did not come to the woods of northern Michigan just to have her follow me."

Tatiana Marise was the lead on my absolute favorite streaming show. She was spunky and gorgeous and seemed so fun. I had no idea the two were dating.

"You're together?"

The news was disappointing, but it wasn't as if he would have been interested in me. He was a movie star, after all.

"I mean . . . kind of?" Arlo shrugged. "She's at the bungalow right now. So, I lied—I told her I had a late-night rehearsal."

Arlo's bungalow was on the bluff, a mother-in-law cottage behind one of the ritzier homes. Private but very secure, with a gate that needed a code. The former theater manager had told me his team spent weeks vetting the location before he would sign on.

"You just left her there?" I asked.

He nodded. "I was planning to make it an all-night rehearsal and sleep on the stage, but now, you've caught me."

"Why wouldn't you just ask her to leave?" I said.

"That wouldn't go over well. She's an actress. Super intense. She'd burn the place down."

"Well . . ." I patted my shoulder bag. "Then, I guess I'll leave you to it."

"No, stay." He touched my arm. "I'm a little scared of the dark."

Outside the window, the trees shifted in the breeze. The branches were bathed in the silver light of the moon and seemed to dance against the night sky.

How often do you get to fly close to the sun?

I looked at Arlo. His intense blue eyes were as black as the night.

"Okay," I said. "For a little while."

~

The bottle of wine Arlo had lounging around his bag was a 100-rated Barolo from Tuscany, one that I'd always wanted to try. He stole some glasses from the bar, and we had a seat on the edge of the stage, the lights up low. He'd also made us a mini buffet with salted seaweed, chocolate-covered macadamia nuts, and protein crisps.

Arlo clinked his glass to mine. "To the Playhouse."

"The Playhouse," I echoed. "And a very successful season."

The wine was sharp with currant and seemed to linger on my tongue long after I'd swallowed it. Just a sip was complex enough to feel like a whole meal.

"This is incredible," I said. "Speaking of your future performance on this stage, I'm supposed to ask if you're okay with the idea of doing two shows on Sundays."

His blue eyes crinkled at the corners. "Business right away? I like your style."

"I thought it was appropriate, since we're wining and dining."

"Yes, definitely," he said. "I'm here to immerse myself in the world of theater, so let's do it."

We clinked glasses again.

Dangling my feet over the orchestra pit, I took in the sight of the red velvet seats and imagined them filled with audience members.

"It feels so strange to sit up here. On the stage." I glanced at him, then took a protein crisp. It tasted spicy, like buffalo wings, but it wasn't bad. "How did you get into all this? Acting, I mean?" Quickly, I added, "And you do not have to answer my questions at all. We can talk about whatever you want; I'm just curious, that's all."

"You can ask." Arlo kicked his feet against the edge of the stage. "Plays with the neighbor kids, puppet shows, that sort of thing. I'd do these monologues that would go on for days, and my mother—bless her—actually sat through them. There was one that went for so long that she burned the baked mac and cheese she'd been making for me. The smoke alarm was going off, but she just opened a window and waited for me to finish my saga. She was a good mom."

I glanced at him. "Was?"

"Yeah." He gave a slow nod. "It was a few years back."

"I'm sorry," I said.

"Me too." He lifted the glass and studied the wine. "I'm glad she was around to see all that's happened with my career. I scheduled myself pretty tight after she was gone because I didn't want to be alone with my thoughts. That's part of why I agreed to be here. I've been going at a breakneck pace for years, and it was time to slow down." He opened the package of macadamia nuts and poured some in my hand. "For a while, at least. I'm headed to Italy for six months in October."

"I could only dream of your life," I said. "At the same time, I wouldn't want to go from place to place. I like it here, and I like to let adventure come to me."

"Well, you're looking at it," Arlo said and grinned.

I pulled my knees up to my chest. It was so peaceful, sitting up on the stage with him. Looking out, I considered the balcony up above and the rows of chairs in the orchestra-level seating.

"Do you get nervous, performing onstage?" I asked. "I don't know if I could do it. That's actually a lie—I did do some theater."

"Where?" he said.

"Oh, some very important shows in elementary school, but my big break was Starlight Cove High." I started laughing because I hadn't thought of this in ages. "One of the Henderson brothers—they're these gorgeous guys who own a hardware shop here—one of them was interested in the romantic lead in *Mamma Mia!* So, every girl wanted to try out because we'd get to kiss him."

"That's pretty much why I got into theater too," Arlo said, grinning. "I was the one hoping to be kissed. So, what happened?"

"I practiced the songs in my room for hours at a time. I was so into it that I could practically smell the Greek sea breeze. Well, the day of the audition, I curled my hair, stole my mom's mascara, and was cast as Seagull #2."

Arlo winced. "Not Seagull #1?"

"It ended my career."

"Heartbreaking." He poured us another splash of wine. "I still feel guilty, like I skated into my career."

"How's that?" I asked.

The sound of his voice was soothing, and he probably had thousands of stories to tell. I could happily listen to him talk all night.

"I moved to LA straight out of high school," he said. "I started working as a stunt double to pay the bills. It was torture being on these sets and not being able to act. My roommate worked at one of the biggest talent agencies and got me a job at the office as an assistant. The guy that I worked for . . ." His expression became intense. "I just happened to be standing in front of his desk the moment a breakdown came through. The agent looked up and said, 'You act, kid? Because they want someone who looks just like you.'"

"Breakdown?" I said, confused.

"The breakdowns are a list of characters the casting director wants to audition. They describe the part, the physical appearance of the character, all of it. So, he sent me in for this audition, and sure enough, I got it. My first credit ever, and I was the supporting lead on a studio film."

"That's amazing," I said.

I didn't know much about how it worked because my grandmother had started her career at the end of the studio system, but I did know it wasn't easy to get a part at all.

"It was pretty great I didn't mess it up." Arlo leaned back on his elbows, displaying his toned arms. "It was my big break, the moment everything started. There have been so many times in my life where I've rethought that moment—where would I be if I'd stopped to use the bathroom, get a drink of water, chat up one of the girls? The guy never would have thought of me if I hadn't been standing right there, at that exact moment. I could have missed my moment. Sometimes, I have actual panic attacks about it."

I laughed.

"Oh, I'm not kidding." His expression was serious. "There are only a few moments in life that matter. Watch for them because once they're gone, they're not coming back."

"This is one of them, for me," I admitted.

He sat back up. "It's good wine, isn't it?"

"I mean, it's fun hanging out with you," I said.

Arlo smiled. Then, he leaned forward, cupped my chin in his hand, and kissed me.

I couldn't believe it.

Electricity shot through me, and I melted into the softness of his lips, the rough stubble on his cheek, and the intoxicating taste of Barolo. The kiss gained in intensity, but an image of him kissing someone on screen flashed through my mind, and I had to pull away.

"I can't." I was embarrassed to be breathless. "Sorry. I can't do this."

He rested his forehead on mine, and those incredible eyes held mine. "Why?"

"Because you're you."

"Ouch." He sat back on the stage with a thud and gave me a charming grin. "So much for 'it's not you, it's me,' folks. She has clarified, it's definitely 'because you're you.'"

I laughed, still able to smell his incredible aftershave somewhere on my face. It would be delicious to fall into his arms right there on the stage, but I was a grown-up, a mother. I had wrinkles, and sometimes my jeans were too tight. Plus, my marriage ended because my husband found someone better. I had no business acting like this superstar wanted anything to do with me.

"Sorry," I said. "I'm not at my personal best these days."

He made a petulant face. "Lies."

"Truth." I took a drink of wine. "Besides, you just told me that your girlfriend flew in from LA and is at your house."

"No, I told you someone I no longer want to be involved with flew in from LA and is at my house."

The thing about Arlo was that we did seem to have some sort of a connection. I didn't know what it was, but we'd had an easy rapport from the beginning. Still, that didn't justify setting myself up for instant heartbreak, which was exactly what this would be.

He leaned back on his elbows again. "So, you haven't dated since the divorce?"

"My daughter and I moved here right after. This is a small town, so once you start dating someone, it can be complicated to untangle."

Arlo nodded. "You're using words familiar to me. *Complicated, untangle* . . ." He ran his hand through his hair. "You forgot *impossible.* It's impossible for me to date. That's part of the reason Tatiana Marise and I keep up. We both have the same issue. I've tried to connect with women outside of my industry, but it never works."

He finished his glass of wine and poured the rest of the bottle, dividing it between us. It smelled like dark chocolate and raspberries. I breathed it in, fully aware that the opportunity to drink a wine like this probably wouldn't happen again anytime soon.

"Out of curiosity," I said, "why doesn't dating work?"

He was staring off into space, but his eyes widened. "Cell phones, privacy issues, but on a deeper level, the women are waiting for me to become their favorite character." He stretched out his legs. "There's always a movie that's shaped their attraction, and if I don't bring that to the table, they're disappointed. I do my best to dazzle them with me, but I fall short. It's impossible to compete with the guy who saves the world."

"Well, I think you're doing a pretty good job." I paused. "It's not you, it is me."

Arlo gave a sexy smirk. "What a relief to hear it." He hopped to his feet, as if getting ready to pull me up to dance, and something fluttered down below our feet into the orchestra pit.

I scrambled up. "Was that a bat?"

There were few things that gave me the creeps more than bats, but the fact that we were practically in the woods, in an old building, made it possible that one had found its way in.

Arlo shone his cell phone toward the pit. "It's papers." He frowned. "Did those fall out of your bag?"

I shook my head.

"That's strange. Where did they come from?" He grabbed the side of the stage and hopped down. "Let me . . ." He went quiet.

"What?" I called. "What is it?"

"Lily, come down here," he said. "You're going to want to see this."

I stared down into the pit. It was a pretty deep drop, maybe nine feet total, and we wouldn't be able to climb back out. I'd have some explaining to do if everyone showed up in the morning to find me and Arlo Majors trapped in the orchestra pit.

"Can we get out?" I asked.

Arlo tried the door that led out under the stage and nodded, his face still buried in the pages. I shimmied over the edge, the ground hard beneath my feet.

He held a collection of handwritten papers in a cardboard folder locked in with brackets. Some had come loose during the fall, and he was sifting through those.

"It's an old play," he said. "Look at this, though."

He handed me the title page.

"The Script Calls for Revenge," I read, then stopped.

"You see it? There at the bottom?"

"Yeah," I said, voice quiet.

The play was written by Belinda Hamilton.

Chapter Fifteen

"It's a practical joke," I said. "I've heard some of the actresses talking. They're new here, they're obsessed with the idea that the theater is haunted . . . this has to be something they put together."

"This doesn't seem like a joke." Arlo was focused as his hands glided through the papers. "The pages are old." He went silent, reading. "This play is actually pretty good."

The warmth of the wine had faded, and a chill went through me.

"Where did it even come from?" I said. "It didn't fall from the rafters."

Arlo clipped in the pages that had come loose. I walked over to the edge of the orchestra pit. I ran my hand along the edges, trying to understand how a play had just magically appeared.

I found it. A small gap between the edge of the orchestra pit and the stage where we had been sitting. It might have been used as a cubby for the conductor to rest sheet music.

So much of the theater had been remodeled, but the structure remained unchanged. Was it really possible that the script had been hiding there all this time? Arlo had leapt up right before it had fallen. The sudden movement could have rattled the wall enough to knock the folder out onto the floor.

I chewed on my lip. "What's the play about?"

"A family," he said, still reading. "There was a big accident—a building collapse—and the sister died. That's as far as I've gotten."

My mouth went dry. "The bridge collapse."

The idea that we had found something that had belonged to Belinda was one thing, but the idea that it was a thinly veiled story about the way her sister died was something else entirely.

"I don't like this," I said. "Belinda Hamilton is the actress that died in the fire here at the theater. There actually was a big accident that killed her sister."

"So, this could be true? Talk about intense." His face lit up. "Lily, this is a true-life, small-town family drama with crime. People love a story like that. Did the mayor . . ." He read for a second, then tapped the pages. "Did he really try to cover it up for his construction buddies?"

"What?" I whispered, peering over his shoulder.

> Mayor: The construction company knew the deadline and they met it.
> Mayor's wife: They skipped the safety check.
> Mayor: Prove it.
> Mayor's wife: The building collapsed. Is that proof enough for you? A woman died because *you* wanted to cut the ribbon at the special ceremony. You forged that inspection!
> *The mayor flies across the room and wraps his hand around his wife's neck.*
> Mayor: If I ever hear you say that again, you won't be able to talk at all. Do you understand me?
> *He releases her.*
> Mayor's wife: I understand it all.

Arlo whistled. "This is intense."

I took a step back, feeling sick. "This is . . ."

"Hey, what's wrong?" He stopped reading. "You okay?"

I stared at the black folder, trying to piece together my thoughts. If the content of the play really did deal with the bridge collapse, it felt almost . . . dangerous.

"People do love a small-town story," I said. "But you've got to understand, this is my small town. I don't know what the play's about, but I've literally read one quick part, and it's throwing out questions that could be really damaging. It could start some pretty intense rumors."

"That's what good theater does, though," Arlo said. "It gets people talking. Gets them thinking."

"Yeah." There was no point arguing about something I hadn't read, but I had to admit, I had a bad feeling about what could be in the rest of those pages.

Three loud bangs nearly made me jump out of my skin.

"What was that?" I said.

Arlo seemed daunted too. "Uh . . . don't know."

Then, there was the unmistakable sound of a phone buzzing. He pulled his phone out of his pocket.

"Oh, great."

Three more loud bangs.

"What?" I said, looking up at the rafters. Was something about to come crashing down?

He slid his phone back into his jeans pocket.

"It's Tatiana Marise." He let out a hearty sigh. "She's at the front door."

~

They say never meet your idols. Maybe that's true. When I unlocked the front door of the theater, the luminous Tatiana Marise, dressed in black athletic wear and gold kitten heels, took one look at me and shrieked. It echoed through the lobby like the screech of a barn owl.

"Where is he?" she demanded.

"He's right here," Arlo said, his voice wry.

Tatiana pushed past me in a blur of glimmering skin and a heavy cloud of hyacinth-scented perfume. "You!" She stomped right up and got in his face. "I didn't come here to be ignored."

He still held the play, and as I watched in horror, Tatiana lunged forward and knocked it out of his hands. For the second time that night, the papers fluttered to the floor. This time, I was the one who raced to pick them up, for fear of what she was going to do next.

"Take me to the airport," she demanded. "I'm leaving."

"Tatiana, please," Arlo said. "Don't be like this."

It startled me to hear him pleading with her, his expression intense but for once, not full of confidence. "I want you to stay. I do."

He glanced at me, and I looked away. Tatiana noticed.

"Who is that?" she demanded. "The janitor?"

"My boss."

"Lily," I said, deadpan "Big fan."

Tatiana appraised me with China-blue eyes, and then they filled with tears. "Where *am* I? There's no food-service delivery, the bugs are ridiculously loud, and I'm *cold*. I don't know what I'm doing here."

One thing I'd learned from my grandmother was how quickly an actress could turn the tables. If I wasn't careful, I'd be bringing her a take-out order and my favorite sweater before I knew what had hit me.

"I have to call it a night." I clutched the play tight. "So nice to meet you."

"Lies," Arlo murmured, and I shot him a look.

Tatiana did not hear, because she was too busy sinking into the comfort of the red velvet upholstered couch in the lobby. Her lashes actually quivered shut, as if she was settling in for the night.

"I have to lock up the theater," I told him.

"That's your cue, darling." He swept Tatiana Marise into his arms. She cooed and laughed, while he gave me a conspiring look. I shook my head, fully aware that I had no right to feel left behind.

"Have a good night," I told him.

"The sunrise is never the same as the sunset," he said as they passed me on the way out.

My cheeks went hot, but Tatiana seemed baffled. "We're not getting up at the crack of dawn. I'm already jet lagged. I'm sleeping, baby."

He carried her all the way to what must have been her rental car. I was surprised to think that she'd driven the big black Tahoe, but she must have; she'd gotten here somehow.

I waited until they'd pulled out of the drive before I locked the theater and made my way to my car. The night was silent except for the symphony of bugs that had outraged Tatiana Marise. It was so late that the moon was high. Still, I knew I wasn't going to get a moment of sleep until I'd read every word of that play.

Chapter Sixteen

I settled into bed with the comforter pulled tight around me, a cup of chamomile tea on the nightstand. It had been the world's longest day, and even if it didn't mean anything, I'd kissed a movie star. The fun fact flitted through my mind but agreed to wait in the wings.

Letting out a breath, I opened the cardboard folder and stared down at the pages.

Belinda's handwriting was neat and precise. Some of the pieces of notebook paper were purple, and the ink was some sort of pastel light blue. There were no text abbreviations like kids used today, and she'd used Wite-Out to correct mistakes. I could only imagine the care and attention she'd showed this project, and I wondered if Benjamin Hamilton had ever read it.

I was curious why Arlo had barely looked up while reading it. Now, I realized that was because it was shockingly well written. There were moments I had to stop and take a breath, because the scenes were so intense, the drama so real. When I got to the part about the building collapse, tears ran down my cheeks, and I dried them on the sheets.

I could only imagine the hurt that must have driven Belinda to write those scenes describing the death of her sister and the pain of thinking it could have been prevented. She painted the mayor, the construction crew, and the development company as criminal and desperate to cover up their mistake.

I had to wonder why Belinda had written this play. What had she planned to do with it?

Most likely, it was a way for her to exorcise the pain she felt about the bridge collapse and the death of her sister. But if there was truth to her words, performing it could have exposed the people involved. The thought gave me a little jolt. Could this play be the reason she'd felt her life was in danger?

One thing was clear: she believed there were several people at fault who got off with nothing more than a slap on the wrist. Based on what she wrote, all eyes should have been on the mayor.

The play suggested he'd skipped the safety inspection because it conflicted with his ribbon-cutting ceremony and that he had forged the safety inspection report for the building. Once it collapsed, the engineer who had allowed the mayor to forge the inspection, and whose name appeared on the inspection report, had taken the fall. Was Belinda suggesting that, in real life, the mayor had done the same with the bridge?

Quietly, I shut the play. The claims weren't likely. The collapse of the bridge had been investigated, but still, the accusations were specific enough to make me question if there were things that had been covered up.

The mayor had been known to help those in his inner circle. My friend Abby had worked for years trying to put together a wine trail to benefit the local wineries, but Mayor Matty had blocked the project until she included a winery that belonged to one of his friends. That story had made me dislike him, but this was something else entirely.

My hands rested on the smooth cardboard of the faded and scratched-up folder. Belinda was either an incredibly good writer who had gotten my buy-in, or there was actual truth in what she'd written. I could only imagine the reaction if this play had been performed in Starlight Cove. It would have been talked about endlessly and would have forced a deeper investigation into the accident.

This wasn't something I could pass along to Benjamin Hamilton. It might send him spinning, looking for revenge.

I turned off the lights. I tried to shift my mind to brighter things, like the kiss from Arlo Majors. That had to wait, though, because I was asleep before my head even hit the pillow.

Chapter Seventeen

Kaia poked her head into my room first thing the next morning.

"Oh, good," she said. "You're here." Her pretty face was cautious in the early morning light. She wore a cute athletic-wear outfit, with her hair down but pulled back with a thin pink band. Her sneakers were huge compared to her thin body because her body hadn't yet caught up with her feet.

I rubbed my eyes and sat up. "You look nice."

"Why weren't you home last night?" she asked.

The words were like a bucket of cold water. "I was." Quickly, I sat up. "What do you mean?"

"I had a bad dream and came in." Her tone held a hint of accusation. "Where were you?"

Guilt rushed through me. "Working. Still at the theater."

"It was one o'clock in the morning."

"Yes, we discovered an old play hiding in the orchestra pit." I held it up like evidence. "I'm sorry. You should always call me if you're worried."

"Okay," Kaia grumbled, but she looked a lot more cheerful.

"Here, let's go eat breakfast," I said, climbing out of bed. To my surprise, she rushed forward and held me tight, enveloping me in the scent of strawberry body spray.

Tears smarted at the backs of my eyes. Probably because I was tired but also because I'd upset her.

It was like she suspected I'd hung out with someone other than her dad. I didn't want to lie, but I was not about to volunteer the truth. It was much too complicated. Besides, she'd never believe Arlo Majors had spent that kind of time with her mother—I had a hard time believing it myself.

I linked my arm in hers. "What should we eat?"

"I already had yogurt, but if you happen to be making sunny-side up eggs with a heavy sprinkle of parmesan cheese and salt, with orange slices on the side, I won't say no."

"What a coincidence," I said. "That exact thing was on the menu."

She looked at her watch. "Tell me about the play."

"I'd rather hear about you and your friends," I said. "How did it go at track?"

Kaia lit up and started monologuing about the high jump. I chewed on my lip, grateful for these brief moments with my girl. Benjamin Hamilton came to mind, and for the first time, I felt sorry for him, realizing this type of connection was one of the things he had lost.

~

Once Kaia had gone off to do her own thing, I went in search of my father. He liked to start the day reading his paper in the study.

"He used to read it at the breakfast table," my mother complained, heading to the laundry room with a basket full of clothes. "Why the sudden need for privacy?"

"Maybe the chair in the study is more comfortable," I suggested, even though I didn't have the slightest clue what drove my father to do the things he did.

My mother made a face and headed down toward the basement, balancing the basket like a pro. She was already dressed for church, and it was good to see her up and in action, instead of lying in her bed.

I found my father in his favorite chair, snoring with his head thrown back. The paper that he must have intended to read rested on his chest. I backed out of the room, but he opened his eyes.

"Come in, come in," he said, sitting up. "I was just reading the news."

"Captivating?" I settled into the couch, enjoying the early-morning breeze from the open window.

"Indeed." He folded the pages. "What's up?"

I explained about finding the play at the theater, leaving out details on what I was doing on the stage so late at night. "It's pretty intense, Dad," I said. "The stuff in there about the bridge collapse. Everyone knew the head of the construction company was related to the mayor, right? Back when it happened?"

He frowned. "It says that in the play?"

"It says a lot of things. It's based on a building collapse, but it's obvious what she's talking about."

"I see. Well, everyone knew they were related." My father took a sip of coffee out of a mug with a picture of a worm and the slogan *I'm the Best Catch*. "Mayor Matty actually made a big point to bring in an outside panel to select the company, and his brother-in-law was still hired. When the accident was investigated and it was announced that the construction company was not at fault, there was trouble in his family for some time. There were reports from the staff in the house that the mayor and his sister had gotten into it, that he'd said her husband was no longer welcome in their home—he should be behind bars, all of it. They left town."

I considered this. "I wonder if that was performative. The fight."

My father gave me a questioning look.

"I mean, Mayor Matty isn't dumb," I said. "He knew the staff would be listening. Maybe he and his sister agreed to have a big blowup so the right message would get out in the world, while they were doing the wrong thing behind closed doors."

"That seems a little far fetched," my father said. "Besides, it would have been hard for him to interfere with the investigation." He peered at me. "The play really has you thinking he's done something wrong, doesn't it?"

"I don't know." Some of the things Belinda had pointed out left me with more questions than answers. "That's why I wanted to ask you about it."

My father sat in silence for a moment. "Mayor Matty's brother-in-law is back, you know. They were awarded the contract for the ski project."

My eyebrows raised. "Really? One would think . . ."

"The accident was over twenty years ago. It changed everything about the company's safety measures, and they've had several impressive, high-profile projects since. They placed a bid on the ski resort, and from what I understand, the committee picked them without a moment's hesitation."

"That seems . . ." I shook my head. "My POV right now is what I read. But they wouldn't award something like that if the company hadn't cleaned up their act. It's just unfortunate that Belinda's family had to go through it the first time."

"Who's read the play?" my father asked.

"Just me and . . ." I hesitated, holding back again about Arlo. "I'm the only one who's read the full thing."

"Probably for the best." My father got up, tightened his bathrobe, and grabbed his coffee mug for a refill. "It seems Belinda's spirit is all around us these days, but the past is past. There's no point in getting everyone upset about something that is most likely complete fiction."

"I know," I said.

My father rested his hand on the doorjamb, deep in thought. "I do remember a couple of guys whispered at the shop that the real reason the mayor's brother-in-law left town was because he was cheating on Mayor Matty's sister, and the mayor found out."

"That's not in the play," I said.

My father shrugged. "Just telling you what I heard."

In the kitchen, my mother sat at the table, eating a bowl of oatmeal. My father walked right past her, but they barely acknowledged one another.

The moment he was out of the room, I pulled up a chair. "Okay, something's going on with you and Dad."

"Nothing's going on." My mother added creamer to her coffee. Then, she said, "He's not doing dance with me."

My mouth dropped open. "What? Why?"

"He doesn't want to." She shook some cinnamon on her oatmeal. "To him, it's that simple."

I took a long drink from my coffee. "Well, he doesn't have a choice," I said. "I'll tell him he's going."

"Lily." The skin under my mother's eyes was puffy. "Trust the person who's been married to him for forty-five years. If he's not interested, he's not going to do it."

"What about you, though?" I was baffled. "I'm sure he'd do it to make you happy."

She shook her head. "That's never been our marriage. Sorry to break it to you."

Living at home as an adult was completely different than it was when I was a child. It was impossible not to notice the nuances and the slights, the things that threatened the heart of every relationship. It was impossible to ignore the fact that my mother was unhappy, which was a surprise.

For years, I'd assumed my parents had the perfect marriage—they did everything together. It had never occurred to me that maybe my mother didn't want to be doing the half of it. There were few women who would choose a lifetime of working in a sportfishing shop selling worms, but that's what she'd done, each and every day.

"I thought retirement would change things," she told me. "It hasn't. Your father puts me in last place, and he has for years."

"Mom, he loves you," I said. "You're not last."

"If I'm willing to do what he wants."

I didn't want to hear this. I'd been through enough relationship drama to last a lifetime, struggling to keep my marriage together and watching it fall apart. The idea that my parents might be going through the same type of thing was too much to take.

"Well, what *do* you want to do?" I said, in an effort to move away from the topic. "That's what we've been working to figure out."

She finished her oatmeal. "Well, I've figured it out. Enough waiting on him."

"That's the spirit," I said, feeling cautious. "What do you mean, exactly?"

My mother sat up straight. "I'm going to take the class by myself and dance with every charming man that passes through."

I wrinkled my brow. "Is that what you want to do?"

"No, but . . ." She folded her napkin. "What else can I do?"

It was a tough call. I wanted my mother to find her independence, but I didn't want to accidentally encourage her to build a life without my father. Part of being a couple meant making time to spend together, and sometimes, I wondered if that's where Jin and I had fallen apart.

I'd thought it through so many times, trying to figure out when he and I had started to go our separate ways. I think it all started when Kaia was born. She was the most beautiful thing I'd ever seen, the complete focus of my attention.

When I had to put her into day care to go back to work, I spent my time away from her feeling anxious, counting the seconds until I could pick her up. Then, shortly after I started back at work, Jin decided it was time for us to start being social again, instead of staying home all the time with the baby.

"We could use a dinner out with friends," he kept telling me. "Some time for us to be together."

The idea of leaving my daughter just to go have dinner didn't make sense to me. She was at day care all week, and I wanted to be with her. I suggested picking a place where we could bring her along, but Jin worried our friends wouldn't feel comfortable with a baby on board. Finally, he decided to go without me.

He was mad about it, but I wasn't, not at all. Maybe I should have bent a little, but in the grand scheme of things, Kaia was only going to be a baby for such a short period of time. The fact that he was unwilling to compromise, knowing how much I missed her during the day, made me even less willing to see his side at the time.

Looking back, though, that was the time where Jin started building a social life without me. Finding new interests like mountain biking and learning how to brew beer, things that might have been fun to watch him explore if we'd been at a different stage in our life. By the time Kaia was older and he started traveling for work, we'd gotten into a habit of spending time apart.

That said, my parents had been together for years. They'd worked side by side for most of their life and had spent every waking moment together. Surely, one dance class wouldn't be the end.

"I think that sounds like a brave idea," I said. "You've wanted to dance for years, and I think it's wonderful that you're thinking of pursuing it, whether he wants to or not. The good news is, Dad might change his mind when he sees how much fun you're having."

"Doubt it." She brushed some crumbs off the table. "Wouldn't it be wonderful, though, if I actually did have some fun?" Her eyes filled with tears.

"Mom." I crouched down next to her chair and hugged her tight. "You deserve some fun."

She laughed, brushing away a tear. "I think so too. I've also come up with another thing I'd like to do—I want to audition for the play."

"The open auditions?" Her words filled me with pride and panic, all at the same time. "Really?"

"Yes." Her cheeks were pink. "Is that silly?"

"I think that's great," I said slowly. "Auditions are this Friday. Do you think Dad will mind?"

"I don't think he'll even notice," she said.

"That's not true," I said. "Mom, I think it's important that you keep talking to him. Communicate. Try and find some things to do together, okay?"

"Yes, yes," she said, waving her hand. "But I want to do this. Do you think there's a part that would be right for me?"

My mind whirred through the small list. Surely, there had to be something that would be a match.

"Yes," I told her. "We'll find a way to make it work."

Even if my family no longer owned the theater, I was still running it. I couldn't let my own mother walk away with nothing. She'd get a part, even if I had to make one up for her.

"I think it's great you want to do this. You could even stick around after rehearsals and help me," I said, starting to feel excited.

It would be nice to have her around. It would give her a sense of purpose, and it would give me the opportunity to get my family involved again.

"Would you want to do that?" I asked. "Help with behind-the-scenes stuff?"

"Yes. I always liked being there back when your grandmother was in charge. It will be fun to have it be you. Besides, I could use a little excitement." She glanced around the house and sighed. "There isn't much going on around here."

Chapter Eighteen

My office door clicked shut as I tapped away at the keyboard.

Looking up, I spotted my favorite sunset walk into the room. He wore a pair of black jeans, a black T-shirt so ratty it looked as cozy as a blanket, and a beanie pulled down low over his eyebrows.

"Good morning, beautiful." My voice was wry. "Did you talk down your girl?"

I was not about to act like I was in awe that we'd kissed because I had no doubt that it hadn't meant anything to him, and besides, it couldn't happen again. Kaia wasn't ready for me to get involved with anyone, so I had to stop thinking of him that way.

It was hard, though, especially when he shot me that grin and sprawled out on the couch, putting his loafers back up on my coffee table.

Sipping from a glass bottle of green juice, he said, "It was a night. I got yelled at for at least two hours. The actresses love the drama, you know?"

"I do," I admitted.

There had been times my grandmother had turned the slightest mishap into a full-fledged stage performance. It irritated my parents but left me entertained.

"Did she go back to LA?" I asked, getting up and sitting in a leather chair across from him.

Through splayed fingers decorated with silver rings, Arlo gave me a sheepish look. "I let her stay. Look, it's hard to date anyone when you're famous. You sort of have to stick within your group." He made a face. "That sounds obnoxious, but it's true. You always have to ask questions like, Is this person secretly recording me or—" He gave an awkward laugh. "Actually, are you secretly recording me?"

I raised an eyebrow. "Are we dating?"

This time, he laughed for real. "I shouldn't complain about any of it. My life is blessed. I have the freedom to invest my passion into projects for months at a time, and I'm grateful for that every day." He took off his beanie and twirled it on his fingers. "In general, I think it all comes down to being grateful. I fall asleep thinking about what I'm grateful for, and I wake up thinking about it. If your life is surrounded with gratitude . . ."

"That's easy for you to say." I ran my hand over the smooth leather of the chair. "You have the time and the luxury to invest in reflection. The rest of us are just scraping by."

"Please." He rolled his eyes. "There are days where I work for seventeen hours straight, then get up and do the whole thing again. I'm living a grind, too, you know. It comes down to what you choose or sometimes, what chooses you. Speaking of, I was thinking about that play we found."

My shoulders tensed. "What about it?"

"Have you read it yet? It's one of those stories begging to be produced, to be seen. It's raw, painful, and it doesn't pretend to ask the big questions—it asks them and demands answers."

"It can't be performed," I said, pushing his feet off my table. "This is a small town, Arlo, and it will start gossip."

"Why would it?" he said.

"Because parts of the play might be true."

He sat up, his blue eyes intense. "Look, theater keeps me connected to the heart and soul of the craft. The audience is a living and breathing entity. We shouldn't lie to them. Let them hear the truth." I didn't respond, and he said, "The scenes I read would captivate an audience. I can even see it going to New York."

"That would be a much better place to perform it than here."

"But here, the audience would really relate to it," he said, leaning forward. "It would mean something to them."

"The people of Starlight Cove will see each other in this story," I said. "There's no way to prove the story is actually true. It would be damaging to present it as fact."

"It's not fact."

"The people in this town would not see it like that."

Arlo tossed his beanie back and forth in his hands. "What if it is true?"

I thought of the neatly kept pages and the terrible claims written in the script. If the construction company had truly been negligent in real life, they would not have been able to get out of being cited, maybe even prosecuted. They would not have continued to get large contracts like the ski resort. If the mayor had forged a document, he would have gotten caught.

Getting up, I took a sip out of my water bottle. "It's impossible that it happened like that."

"Perfect. They'll know it's fictionalized."

"Arlo, it wouldn't be considered entertainment here," I said. "It would be destruction. I'm sorry. It's not going to happen."

"Then, what are you going to do with it?" he asked. "Let it linger in the shadows for the next fifty years?"

Gesturing at the stack of papers on my desk, I said, "I love batting ideas around with you, but I really have to get back to it."

"This conversation isn't over," he said; then he stretched out on the sofa and pulled a pillow over his face.

I stared at him in disbelief. "What are you doing?"

He lifted up the pillow so I could see one eye. "Taking a nap."

In two minutes, his breathing slowed, and he was fast asleep. I stared at him, baffled. I had Arlo Majors—*the* Arlo Majors—lecturing me about the heart and soul of theater, and moments later, cozying up to take a nap in my office.

When had my life gotten so bizarre?

Chapter Nineteen

On the day of the auditions, Piper burst into my office, her face lit with excitement. She pulled back the shade on my window.

"You might want to take a look at this," she said, pointing outside.

Typically, the front lawn of the theater was empty, with only the trees and antique gas lamps for company. Now, a line of locals stretched from the front door to the parking lot. The people of Starlight Cove had turned out for the open call as if they were auditioning for a national televised singing show.

My heart leapt. "That is incredible!"

I knew most of these people; I had grown up with them. It was fascinating to see so many interested in performing—or, more likely, spending time with Arlo Majors.

"This is great," I said, taking a hearty gulp of coffee. I got to my feet and started to pace. "First, can we handle that many people?"

"Sure." She adjusted her horn-rimmed glasses. "Our illustrious director is in a panic, but I can usher them in and out pretty quickly."

I laughed. Sebastian, I'd quickly learned, was always in a panic about something, so I wasn't too worried about that.

The small clock on my desk read 9:15 a.m. Forty-five minutes until go time.

"What can I do to help?" I asked.

"Hand out numbers," Piper said. "It's the only way we'll be able to keep track. Have people sign in next to their number and tell them it will be their name for the audition. Do you need me to print the numbers out?"

"No, I can do it," I said. "I'm also going to order coffee, some fruit plates, and doughnuts for the lobby. Can you get the stagehands to set up tables? Put some cloths over them? It's starting to occur to me that most of these people won't get a part, so we should make it feel like more of a celebration."

"Sure thing, boss." She handed me a headset. "Put this on when you go outside. Press this button, and it will be like talking into a bullhorn."

I pressed the button. "That's easy enough." My voice blasted through the room, and Piper gave me a high five. "One more thing. My mom said she was going to audition . . ."

"Put her on the list as number ten," Piper said. "That way, she won't be stuck waiting in line all day. Don't make that face—there's no reason to feel guilty. You're going to give enough blood, sweat, and tears this summer to earn that small perk."

"Thank you," I told her.

"You got it."

I called my favorite doughnut shop, the one that always smelled like spun sugar, and they said they could have the fruit and doughnuts up at the theater in ten minutes. The coffee would take longer, so we skipped it. Once the food had been handled, I called Gillian G. Smith.

"It's Lily," I said when she picked up. "Listen, there's a line to the Sweetery for these auditions. Do you want to send a news crew?"

"Yes, please," she sang.

Excellent. Having the news here would also make this a festive occasion, not to mention the boost of publicity we'd get for the theater.

I texted my mother. Auditions are slammed. You're officially number ten, okay? Be here on time.

Her text back gave me hope for her general spirits.

Thank you!!! Excited!!!!

I was glad to hear it. She'd surprised me the other day with her sudden resolve to get on with her life, and I'd hoped it wasn't a momentary thing. The fact that she still planned to come was a good sign. The excess of exclamation points was promising, too, unless she just didn't know how to text without them.

I got to work printing out the numbers and the list that Piper had asked me to put together. It printed without a problem, but cutting up the numbers took a little longer than planned. By the time it reached ten o'clock, I was actually sweating.

Still, the smile on my face was genuine as I pushed open the front doors to start the auditions. The fresh air felt great, as did seeing so many familiar faces. Gillian's crew had set up, and the cameraman was already filming the crowd.

Pressing the button on the headset, I called, "Welcome to the Starlight Cove Playhouse!" The words almost made me get emotional.

Over the past few days, I'd learned that I loved being with the theater. It connected me to my family history in a way I hadn't expected, and it gave me a sense of pride to be in charge of something so important for our town. It meant a lot to me that so many people cared about it too.

Over the mic, I said, "This turnout is incredible, and we're so happy you're here. You're welcome to wait in the lobby or outside while you wait for your turn. You'll only enter the stage area when our stage manager calls your number, which one of us will hand out as you walk in. Results will be posted online tomorrow. We look forward to seeing your audition, and we'll get started here very soon!"

There was a rumbling sound, and I glanced out at the parking lot. To my dismay, I spotted Benjamin Hamilton sitting in his old white pickup truck. His jowls were sagging, and he gripped a Styrofoam coffee cup tight while glowering at me.

I hesitated. Should I go talk to him? There were so many things written in that play that had left me conflicted on how I should feel for this man, but he was just sitting there, looking unhinged. It made me nervous that he might be planning to do something, to get that revenge he'd talked about. Especially since I hadn't heard from him until now, when there was a big crowd of people. That thought alone made me reach for my phone and call Dean.

"Lily, you okay?" he said, picking up on the first ring.

"Yes," I said, touched by the greeting. It was nice to have someone looking out for me. "Listen, we're having that big casting call, and Benjamin Hamilton is here in the parking lot, just hanging around."

"I'll call dispatch," he said. "Tell them you need someone up there for crowd control right away. That should scare him off."

"Thank you," I said and slid the phone back into my pocket.

I'd been nothing but kind and cordial when I'd sent that letter to clear the air. That did not mean I was going to let Benjamin Hamilton come here and intimidate me or anyone else.

Maybe he'd guessed what my phone call was all about because moments later, the motor of his truck roared back to life. He peeled out of the parking lot, muffler popping, hardly looking to see if anyone was in his way. The sheer recklessness made my blood boil.

I propped open the doors and let out a breath. Pasting the smile back on my face, I pressed the button on the headset.

"Shall we get this party started?" I asked the crowd, and they roared their approval.

It gave me joy to hand out the very first number to none other than Frannie Gussie, an old friend of my grandmother's. Frannie had become a widow a few years back, but even though she had to be pushing eighty, I heard she still shoveled snow off her sidewalks each and every winter. She definitely came across as a character from the stage, dressed in a sequined cocktail dress and a pair of tennis shoes, and her hair perfectly combed and sprayed.

"Honey, is Arlo Majors here?" she asked, giving me a lipsticked kiss on the cheek. "I'll do that silly speech you posted on the internet, and I'll warble my way through 'Happy Birthday,' but I'd really just like to get a glimpse of that man."

I pretended to be shocked. "Frannie Gussie. This is an audition, not a dating service, and thank goodness for that, or you would sweep him off his feet." I held out the clipboard. "Now, sign in for me here."

Once she did, I whispered, "He's not here, but I'll make sure you get to meet him if he shows up, okay?"

Frannie winked. "I hope he likes selfies with cute old ladies. Now, show me that stage." She sashayed through the front door like she was born for the spotlight, and I turned to the next person in line.

It was a younger guy in his twenties with a full beard. He seemed vaguely familiar, maybe from the bike shop.

"Welcome to the Playhouse," I said.

"My girlfriend is making me do this," he grumbled. "That's the only reason I'm here."

I laughed. "Well, should I tell you to break a leg or not?"

"Not." He scratched his beard, looking panicked. "The odds are good I'm going to pass out and fall off the stage, so let's try and forget this ever happened, okay?"

"That's the spirit." I pointed at the table in the lobby, heavy with glazed and powdered doughnuts. "Grab a treat. You're going to need it."

I greeted the next few people and then spotted my mother making her way across the lawn. She walked right up to the front of the line, and no one cared at all because each and every one of those people had most likely bought worms from her at some point in their life.

"You look great," I said, surprised to see she was wearing makeup and a starched, pale-blue dress.

Tugging at the short sleeves, she said, "Is the mascara too much? I didn't really know what to do."

"It's perfect," I said.

Opening her purse, she gestured at a Tupperware container. "Look, I brought a cupcake, and I'm going to light it right before I sing 'Happy Birthday.'" She flicked the lighter as if to demonstrate, and quickly, I swiped it away.

"I love the ingenuity, but let's keep fire away from the theater," I whispered.

She grimaced. "Didn't even think about that." Taking the number ten, she said, "Do you plan to watch?"

My mother had sat through each and every one of my school plays and had even sewn the costume when I played the lead role in *The Giving Tree* in the second grade. Of *course* I was going to watch.

"Absolutely," I said. "Just let me get one of the ensemble members up here to handle the front door."

Once I got one of the young actors set up at the entrance, I headed inside. The lobby was getting crowded, and the auditions were underway. In spite of what I'd said about waiting in the lobby, some people had posted up in the audience like it was a talent show. I stationed another one of our ensemble members at the door of the auditorium to make sure no powdered doughnuts joined the viewing party.

Everything set, I slid into a seat next to our production manager and Sebastian, fascinated by his thick binder and red pen. Even though today's talent was at the community level, he was as focused as ever.

"Hello, there," the production manager called, when number nine was ushered onstage. "What's your name?"

I was silencing my phone but tuned right back in when a voice said, "Cody Henderson."

Cody Henderson was Emma's boyfriend and one of the owners of Henderson Hardware. Cody was built like the Incredible Hulk, tough as nails, with a heart as soft as a marshmallow. I couldn't believe he'd shown up to audition.

"Which speech are you doing for us today?" Sebastian asked, barely hiding a yawn.

The two speeches that were posted on the website were very simple. Four lines each. A greeting, a conflict, an emotional outburst, and at the end, a resolution.

I was excited to see Cody act one out because it would be fun to tell Emma all about it. But when he stepped forward, something about his posture changed. He stood up straighter, which made him appear even more commanding than usual.

Looking just above the crowd, he said, "Hi, darling," with a sweet, flirtatious smile. His face changed, and he drew back. "No, I don't have your money. Is that all you care about?" he cried, his voice practically breaking. Then, with the purest sincerity, he said, "You know what I care about?" He gazed off into the distance, and everyone in that theater held their breath. "You."

My mouth dropped open, and I looked over at Sebastian, who had put a large check mark by Cody's name.

Cody grinned and said, "This next part is going to be really embarrassing." He turned his back to the audience, did jazz hands, and snapped back around, singing as quickly as possible, "Happy birthday to you . . ."

It was funny, it was cheerful, and it was the complete opposite of what he'd shown with the drama. The audience burst into applause. The guy could act, and he could sing. Most of all, he could entertain. I swear, if he'd tap-danced his way offstage, I would not have been surprised.

I texted Emma:

Cody was born for the stage but I would expect nothing less from a Henderson brother.

Emma replied with a series of delighted emoji.

My mother was next up. I held my breath as she sashayed onstage in her blue dress, with a big smile on her face.

Now, I'd grown up seeing my grandmother up there, but I could not remember one time where my mother had been involved. Even though I didn't want to embarrass her, I burst into applause. She squinted in the stage lights and gave an enthusiastic wave.

"That's my mother," I told Sebastian.

"I see." His voice dripped with disdain. "I guess my free will has flown out the window with this one, yes?"

"You betcha," I said cheerfully.

He gave a hearty sigh. "Hello, Lily's mom," he called, flipping his neck scarf. "What will you be titillating us with today?"

My mother smiled, putting her hands in the pockets of her sundress. "Well, gosh. I'd planned to do the speech Cody just did, but he's a tough act to follow. I think I'll just do it in French." With a toss of her hair, my mother launched into a perfectly accented recitation that made Sebastian light up like a candle. Then, she sang "Happy Birthday," pulling out the cupcake and bringing it to the edge of the stage.

"Sweets for the sweet," she said.

To my absolute shock, Sebastian practically scrambled out of his seat to retrieve the cupcake. I applauded long and loud as my mother left the stage.

Sebastian sat back down and took a frosting-filled bite. The look he gave me was much less sour than before. "Your parents are divorced, no?"

My mouth dropped open. *"No."*

"Pity." He made a note in his book, and the production manager hid a smile.

~

The day rolled along, and around noon, I went to find Piper backstage.

"How's it going?" I asked. "What do you need?"

"I'd love it if you could turn up the air." She wiped the back of her hand over her forehead. "The stage lights and all these lookie-loos are making it stuffy."

The audience area had been a revolving door, with the locals continuing to watch and cheer one another on. She was right, though. It was starting to smell a little stale.

"It's been so fun," I said, handing her a bottle of cold water. "I knew the town would want to get involved."

"It's good to know," Piper said. "It's a good lesson on how to manage opening night, since this is the first and only time we'll have this many bodies here until then."

I was just about to duck out and turn up the air when there was a small disruption by the door. My shoulders tightened. I'd stopped worrying about Benjamin Hamilton because the police had sent an officer to sit in the parking lot, but I turned to the door, afraid he'd found his way back after all.

It wasn't Benjamin Hamilton—it was my grandmother. She had her hair up and wore a stunning black dress, a sparkly diamond necklace, and a floor-length mink coat.

"Wow." Piper stopped in her tracks. "What is she doing here?"

"She probably came to watch my mother. Grandma," I whisper-called. "Hi! Did you come to watch? Mom went on hours ago."

The ensemble member who had helped assign numbers at the front door was right behind her and gave me a delighted smile. "Your grandmother has decided to audition."

The people sitting in the nearby seats actually gasped. I narrowed my eyes at my grandmother.

"Audition," I said to her. "Really?"

"Yes, darling."

I sighed. My grandmother had played supporting roles in at least fifteen studio films and had starred in two Broadway shows, not to mention all the touring shows she'd performed in. If she wanted a part in a play, the only thing she had to do was ask.

"Okay," I said. "That's fine."

The ensemble member squeezed my grandmother's arm. "The stage is yours."

The word must have gotten around that my grandmother was going to perform because everyone was heading into the theater, including the cameraman from the local news. I raced out to the hall to turn up the air. By the time I got back, my grandmother had made it up the stairs and to the stage. The theater was packed.

Gazing out at the crowd, she said, "I believe that, before we can start, I need to find my light."

The younger actresses had crowded in toward the front. They gave eager nods, drinking in her words like they were attending a master class.

My grandmother stepped into the spotlight. It caused her diamond necklace to sparkle like her sudden bright smile.

"I will be performing a brief monologue from *Antony and Cleopatra*," she said.

"So much for the four-line speeches," I said to Piper, who shushed me.

Once my grandmother's extensive monologue was complete, leaving the audience riveted, she took a step forward. "Now, I'd like to sing for you." She dropped her coat onto the stage like Barbra Streisand in her famed first audition, saying, "I think I like it here."

My grandmother belted out the first, sassy bars of "All That Jazz." I leaned against the wall, thinking back to all the times when I was young, watching her onstage. Her voice was as captivating as ever.

Once she reached the final chorus, Arlo Majors wandered into the auditorium. He seemed to be trying to appear incognito in a navy sweatshirt and a baseball hat tugged low, but his presence was undeniable, and right away, people started to notice that it was him.

I groaned. "What is he doing? Does he want to start a riot?"

No sooner than I'd said it, he climbed up the stage-left stairs, snapping his fingers. Without missing a beat, my grandmother crooned, "Arlo Majors, ladies and gentlemen!"

Arlo held his hand out to my grandmother, and the two did what appeared to be an impromptu soft-shoe dance that he somehow made look both sexy and cool, before he swooped her up and spun her around. My grandmother laughed as he lowered her to the ground, draping her coat across her shoulders. The audience burst into thunderous applause.

My grandmother lifted her chin, contemplated the crowd, and said, "Did we get the part?"

The cheers nearly brought down the house.

Chapter Twenty

My grandmother beamed as I escorted her offstage and to the green-room, followed by a full court of adoring ensemble members, headed up by a twentysomething actress named Millie. She was striking, with sharp cheekbones and enormous cat eyes, and had the lead in four of the six performances.

In a sweet but raspy voice that made everyone hang on her every word, Millie said, "Please tell us everything about your career, Maxine. Like, every detail."

The actress who liked to wear black, including nail polish, echoed, "Every dramatic detail, start to finish."

"Yes, please," Jade said, walking into the room. "But first, I'm going to require a hug." Jade's hair was pinned up, her face was without a trace of makeup, and she wore a summer dress in her traditional shade of plum. "I heard you were in the building and came running. It's so good to see you again."

My grandmother beamed at her. The young actresses helped her back to her feet, and she and Jade embraced, holding each other tight.

The ensemble members quickly made room for Jade on the couch. She and my grandmother took a seat.

"Grandma, do you need anything before I get back to work?" I asked.

She brightened. "I'd adore some lunch."

I ordered my grandmother the lemon chicken soup from Towboat. It arrived right around the time of the last audition, and I brought it in, surprised to see that the same group was still in the greenroom. Once she'd eaten, my grandmother and Jade started to flip through some old photo albums, the group of young actresses hanging on their every word.

"Look at this one." Jade held up the book. "There are some oldies but goodies in here."

The ensemble members oohed and aahed, gathering around.

"Darling, look," my grandmother said to me. "There's your grandfather."

"So dapper," I said, peering at him.

My grandfather was dressed in a suit, with his silver hair perfectly combed and his shoulders thrown back. My grandmother had a white fur stole draped across her shoulder and was leaning against an eighties Porsche. I vaguely remembered the car—my grandparents had driven it during the summers.

"Where did you find those albums?" I asked.

It was interesting to find a picture of my grandparents that I'd never seen before. It wasn't in any of the family photo books, and I knew my father would like to have a look at it. I'd have to make some copies.

"One of the stagehands was cleaning out a closet, and they were stacked there," Jade said. "You might want to consider putting someone in charge of searching the theater for relics, because there's an exceptional section of older items down in the basement that should be sorted."

I hadn't even been down to the basement, but someone—maybe Piper—had mentioned the same thing.

"Thank you," I told her. "I'll put it on the list."

One of the actresses giggled and held up a book. "Jade, is this you?"

Jade's expression changed. She held out her hands, and obediently, the actress passed the photo album her way.

"Yes," Jade said, flipping through the pictures. The frown line in her forehead was deep. "This is from another lifetime."

One of the girls let out a catcall. "It looks like you found the hottest guy in the bunch."

We all leaned over to see who it was. The man in the photo had a strong jaw, sharp eyes, and one of those yachting sweaters draped over his shoulders. The way Jade was nestled in the crook of his arm, it appeared as if they were a couple.

"If you're talking about the best-looking boy in the bunch," Jade said, securing the clip in her hair, "you must be referring to my son."

"Your son?" I said, interested. "Which one is he?"

In spite of my best efforts, Jade had remained tight lipped about her life. This was the first time I'd heard her volunteer personal information. I didn't even know she had kids.

Jade pointed at a striking boy who couldn't have been older than twenty-five in the back row of a group photo. He had his mother's bone structure and cat eyes. In short, he was beautiful.

"That's Ryder," she said.

"Goodness." The redheaded actress fanned herself with a photo album. "I should have been born twenty years earlier."

"He is handsome," my grandmother agreed, patting Jade's hand.

The actresses cooed, and I smiled, studying his picture. He had nineties hair and wore a flannel, giving a good-natured glower to the camera. I vaguely remembered him, since I'd been fifteen that year and had a crush on pretty much every good-looking guy in the cast. The girl next to him was stunning, and suddenly, I realized who she was.

"That's Belinda," I said.

"Yes." Jade's voice was tight. "They were together. So in love."

"The girl who died?" one of the actresses said, leaning in.

The group studied the picture in silence, and I tried to see the resemblance between Belinda and her father. It was a hard comparison, but it was there, around the mouth. Her expression was so bright, so vibrant, that it was hard to believe that, in a few weeks after this picture was taken, she'd be gone.

"I feel so sorry for her." The redheaded actress twisted her hair around her hand. "She has no idea that it's all about to end."

"It was a hard time." Jade closed the book and rested her folded hands on it. "My son had some pretty serious burns from trying to save her. His arms, his back. The firefighters found him with her collapsed on top of him. He'd almost made it to the exit."

"Oh, Jade." I couldn't believe no one had mentioned that part of the story. "I didn't know."

"How would you?" Jade's voice was light. "No one talks about it, which is understandable. He survived, and he's just fine. He had skin grafts to repair the damage on his arms, so you'd never know from looking at him. He was very lucky." She got to her feet and gave a tight smile. "I should get back to work. It was wonderful to see you, Maxine. Excuse me."

Jade swept out of the room. The silence in her wake was as quiet as a tomb.

"I'm going to see if she's okay," I said quickly. "Grandma, would you like to go to my office?"

"My new friends will entertain me," she said, and the actresses gave eager nods. "Now, who here is living in New York? I used to adore the bustle of that city."

I rushed out of the room, texting Piper a request to check on my grandmother in ten minutes. I couldn't believe no one had mentioned that Jade had been impacted by the fire. Her poor son.

I grabbed a fresh cup of coffee for her from the break room and brought it to the costume shop, the large section in the back of the theater where the costumes were made. It had such a particular smell, of old fabrics, spray starch, and freshly washed clothing.

Jade had a small office in the back that she'd personalized, even though she did the majority of the work in the main room. Letting out a breath, I rapped on the door.

"Come in." There was a lump I could hear in the word, but when I walked into the room, her gaze was strong and steady.

"You okay?" I set the mug on the table next to her.

"That was a disaster out there." She rubbed a lotion that smelled like eucalyptus and rosemary into her hands and tapped it around her eyes. "Sorry to be a downer. I should have kept my mouth shut. Here, have a seat."

She moved a shimmering array of fabrics off a folding chair, then draped them over a small clothing rack. The green and blue sequins reflected in the overhead lights in a way that seemed much too cheerful for this conversation.

"Jade, I'm glad you told us about your son," I said, sitting down. "I'm really sorry that happened to him. What can I do to help?"

"Nothing." She sighed. "Time—it's such a tricky thing, isn't it? You step into the same place where you were so many years back, and you expect it to be the same. Especially if it looks the same. The wallpaper looks the same. The lamps on the wall. The lake, the forest . . . even your grandmother, in some ways. Not my son, though. He'll never be the same. Oh, he is on the outside. Charming, fun, well loved, but his time here, in this place . . . it still affects him."

"How?" I said.

"He's so guarded now. He won't let anyone get too close." She ran her hands over the frayed edge of a piece of fabric. "His first experience with love was as painful as it could be. It left him searching, you know. Trying to understand why things happen the way that they do. Who's to blame, all of it."

"I'm so sorry," I said.

She shrugged a thin shoulder. "Me too. He's had such a struggle, and to be frank, it hurts that no one talks about him. It's all about

Belinda, and I get that, but he was in the hospital for three months. Do you know how long that is? So, to step back in time and see his ghost, the time before it all happened, it's . . ." She winced. "I'm so sorry, Lily. This is unprofessional."

"No, it's not," I said. "It's horrible what he went through. What you had to have gone through, standing by his side."

"Yes." The word was short. "It was a challenge."

My heart broke to see her attempt at dignity in the midst of such pain. We were years apart, but we were both mothers. I reached out and took her hand. She clutched mine hard, as if falling, and I squeezed back.

I wanted to ask about her son. The things that made him laugh, the things that she loved about him, the things that made him unique. He must have been an extraordinary man to have overcome that experience. I wasn't brave enough, though, to broach those topics. I didn't want to cross a line.

"I came back here because Starlight Cove was so kind to me in the aftermath of the fire," Jade said. "It's been long enough now that I thought I could handle it." She took a sip of coffee. "I'm starting to believe that everyone has that moment in their life, a decision that might have been wrong. This was mine. I spent years thinking how selfish I was to bring him here. He could have spent the summer on a fishing trip with his college roommates, and this never would have happened."

"Jade, it's not your fault," I said.

She stared down at the table. "What if it was, though?" she asked in a voice that was barely a whisper.

"It wasn't." I told her this with the deepest resolve in my heart. "Besides, you don't know what would have happened if he took a different path. The boat could have capsized on the fishing trip. His friends could have crashed the car on the way there. It was not your fault that he fell in love with Belinda, that he was here that night, and that he tried to save her. Your son sounds like a hero."

"A hero who failed." She rubbed her arms. "That's not my take, it's his. Nothing I could ever say to him will change that."

"At least he got to experience true love," I said. "When he still had an open heart. That doesn't happen a lot."

"True." Jade thought for a moment. "I hope that one day, he'll let someone else in. I don't know if it will ever happen, but yes, it is comforting to know that he had the opportunity to experience love without all the baggage he puts into it now."

She pulled a piece of fabric to her and began tearing out a stitch.

How strange to think that this accomplished woman had been battling ghosts from the moment she walked through the front door.

"I think you're brave for coming back," I told her.

"Thanks. Even that makes me feel guilty because I know he'll never come here to see me." Her gaze was frank. "I had to do it, though. I need to learn how to move past it all. Or at the very least, replace those memories in my mind." She crumpled up the fabric and pushed it aside. "This conversation won't solve a thing. This isn't something that can be fixed in a day. I appreciate you coming to talk to me, but I will be fine, Lily. You really should get back to your grandmother. Those young actresses can be quite intense."

I got to my feet. "If you need anything, please let me know."

She gave a curt nod.

I made a quick detour to my office and was grateful to not see a soul on the way. There, I shut the door and collapsed into my chair, trying to process it all.

The hurt radiating off Jade was as heated as the anger from Benjamin Hamilton. I wondered if the two had talked or shared in their grief together. Years ago, maybe. I wondered if it would help for them to talk again.

No. I could see, in some ways, how they would take it out on each other.

My heart ached for Jade, as a mother, but my feelings for Benjamin Hamilton were more complex. I'd been frightened to see him out in the parking lot this morning, but I also felt for the man and all the heartache that he'd been through. Especially now that I'd spoken to Jade and seen the grief that she carried, even though her son was still alive.

These questions made me wonder if I should show Benjamin Hamilton the play. It would at least give him a small piece of Belinda back, a part of her that he might not know. It was something to think about, but it wasn't a decision that needed to be made right away. The play had been hidden away for the past twenty years; a few days or weeks wouldn't make a difference.

It was getting close to the time the ensemble would have to get to rehearsal, so I headed back to the greenroom to retrieve my grandmother.

"You can't *really* believe there's a ghost in this theater," I heard her saying. Peeking in, I saw the actresses nodding. They'd been joined by a smaller group, including one of our most talented male leads.

"There is definitely a ghost in this theater," one of the girls said. "This place is haunted."

"You know she's nearby if you smell the faint scent of a campfire," Millie sang, crossing her long legs.

The girl in black gave a solemn nod. "Or if you hear the sound of crying on the wind."

"Do you know what I heard?" the actor said, and everyone turned to him. "That there are nights where you can hear actual chains clinking in the orchestra pit, keeping time with the music."

"How remarkable." I strolled in, making everyone, including my grandmother, jump. "Especially since the orchestra has not yet played a bar of music, and this is not a castle with chains. My friends, it's nearly time for rehearsal."

My grandmother lifted her hand in a cheerful wave. The actors streamed out of the room, one of them saying in a low voice, "I've already had that feeling that someone is watching me like, a hundred times. Even though I was alone. You know what I mean?"

"So young, beautiful, and entertaining," my grandmother said, stretching. "Hard to believe that once was me. How is Jade?"

"Upset," I said, thinking about the grief on her face. "I wish I would have known that about her son. Why didn't you tell me?"

My grandmother rested a hand on the soft fur of her mink coat, which was draped over the back of the couch. "It was such a tragedy. It shut down the theater, ended one life, and caused so much pain to another . . . What's there to say?"

"But you'll talk about ghosts?" I asked. "I can't believe you were letting those kids tell those stories."

"Oh, they're young," she said. "Let them have their fun while they believe life's innocent."

I studied her. "You were captivating up there today."

My grandmother gave me a coy grin. "My darling, I was simply delighted Arlo Majors didn't take one look at me and forget how to dance. It's been known to happen."

Laughing, we headed out to the car. My plan was to take my grandmother back to the assisted-living facility and return to help with cleanup before heading home for the night.

When my grandmother and I stepped into the sunny afternoon, Benjamin Hamilton was back in the parking lot, his loud motor puttering away. The police had left hours ago. The sympathy I'd been feeling for him drained out of me, but my grandmother waved at him, like they were the best of friends.

My shoulders were tense as I held her hand to help her get into the car. She gave me a slight nod, as if I were a chauffeur.

"It's such a shame," she mused, "how heartache can light a fire—forgive the expression—under some people but freeze others."

I tilted the rearview mirror to look at Benjamin Hamilton. He was staring right at us.

"He didn't want the theater to reopen," I told my grandmother.

"He really just wants to turn back time." She pulled on her seat belt. "That can't be done."

Jade wanted the same thing. I sat for a moment, considering that, and my grandmother gave an impatient sigh. "If you would prefer, I could call a driver."

I started the car, the air-conditioning stirring the scent of my lemon-mint air freshener. "I was just wondering if I should talk to him."

"It's not your fault, and it's not your problem. Now, let's go."

I watched the truck in my rearview mirror as we pulled out. He still sat in the lot of the theater, which made me nervous.

"I wish I knew what he was up to," I said. "What does he hope to accomplish by sitting there?"

My grandmother sniffed. "Perhaps he's working up the nerve to audition."

I laughed. "I can't believe you auditioned. Was it the same as the old days?"

"Oh, heavens no. The sooner you accept the fact that life moves forward, the less likely you are to get left behind. I have no illusions that I still hold the same ability to captivate as those young girls."

"I disagree," I said. "Every single person in there was hanging on your every word. You could have just told us you wanted a part."

"Oh, darling." My grandmother waved her hand. "I have no intention of accepting a part. I'm too old for that nonsense."

"Wait, you're not going to do it?"

"Gracious, no. I just wanted to show them how it's done."

I couldn't believe this. "You have to! The entire town would come to see you perform."

"That's the problem, though, isn't it?" My grandmother folded her dainty hands. "The ensemble is such a small part. I'd be a distraction because I am not a small actor."

The news was disappointing, but I knew that arguing with her wouldn't change a thing. The sun reflected off the windshield, and I slowed down, as the road from the theater into town took some focus to drive safely.

"The thing with Jade threw me," I admitted. "I had no idea her son had gone through all that."

"Oh, yes." My grandmother sounded sad. "That poor man. He was at the hospital here until he was stable enough to be transferred."

"Did Jade's husband stay in town with them?" I asked.

"Oh, she wasn't married, but . . ." My grandmother lifted her eyebrows. "Her boyfriend certainly was. Jade made a point to change the subject when the girls brought up that man in the photograph. I have to admit I'm a little curious about whether she's going to get in touch with him now that she's back. Their relationship was quite dramatic. It kept us all watching to see what would happen next."

"You think she would rekindle that?" I loosened my grip on the steering wheel as we got closer to the bottom of the hill. "That was twenty years ago."

"Oh, life is long," she drawled. "Twenty years is nothing in the blink of an eye."

"So, who is he?" I asked. "Who was her boyfriend?"

The man in the photograph had been attractive but also vaguely familiar.

"I couldn't tell you that," my grandmother said. "That would be gossip." She lifted her chin slightly and stared out the car window.

I hid a smile. "You really should do the show. I think it would be—"

In the rearview mirror, headlights were coming up fast. Some instinct made me stop talking and pull off onto the shoulder, and I did it just in time. Benjamin Hamilton went barreling down the hill at top speed.

"What in the world?" I cried. "Is he trying to kill us?"

My grandmother stared after the taillights, glowing like embers in the hazy light. "He's trying to kill himself, darling. That poor man has been trying to kill himself since the day his daughters died."

Well, I was not about to let him take out anyone else in the process. I picked up the phone.

My grandmother grabbed my hand. "Don't."

"He needs to get off the road."

"You need to get off his radar," she said, just as I dialed emergency services. "Lily, put down that phone."

The emergency response unit picked up. Everything in me wanted to report him. If I hadn't pulled off the road, or if that had happened higher up where there wasn't a shoulder, there was no telling what could have happened. The truth behind my grandmother's words was just as chilling, though.

"What's the nature of your emergency?"

"It's Lily Kimura," I said, my voice shaking. "I just called to thank you for your help at the theater today."

"You're so welcome," the dispatcher said. "I'll pass it along."

"Have a good night."

Hanging up, I looked at my grandmother. Her face was tight with concern, but she gave a sharp nod.

"You are strong, Lily," she said. "That man is understandably not. Stay away from him."

We drove in silence the rest of the way.

Chapter Twenty-One

When I walked in the door with Kaia's favorite takeout—yellow chicken curry with white rice—I was surprised to hear my parents fighting.

Kaia was sitting at the table, working away on her computer with her earbuds in. She pulled them out and gave me a helpless look as soon as I walked into the kitchen.

"They have been arguing ever since you called about Thai food," she said, in a low voice. "Grandpa accidentally nicked a pipe trying to install the crown molding, and there was a momentary rain shower in the living room."

"How do you accidentally nick a pipe?" I said, setting down the bags with a thud.

Kaia shrugged. "Don't ask me. Carter Henderson's going to come over and fix it tomorrow, but he's already been here three times this week. I'm more than okay with that, but Grandma's getting super annoyed."

It was hard to imagine anyone getting annoyed with the presence of a Henderson brother. That meant she really was fed up.

"Why didn't you tell me this type of thing has been going on?" I whispered.

My parents rarely fought when I was growing up, and I could only remember one really big fight. My mother was mad because my father had convinced her to leave the turkey in the oven too long at Thanksgiving, and then he had the nerve to complain at the table—in front of my grandparents—that it was too dry. My mother had fumed in silence, but once they'd gone to the kitchen to get the pies, he'd gotten an earful. We could all hear it in the dining room, and my grandmother had burst into loud applause.

Now, I put my hand on Kaia's shoulder and gave it a comforting squeeze. "I'm so sorry," I said. "They shouldn't be fighting like this."

"Everyone fights," she said, her voice light.

The words filled me with guilt.

"Well, I hope that—"

She gave a pointed look at the brown bags. "Hungry."

I got the hint. Quietly, I started pulling out bowls and unpacking the food.

"You auditioned for the play?" In the next room, my father sounded outraged. "What am I supposed to do all alone in this house? This is not why I agreed to sell my store. I thought we'd be doing things together."

"Well, I did too." My mother was trying to keep her voice low, so I stopped rattling the bags. Right or wrong, I didn't want to miss a word.

Kaia and I both leaned in, waiting for my mother to speak. When she finally did, her voice trembled. "You said that we would hike every day. That we would drink wine and watch the sunset. Plan a trip to the mountains. The only thing you've done since we sold our store is fish and putter around this place, fixing things and, quite frankly, making them worse."

Kaia snorted and clapped a hand over her mouth. I would have laughed, too, if I didn't know how much those words would hurt my father. He wasn't doing a great job with the home repairs, but I had to give him credit for trying.

"The fact of the matter is, I am not about to sit around here waiting for you to entertain me." With that, my mother swept into the kitchen. She stopped short at the sight of me and Kaia, hanging on every word.

"Were the two of you spying?" she demanded.

Kaia grabbed for her phone and pretended to look at an app. "Nope."

"No way," I said and dumped the yellow coconut curry into a bowl and added a serving spoon. The spices tingled my nose as the sound of the electric drill rang out from the living room, followed by insistent hammering.

"Hey, Mom. Carter was here three times this week?" I whispered.

She held up her hand. "Five."

The three of us giggled quietly.

I got to work spooning up rice onto the plates and set them on the table. The carrots and potatoes looked especially fresh, and the sauce, inviting. My parents were sometimes reluctant to try spicy foods, so I hoped this dish wouldn't add to the drama in the house.

"Dad," I called. "Come on in for dinner."

My father came into the room looking tired but still a little annoyed. He waited to bring up the theater until we were all seated at the table, the strong spices rich in the air.

"This looks good," he said, and my mother nodded.

At least no one planned to give me a hard time about the food.

"I heard Gigi also auditioned today," he said. "How was that?"

My shoulders tensed, thinking of the car ride and what could have happened if I'd not pulled off the road when Benjamin Hamilton came roaring down the hill.

"It was fine." I didn't want to bring up the issue in front of Kaia. "She said she's not going to do the play. She just wanted a moment in the spotlight."

"If she wants a moment in the spotlight, she should do social media," Kaia suggested. "The interview I did with her was fascinating. I'm sure thousands of people would love to hear from her."

The thought made me laugh out loud. "I can't even begin to imagine how that would go. Have you seen her texts?"

My parents groaned. "The best one," my mother said, "was when she texted to say she was having the worst cracked ribs."

Kaia looked puzzled. "She broke her ribs?"

"Oh, she was fine," I said. "Right as rain. Turns out, the assisted-living facility was serving baby back ribs. It was supposed to be the worst baby back ribs. Of course, she didn't text back when Dad panicked, and since it was the middle of an ice storm, the phones at the facility were dead. Dad assumed the worst and rushed over there in spite of the ice. The roads were so bad that he was stuck, and so he had to sleep on their couch."

He nodded. "There were lots of ribs, though. They tasted pretty good to me."

The mood had improved. My parents were both eating, my father spooning up the rice and sauce with gusto. I didn't want them to start arguing again, but I did want to congratulate my mother. There wasn't much point holding back, since she and my dad had already been talking about it.

"I have news," I said after wiping my mouth. "We all know that Mom auditioned today too. She did fabulous and . . ." I did a drumroll on the table, and she gave me an expectant look. "You got a part!"

"I did?" Her cheeks flushed a pretty rose color. "Really?"

To his credit, my father actually seemed proud. "Good job, honey," he grumbled. "Is it a big time commitment?"

"It's not that much," I said, "unless she wants to help with other things at the theater too." My dad appeared ready to protest, and I said, "Dad, she needs to be active."

"That's right," my mother said. "Not sitting around the house waiting for you to finish your projects."

I winced. "Mom, let's not get into all that right now."

"I don't see why not." She set down her fork and looked at him. "You don't want to spend time with me, but you want me to sit around doing nothing?"

"I never said that I wanted you to—"

"I asked you to go dancing with me, and you weren't interested."

"I'm not ready to do that yet," my father said. "Let me have some time to get into the things that I want to do. I've worked for years."

"So have I!" My mother stabbed a potato. "It's one hour of your time, but more than that, you promised you would."

"That's enough," I said. "Not in front of Kaia."

Jin and I had done our best to not argue in front of our daughter, but there had been a few times when she'd seen us at our worst. I'd actually found out about Norah right in front of her, thanks to Jin's new phone automatically linking to my computer.

Kaia and I had been working on a school project when a text thread popped up on the screen. The air had left the room as I stared, horrified, at the intimate conversation taking place between my husband and another woman. Even worse, that he was in the next room.

I had been grateful for two things that day: One, that Kaia had been busy working on the poster for the school project, so she didn't see those texts. Two, that Jin had the presence of mind to send her to the neighbor's house to play the moment he saw my face.

We began fighting in earnest after that day, as our marriage quickly fell apart. It must have been hard on Kaia. I didn't want her to relive that time simply because my parents couldn't agree on dance lessons.

"Let's move on from this, okay?" I said.

My mother pressed her lips together. Kaia pushed her food around her plate, and the tension in the room felt thick.

"You know," she said, her voice quiet. "Grandpa's right in some ways. If you and Grandma are both at the theater all summer, who am I supposed to hang out with?"

"Don't worry, kiddo, you can hang out with me," my dad said.

"Sounds good," she said, but the look she gave me was heartbreaking.

Her summer was supposed to be an international getaway in Japan; now it had turned into being stuck at her grandparents' house.

"Well, what about this?" I said, as an idea hit me. "Kaia, how would you like to be an intern?"

She raised her eyebrows. "What do you mean?"

"The theater is super busy, and we need help," I said, delighted to have come up with a way to spend time with her while I worked. "I'm not sure whether or not it can be a formal thing, but school's out in just a few days. I was thinking you could come and work with me."

The idea hadn't crossed my mind until that very minute, but it was brilliant. There were a thousand things that needed to get done—Jade had just commented on the closets and the basement. It would give Kaia something of value to do with her summer, but most important, we would be together.

"It's fun over there," I said. "You could help with anything that you were interested in. Building sets, painting sets, sewing, working in the box office . . . plus, you could be around the actors, learn about scene study, performance, all of it. I spent a lot of time there when I was your age, and it was special."

My father grunted. "I seem to remember you complaining a lot and calling it boring."

"You live and you learn," I said, pouring some more water from the pitcher.

"I'd like to go to the theater with you." Kaia dipped her fork into the curry sauce. "If I don't like it there, though, I'm not going to do it, okay?"

"Of course," I said. "But this is one way we could spend some time together. If there's any point you'd rather be reading, swimming, or hanging out with friends, you are not obligated to stay and help. It will all be completely off the books."

"Because child labor is illegal," Kaia pointed out.

"You won't be getting paid."

"That's what you think," she said cheerfully. "I'll start the second school's out, okay?"

My father frowned at his food. "I don't know how I feel about all of this. You're all just going to leave me here alone again for the day?"

"Dad, you can come too," I said. "There's all sorts of things that need to be built and—"

He held up his hand. "No thanks. I spent enough time at that place when your grandmother had her day in the sun. You all have your fun. Don't worry about me."

We finished up dinner, and my mother suggested heading out for ice cream. Kaia and I were interested, but my dad shook his head.

"Bring me something back." He headed to the garage. "I've got work to do."

"I do worry about him," my mother admitted, on the way to the car. "Do you think he *will* be lonely? Maybe I should—"

"Mom, he has a choice," I said. "It's not your job to make him happy by making yourself unhappy."

It was my job, though, to make sure Kaia was happy. Looking back at her as she buckled in, I said, "Does this really sound okay to you?"

She pulled her headphones out of her ears, and I repeated the question. She gave me the thumbs-up. "I already texted all my friends."

My mother gave me a sideways look. "The seal of approval," she whispered.

It had been an eventful day, but in spite of everything, the idea that my daughter would be by my side made everything a little bit easier to manage.

Chapter Twenty-Two

"Look at this," Kaia said when I came down to breakfast on Monday morning. She held out her phone and played a clip of my grandmother and Arlo Majors performing their little dance number at the audition.

"Oh, wow," I said. "Where did you find that?"

"It's on social media," my mother said. She handed me a plate for the pan of cheese eggs she'd whipped up. There was also a bowl of cut melon and strawberries sitting in the middle of the table.

"Thank you," I told my mother. "I promise I didn't move back home for the food, but it's really starting to be a perk."

My mother rumpled my hair before peering over Kaia's shoulder. "Is that really how many people have watched that since Friday?"

Kaia nodded, drumming her neon-painted fingernails against the table. "You know, you guys were making fun of the idea the other night, but it really wouldn't be a terrible idea for Gigi to do some social media. She's bored at the home and doesn't want to do the play because it's such a small stage but—"

"Gigi doesn't want to do the play because she's starting to forget things." My father walked in and poured himself a cup of coffee. "She'd never admit that's the reason, but I've seen her lose her train of thought a few times in the middle of a sentence lately, and she's embarrassed. If that happened onstage, she would not handle it well."

"With social media, she can control her content," Kaia said. "Little film clips, quick live performances . . . I think she'd love it."

"Mention it to her." I bit into a strawberry. "You could be her social media manager as part of your summer duties. You only have a few more days of classes—are you excited?"

"I'm excited to get started at the theater." Kaia played the video again and grinned. "Do you think I'll get to meet Arlo Majors?"

I nearly choked. It hadn't even occurred to me that she would be around him. He would be kind to her, I knew that, but I didn't want her to pick up on my attraction to him, especially after how she reacted to that picture in the paper.

"I met him," my mother said. "He's such a nice guy. Beautiful blue eyes."

My father grunted. "Blue eyes are your thing now?"

"I never said that." My mother considered my father's brown eyes. "Come to mention it, maybe they are."

I winced. "Mom."

"Time for the bus," Kaia said and took her plates to the sink.

I got up too. "I'll give you a ride to school. I don't have to be in quite yet."

Outside, the sun was bright, and the mist looked pretty settled over the woods. My father had cut down the scorched trees and planted saplings in their place. It was nice to see that some of his improvements around the house were working.

"Do we have time to stop for hot chocolate?" Kaia asked, buckling herself in.

"For you?" I said. "Always."

∽

The theater was much quieter now that the auditions were over. The sun was hazy over the deep blue of the lake and reflected off the bright white of the lighthouse. The gulls cruised overhead, looking for breakfast.

I headed up to the front door, relieved that there was no sign of Benjamin Hamilton. I hadn't reported the incident on Friday out of respect for my grandmother, but if Kaia was going to come to the theater, I would not tolerate—not even for a second—anyone or anything that made her feel uncomfortable.

Thinking of Benjamin Hamilton at all reminded me that the play Belinda had written had left me wanting to research some things. There were too many details that seemed to ring true, and the best way to prove them false was to find out for myself. That would quiet the nagging voice in my head that made me wonder whether or not I was holding the most dangerous collection of truths in all Starlight Cove.

When I walked into my office, I stopped in surprise. There was a small purple orchid sitting on my desk. A pale lavender envelope rested against it.

The card inside read:

It takes a strong woman to look tragedy in the eyes without flinching. Thank you for being strong, but most of all, thanks for being there.

—Jade

I rested my hand on the orchid for a moment, brushing my fingers against its fragile stem. It was so kind of her to leave me flowers, but at the same time, she was the one who'd suffered through all this.

The casting meeting wasn't for another twenty minutes, so I powered up my computer and got online. I logged onto my email to send her a quick note and froze.

The subject line read Tragedy at the theater?

Sounds like a comedy to me.

My mouth went dry. The message was a total threat and a sinister one too. It was jarring because I'd stopped expecting to find something like this in my email, and I had to read it a few times to believe what I was seeing. Finally, I picked up the phone and called Dean.

"This one scares me," I admitted once I'd sent it to him. "It sounds like it was written by someone with serious anger."

"Or a teenager who's good at playing with words," Dean said.

I couldn't tell if he meant it or was just trying to keep me calm.

"We'll try to trace it again," he said. "See if there's been any mistakes this time around."

"What can we do beyond that?" I asked.

His answer wasn't comforting.

"Nothing."

~

The idea that there was still a threat to the theater put me on edge for the next few days. I kept careful watch of the cameras, scrutinized the key card check-in every fifteen minutes, and refreshed my email. The whole thing made me so angry. It made me want to take action, and since there was nothing I could do about this, I decided to try and right a wrong by moving forward with my research on the play. My father had mentioned an article about the bridge collapse, but since it was twenty years ago, it might take some digging.

It was easier to find than I'd expected. I clicked on it in the archives of the *Town Crier*, and sure enough, it hinted at the same questions the play had asked. Mainly, whether the bridge had been rushed and the safety check compromised as a result.

I'd worked with the *Town Crier* through the Tourism Council. The lead writer on this article wasn't someone I was familiar with. I clicked on his bio. He'd started his career writing features. Now, he managed the online presence of the paper.

I picked up the phone to call him but set it back down. It would be more effective to read his expressions than try to guess about the things he might not be comfortable saying over the phone. I sent him an email asking for a quick meeting and unwrapped a piece of mint gum.

It took less than a minute for him to respond:

Today at 2:00 works.

Perfect. I'd started taking my lunch right about then since I usually stayed through dinner. It would give me time to meet with him and still get back to see part of the rehearsal. Regardless, the whole thing made me nervous, as I wasn't sure I should be asking questions at all.

Before I could change my mind, I said:

See you then.

The day raced by, and before I knew it, I was headed to the newspaper office on the outside of town. It had started to get hot, and I had the windows down, the breeze a mix of warm and cold on my cheeks.

I'd just turned onto the main road when a blaring siren made me check my mirror. A fire truck was approaching fast, and I moved over. Moments later, it streaked by, followed by another.

In the distance, thick black smoke that hadn't been there moments before billowed toward the sky.

The fire was at least ten miles out, on the same side of town where I was headed. I flipped on the radio, and within minutes, the DJ reported that one of the old, abandoned log warehouses was in flames.

The smoke got thick the closer I drove, and I started to feel nervous. We hadn't seen rain in weeks, and each blade of dry grass could serve as tinder. It would be a disaster if the fire spread through the warehouse section to the tree farms that were nearby.

I pulled up to the news office, my throat dry from the smoke. Inside, I waited in the reception area in a black leather chair, relieved at the cheerful smell of a sunflower-scented room freshener. Familiar faces passed through the office, and there were lots of questions about when I'd be back at the Tourism Council.

"In the fall," I said. "October, I think. Our last performance is mid-September."

Trent Brady came out a few minutes later, eating the last pieces of a mandarin orange. He was tall and wiry, with slightly stooped shoulders and a weary expression.

"That fire looks like a big one," he said, leading me back to his office.

"I know," I said. "The dry weather isn't helping."

"True," he said. "Coffee?"

"No, thank you." I took in the details of the room. His desk held a small computer, a classic green banker's lamp with a chain, and a few framed photos of his family. There were articles all over the wall, and a window close to me had paisley curtains that were shut.

"Thanks for meeting with me," I said.

"Yeah, no problem." Trent had a small goatee and silver wire-rimmed glasses with rectangles for lenses. "I heard you say you're with the theater?"

"I work for the Tourism Council," I said, "but right now, I'm helping out over at the Playhouse. The theater manager had to step aside, and they were in a bind."

We made small talk; then I got down to business. "I won't take up much of your time. I just had a few questions about an article you wrote like, twenty years ago, so you might not remember much. It was about the bridge collapse?"

Trent sat in silence for a moment. Then, he got up and shut the office door. "What brought you in to ask these questions?" he said, settling back into his chair.

"The Hamilton family came to my attention when I started at the Playhouse," I said. "I'm concerned about some of the details of that story, and I'm curious why our town didn't make it more of an issue."

"In my opinion? It's because the owner of the construction company was the mayor's brother-in-law. I addressed that in the article, but much of what I wrote was changed before the article went to print. My biggest question: Why wasn't the construction company held liable?"

"Do you believe they were responsible for the bridge collapse?" I asked.

"They built it!" His eyes blazed. "That right there makes them responsible. There was wrongdoing there, corruption, but as to how much, no one will ever know."

"They have the contract for the ski resort," I said. "No one's asking questions."

He gave a bitter laugh. "Nobody dares. Everett Ferris ditched town and came back with a glowing list of successful projects that were highly publicized. When it comes down to it, though, most people don't get to make mistakes that big and bounce back from them. Most people would lose their license and never get to do it again. The rules change, though, when you're not most people."

"Do you think the ski resort will be safe?" I asked.

"I'm not putting my family on a ski lift, if that's what you're asking."

"Then, as a reporter," I said, "couldn't you reopen that conversation? Public opinion carries weight these days."

Trent had a Newton's cradle on his desk and flicked one of the metal balls, setting off the rhythmic movement. We both stared at it for a moment in silence before he stopped the motion.

"Do you know what happened to me when that first article came out?" he asked.

"What?" I said.

"I went from being the lead feature writer to five years in obituaries." He gave a bitter laugh. "I should have left town, gotten a gig somewhere else, but my dad was sick at the time, and he needed help with the bills. Life rolled on. Now, I've got two kids in college, and I'm no longer young and stupid." He looked down at his desk. "The ski resort will be fine. To be quite frank, it has to be. Things like that don't happen twice."

He stood up. I thought it was a dismissal, but he said, "Hold on for a second."

Trent left the office, and I walked around, reading the different articles on his walls. There were some old ones he'd written, but most were current. The one that caught my attention hung next to a picture of Captain Fitzie Conners, once considered the outlaw of our town. The article featured the Conners family, back when they'd cleared Captain Fitzie's name.

I had just finished reading it when Trent walked back in carrying an old brown file folder, the accordion type, stuffed with papers.

"This is all my research," he said. "If you can find a way to get the information out there, do it. What's the expression? Justice is best served cold?"

"I think that's revenge."

He held out the file folder. "It's all yours." Settling back into his chair, he said, "When I first heard about the contract for the ski resort, it felt like a slap in the face. I'd half lost faith in humanity. To have you show up out of nowhere, though, asking me about this?" He gave a tired smile. "The great thing is that life never stops trying to right the wrongs. Good luck."

Outside, I set the folder on the passenger seat of my car. The heat of the sun brought to life the scent of the old newspaper clippings and the waxy cardboard file, mingling with the ash still in the air. The huge plume of smoke had faded from the sky.

The ski resort was on my mind for most of the drive back into town. It was projected to bring in millions in revenue, which would be a big help to our economy during the winter months. The summer saw the majority of the tourism, and winter had always been about living off those proceeds. The ski resort could change all that. If anything happened to slow down the construction, our town would have to wait on that money. They hadn't broken ground yet, but it was supposed to happen in the next month or so.

I wanted to let this go, but there was a big question that lingered in the back of my mind. Both Belinda and the reporter believed the bridge collapse was due to negligence. When Trent asked questions about that, he was relegated to obituaries. Belinda had written the play and then told her father she felt her life was in danger. She died weeks later.

Looking at both of those things, I had to wonder: Was her death really an accident?

Chapter Twenty-Three

Back at the theater, I walked into the middle of a fierce debate that was going on in the rehearsal room. The actors stood around with their scripts, while both Piper and Sebastian argued with each other.

"Hey, what's going on?" I asked them.

Sebastian tossed up his hands in a fury and stormed off to a table and chairs by the windows. Piper beckoned me to the opposite corner, shoving her hands in the pockets of her baggy jean overalls.

"The electricians showed up without warning to hang the chandelier. Our persnickety director won't start rehearsal until it's done." She hesitated. "Sorry. That was unkind."

I smiled at her. "Sounds like it's been a tough afternoon. That's great news about the chandelier, though."

The chandelier was six layers of hanging crystals and electric candles, donated by one of the shipping families in the early 1900s. It was worth a startling amount and had been put into storage while the theater was shut down. I was thrilled that it was finally getting hung, but a bit of notice would have been nice.

"So, he doesn't want to rehearse here until they're done?" I said, taking in the wide space of the rehearsal room. "Isn't that what this room's for?"

"One would think." Piper unwrapped a piece of gum and shoved it into her mouth. "But he wants the production to start where it began. He's such a diva. Ughh. That wasn't nice, either."

I laughed. "I'll talk to him. I actually have to take off at five because my daughter has a dinner planned for us with her friends, so I do hope I can get him to see logic before then."

"You and me both." Piper tapped her clipboard. "Oh, and Arlo's taking a nap in your office. Hope that's okay."

"Of course." He must have felt like it was a safe place, which made me happy.

"Oh, my favorite director," I called.

Sebastian was sulking in the corner, eating a muffin and furiously writing notes on his script. He didn't even look up, so I slid into the wooden chair across from him.

"Hey, let's get to work," I said. "You're brilliant. You can do this in here. There's no reason to wait for the stage."

Dropping his pencil, he glared at me. "There is," he insisted. "We have already held practice on that stage. It sets the tone of the performance. It needs to feel professional."

"Professional would be getting to work, regardless of the perfection of your circumstances," I pointed out. "I know you have a vision for what you want it to be but—"

Piper rushed over and showed me her phone. "The electricians will be out of there in ten minutes."

Crisis averted.

"Great! We'll move straight to rehearsal when they're out." Looking at Sebastian, I said, "Can she inform the cast?"

He wasn't wearing a scarf today, so he settled for flipping the pages in his script before giving a curt nod.

"Okay, everyone," Piper said, clapping her hands. "Ten min—"

There was a loud shriek.

Everyone turned to look at Millie, who was clutching her heart. "There was a face! You guys, I just saw a face in that window," she squealed, pointing at the glass that looked out into the hallway. "Then it vanished."

One of the dancers leapt out the door. "No one's there," he reported, rushing back in.

Piper walked over and studied the window. Returning to me, she mumbled, "I was born for true crime, and there are no smudges on that glass." Raising her voice, she said, "Millie, let's stop getting everyone stirred up about nothing, please."

Millie stalked over to the window with a sour expression on her striking face. Since she was the ingenue of the season, everyone hung on her every word, I'd noticed, but Piper had told me that Millie caused drama whenever she could.

"I saw somebody." She put her hand to her heart. "This place has to be haunted."

"It is!" One of the actresses gave a vehement nod, her eyes as big as ever. "I was in the dressing room, and I had this feeling that someone else was there. I could hear someone breathing. You know how you can sense it if someone's present? Someone was *there.*"

Everyone started telling ghost stories again, and Millie's face looked a little too satisfied.

I rolled my eyes. "There's no ghost."

"Wait until that chandelier comes crashing down," the dancer said. "Then, we'll all be singing a different tune."

"Like this?" Our best soprano trilled out a line from *Phantom of the Opera* to great applause.

"Here's another theory." The redheaded actress waited until the group fell quiet; then she said, "The theater was abandoned for years. We could have a squatter. Someone living in the rafters."

It was possible. In the time period before the theater was remodeled, it had sat vacant. I remembered kids coming up here in high school and returning to school smelling of ash and soot, their heads full of scary stories. But no one could have remained here through all that construction. They would have been detected at some point. Still, nervous giggles spread through the crowd.

"Let's go on a hunt," Millie suggested. "Find him!"

Even though I didn't want the actors stomping all over everything, it would give them something to do while we waited.

"If you find anyone, let me know," I said. "Don't go near the stage yet, though, please—they're not done."

I was about to go peek in on Arlo's nap when Sebastian beckoned me back over.

"Now that we have the space, we'll need to make up the time that was lost," he said. "I'd like for you to tell the cast we'll be staying late because of this delay."

"Sorry, no," I said. "It wouldn't be appropriate to keep them here."

"There are pages of scenes we need to get through," he insisted. "I need an extra hour, at least."

"The schedule is already set," I said. "You can ask for volunteers, but we can't require anyone to be—"

The scream that cut through the air chilled me to the bone, and Sebastian nearly jumped into my arms.

"What was that?" he cried.

"It came from the lobby," Piper said, halfway out the door.

Quickly, we ran down the hall, our feet thundering against the thick carpet. A handful of actors were ahead of us.

"Oh, no," someone gasped.

We came to an absolute stop at the sight of Millie's body propping open the bathroom door, blood gushing from her head onto the white tiled floor.

"Call 911," I ordered.

My mind went into panic mode. It would take emergency services at least ten minutes to get up the bluff. We'd have to apply pressure to stop the bleed—

"Gotcha," Millie cried, with a trill of laughter. She sat up, proudly displaying a prop blood bag. "Ta-dum!"

The roar of laughter from the other actors was intense, followed by hoots, hollers, and reenactments, but I was stunned and then furious. Piper must have felt the same because she clapped her hands together.

"Millie, you're out for today."

"What?" Millie's face shot daggers. "That's not fair!"

"That was terrifying." My heart was pounding, and my whole body was covered in sweat. "I agree with Piper."

"It was a *joke*," Millie said, getting to her feet.

"Well, this isn't a comedy," Piper said. "You're out. Everyone else, get to the stage."

There were grumbles, but I had to give Piper credit. The terror I'd felt thinking someone had actually been hurt wasn't funny at all. If Piper had let that slide, the actors would have spent the rest of the season trying to one-up one another, and who knows what they would have come up with. Things were stressful enough without having to step over dead bodies on the floor.

"Ma'am?" A man in a blue work shirt approached me, holding out a clipboard. "I need someone to sign off on the installation." He gestured at the ground, where Millie had left a pool of fake blood. "You guys doing one of those dinner theater murder mysteries or something?"

"Feels like it," I said, my voice bright. "Let me take a look at the chandelier."

I followed him to the orchestra, where the other actors, including a deliciously disheveled Arlo, had started to assemble on the stage.

"The controllers are here on the wall, protected by a code," the electrician said, demonstrating. "Once the box is open, it illuminates with a pretty simple slide system. It's wired in so you can pull it up through your lighting system or manually, like this."

The chandelier was resplendent, shining with a golden glow that reflected off the gilded accents of the room. The actors cheered, bursting into hearty applause and high fives. My phone lit up with a text.

Arlo said:

Glowing up there like starlight. So, why are you the one who looks like heaven?

The words made me flush all the way down to my toes. I looked right at him up there on that stage, and he smiled that perfect, innocent smile. I wouldn't—I couldn't—walk this path. No matter how good it felt in the moment.

It was time for me to leave for the dinner Kaia had planned, and I was grateful because I didn't dare stick around.

My phone lit up with a text halfway to the car.

Considering the theater is haunted, I'd prefer you didn't ghost me.

The text made me laugh. I was tempted to go back in just to shake my finger at him, but instead, I hit the gas. There needed to be serious distance between me and the heartache that would come—without question—from falling for someone like him.

Chapter Twenty-Four

My grandmother and I met for an early coffee date at Morning Lark the next day. She hadn't started drinking lattes or any of the "fancy coffee" until last year, when one of the managers at the assisted-living facility brought in an espresso machine for the workers. My grandmother figured out how to use it, and in spite of the increase to her heart rate, she insisted on starting most days "Italian-style."

That meant an espresso with a perfect lemon rind.

"That looks delicious." I took a seat at a table over by the window, where she had our espressos hot and ready.

"I made it myself. Otherwise, they get sneaky and try to sub it out for decaf."

Her eyes lit up as I pulled a selection of cream puffs, chocolate éclairs, and a ham-and-cheese brioche out of the bag.

"Cut them up and share?" I suggested.

"Let's start with the cream puffs and éclairs," she said. "Otherwise the diabetics will sniff them out. I don't want them over here pretending to have a sugar dip just so they can get a taste."

"Grandma," I scolded.

"You think I'm joking," she muttered, cutting up the cream puff. "So, tell me everything about the theater. Will the show be stunning?"

"I think it's going to be wonderful," I said. "The dance numbers are steamy, but it's all in good fun, so I think people will love it."

Even though Sebastian had been difficult the night before, the rehearsals had been going great. The cast was exceptionally talented. It would be fun to blend in the locals—the audience was going to enjoy seeing people they knew from town.

"Mom's scheduled to come in sometime tomorrow for her first rehearsal," I added. "She's *so* excited."

"I'll be rooting for her," my grandmother said, licking some cream off the edge of a puff.

"Grandma, can I ask you a question?" I asked. "Do you remember much about Belinda Hamilton?"

She raised her eyebrows but didn't answer.

"We don't have to talk about it," I said.

"We can. I'm gathering my thoughts." She took a sip of espresso. "I remember Belinda well. She was a lovely person with so much talent. It seemed like she was always watching, trying to figure things out. Then, she fell in love with Jade's son. That's one thing I remember vividly, the way she lit up every time he walked into a room. I had a lot of guilt when . . . well."

My grandmother turned her focus to a robin with a bright-red chest hopping across the yard outside, pecking at the ground for worms.

"Life goes on," she said. "Still, there were several times after the incident at the theater that I felt intense regret for ever starting that place."

I thought back, trying to remember when the fire had happened. I was fifteen or so at the time, and I lived at my parents' house in town. They'd heard the news from a neighbor during breakfast, and my father had rushed right away to my grandmother's house. She'd been inconsolable at the entire situation.

"The Playhouse brought so much joy to our town," I said, thinking of the guilt that Jade carried, as well. "It's terrible that it ended that way, but now, it has the power to be a whole new beginning."

My grandmother wiped her hands off on a napkin. "Sometimes, when things end, there's no need to start them back up again. I certainly would not have."

Her words made a bite of whipped cream go dry in my mouth. This entire time, I'd suspected and then assumed that my grandmother was the reason the theater was back in business, even though she had claimed that she was not behind it. This was the first time I almost believed her.

"Grandma, I thought you were excited to see the Playhouse reopen."

My grandmother shook her head. "It's a mixed bag. Do you think it's fun for me to see a stage where I can no longer perform?"

"I hadn't looked at it like that." My mind was going a hundred miles a minute. "Who do you think started it, then?"

"Someone interested in the arts, I suppose." She smoothed her hair. "It shouldn't be difficult to research. Running the theater would require a business license, liability insurance, a paper trail with Equity . . . it should be simple to find out."

"It's not. I've tried."

As the theater manager, I had access to all that information, but everything was listed under a private investment company. "It seems deliberately set up so that no one will know, which is a little mysterious, don't you think?"

"I can think of several reasons investors would keep their name separate," she said, using a knife to cut into the brioche. The cheese spilled out of the sides. "If it's a success, they might not want other arts groups asking for money. If it's a failure, they wouldn't want it attached to their name. The list goes on."

"All good points," I said.

The way my grandmother explained it, there didn't seem to be much heat behind the secret at all.

"Did you know that your performance with Arlo is all over social media?" I asked, switching gears. "Kaia thought it might be fun for you to create an online presence. What do you think?"

My grandmother blinked. "I'm sorry, you lost me."

I took out my phone and pulled up some quick videos posted by some of her favorite older actors. She flipped through the phone, her forehead wrinkled in amazement.

"Who is watching this?" she finally said.

"Kaia's entire generation." I finished my part of the brioche, relishing the saltiness of the ham. "Mine too."

"I wonder if . . ." My grandmother continued to flip through the videos. "Grace is always cackling at something or other on her phone. This must be it."

She took a drink of water, completely engrossed. After landing on a stand-up comedy act about aging, she chuckled. "That's true," she said. "That's funny because it's true." She set down the phone and tapped the table with her fingers. "Why is Kaia interested in doing that?"

To me, the answer was simple. "Because we're here, and she wants to get to know her great-grandmother."

The first few years that I was married to Jin, we spent a lot of time in Starlight Cove, but once I'd had Kaia, life became complicated. There were changes with Jin's job, and eventually, he was traveling all the time, so we rarely made the trip to Michigan. Instead, my parents would visit us, but my grandmother didn't like to travel. As a result, Kaia never really had the opportunity to get to know her.

"Kaia wants to spend time with you. She absolutely loved doing that interview with you for her English class. I think it's important for her to develop her relationship with you and her grandparents, since Jin decided to jump ship." I held up my hands. "I'm not trying to guilt you into spending time with her by any means. I just want you to understand why it means so much to me when it happens."

"I adore spending time with her," my grandmother said, polishing off her espresso. "It's fun to be around someone young and lively. Lately, I've been feeling a little . . ."

"What?" I asked.

Her lashes cast shadows on her cheeks. "Visiting the theater showed me that I've become irrelevant."

"Grandma," I scolded. "That's not true. Everyone loved your performance."

She waved her hand. "It was a moment, and that was it. I suppose that's the same with any accomplishment. You get to the finish line, and you think, Was this all I was trying to do? I'd meant to do more. When the theater burned down, it took a lot of the plans I'd made with it."

"What do you mean?" I said.

"Well, I opened the theater after I gave birth to your father. Being an actress often means adjusting your life to fit into the opportunities that become available. To give him stability, I created my own opportunities through the Playhouse, and I'd planned to do that for years to come. But . . ." She gave a little shrug. "When the theater was destroyed, that was the end of that. It's not easy for an older woman to get work, especially from here. Plus, I felt responsible for Belinda's death, and that took the fun out of it for quite some time. I'll never get over that, but it's time to move on. I have more things to say, Lily, but nowhere to say them."

"Well, you're in luck," I told her. "There's a whole world out there now, ready to listen."

∼

The sky had darkened, and the breeze had picked up once I'd left the assisted-living facility. The wind blew my dress all around, and I had to hold the skirt in place on the way to the car. On the drive to the theater, more than one tree branch fell to the ground alongside the road, due to the heavy winds.

"Well, on the bright side, we might finally get rain," I mused, peering out the car window at the quickly graying sky.

Once parked and out of my car, I was startled to discover the temperature had dropped at least ten degrees. The abruptness of it all made me nervous, and I checked my weather app. It only reported approaching rain, but the trees were whipping around, and the lighthouse was on, flashing across the water.

I called my mother. "The weather seems weird. What do you think?"

I heard her step onto the porch to look outside. "Rain's coming. I think we forgot what it looks like."

Sure enough, the rain arrived just as I made it to the theater's front steps. I darted up, barely missing the torrential downpour. The door shut tightly, and I was grateful to make it inside without getting soaked.

Rehearsals were underway, so I headed into my office and turned on the lights, since the room was so dim. Outside, the trees waved frantically, as if trying to get my attention. A huge limb cracked and fell, tumbling to the ground and rolling several feet through the pelting rain.

My phone chimed. Kaia.

They're having us sit in the hallway for a tornado??

Thunder suddenly shook the theater, its vibrations rolling through long past the initial clap. The lights flickered. Outside, the sky had turned from gray to green, and Lake Michigan had gotten rough fast.

The telling sound of hail began to patter on the roof. Immediately, I called Piper.

"Get the cast down to the basement," I said. "Right away."

There were dramatic shrieks from the stage, followed by titters of excitement. I reviewed the key card check-ins to find out who was here. Quickly, I contacted Jade, the set designer, and the set crew and told them we needed to take shelter.

I tried to keep the mood light as I texted Kaia, but I was worried.

Yes, it's looking bad out there. Not how you planned to spend the last day of school, huh?

She sent a series of lightning emoji.

I knew my grandmother was fine at the assisted-living facility, as they had an emergency protocol for every situation possible, so I called my mom again while rushing out to the hallway.

"So, Kaia's in a tornado hall, and we're headed to the basement at the theater. What about you and Dad?"

"Yes, we'll go to the basement." In a whisper, she said, "I really hope he doesn't try to repair anything down there."

The cast streamed out of the theater, and I held open the trapdoor. Millie, who was at the front of the line, screeched to a halt.

"You expect us to go down there?" she demanded, adjusting her pink headband.

"Yes," I said. "Right now."

It looked like she was going to argue, but Arlo took care of that for her. "Sorry, that's not going to happen."

"What?" I demanded.

Hail was pelting the roof at an alarming rate. It sounded like tap dancers making their way across the stage.

He peered down the steps. "It looks like a tomb."

I gave the cast a bright smile and pulled him off to the side. "Imagine if you were in California, and this was an earthquake. Would you stand here debating about this, or would you try to get everyone to safety? This cast looks up to you. If you refuse to go, no one will."

The pupils in his ice-blue eyes were little black points. "I'm not comfortable in dark underground spaces."

"You said you weren't scared of anything."

"I lied."

"Arlo, please," I whispered. "The roof could come off. Those trees could fall on the theater. It won't be dark when we get down there." I held out my hand. "Take it. I won't let go."

He still hesitated. "There's light down there?"

"Yes," I said, praying the power wouldn't go out. "I promise."

He took my hand. My very own jolt of lightning shot through me as our skin touched, and I couldn't help but think about the kiss we'd shared on the stage.

"Come on," I said and led him down the steps.

The other actors were right behind us. Downstairs, I gave him a half smile. "Thank you for being a hero."

He shrugged. "It's what I do."

~

The basement smelled like mold, rocks, and a million different species of spider. Dim overhead lights buzzed on the ceiling like flies as lightning flashed outside the low windows.

Everyone at the theater was now underground, which gave me a sense of relief, in the event that the tornado had something to prove. In spite of the possibility of danger, everyone seemed calm.

Piper listened to music or a podcast on her phone, Sebastian talked set ideas with the stage crew, and Jade sat under the brightest light in the basement, quietly reading a book. The cast was giddy with the excitement of it all. Since the room was enormous, they immediately started in on a series of dance competitions.

I sat with Arlo by the wall, even though we were no longer holding hands. The stone was cool against my back, and I rubbed at the goose bumps on my arms.

"Here." Arlo handed me his pullover.

It was soft and warm and smelled like him. What was it Abby had said? Leather and sunshine? That might sum it up. I pulled it over my head, trying to pretend such chivalry was an everyday part of my life.

"Thanks," I said. "How's rehearsal going?"

"Excellent." Arlo's expression got intense. "We have a skilled cast, Sebastian's a strong director, I just . . ."

His voice trailed off.

"What?" I said. "If there's something we need to fix, tell me. The show's only two weeks away."

It was hard to believe things had clipped along that quickly, but they had. The moment this show went up onstage, the cast would start rehearsing for the next one. It seemed like a grind to me, but Arlo and every other actor here loved the pace.

"It's just nerves. I get worried about people being disappointed, seeing me live instead of on film," he said. "It's all right, though."

"Everyone will be thrilled to see you perform," I said, surprised. "People will be lined up around the block. I've caught a few of the rehearsals, and you're amazing."

"You think so?" he asked.

Outside, thunder boomed.

"I know so." I almost took his hand again but instead surveyed the room. There were a few actresses that seemed to be watching us, Millie in particular.

I pulled out my cell phone to check for any messages from Kaia. "My daughter's at school. Their tornado shelter is the hallway."

"Are you worried?" he asked. "I'm sure she'll be fine."

"I know, but I'm a mother," I said. "Mothers worry. I promise, your mother was thinking about you every second of every day."

Arlo looked down at his hands. I'd been speaking generally, but now, I remembered that she'd passed away.

"I'm sorry. That was presumptuous."

"No." He cleared his throat. "It's what I've always wanted to hear."

This time, I did reach over and squeeze his hand.

"Ooh, who wants to tell ghost stories?" one of the actresses cried. "Let's all sit in a circle. Come on, you guys."

The group of actors gathered around her.

"This seems like a bad idea," I said, watching.

"The fact that you're still holding my hand?"

Quickly, I let go, and he grinned. He pulled up the weather on his incredibly fancy phone and showed me. "The tornado warning is gone. It's back to watch, so you don't have to worry about your daughter."

The kindness warmed me. "Thank you. I'm going to keep everyone down here a few more minutes, just in case."

"You know, I'm still thinking about that play we found," he said, resting the back of his head against the wall. "When are you going to let me read it?"

"I keep meaning to bring it back in."

He studied me. "You know, I'm pretty good at reading people. I can tell when you're lying."

I made a face.

"It really concerns you, doesn't it?" he asked.

"Yes." I thought of my meeting at the newspaper office. "Because I'm starting to wonder if Belinda's death was really an accident."

His forehead wrinkled. "Her sister's death? The one in the play?"

"No, I mean hers," I said. "Since she wrote the play."

"That's serious. Do you really think that?"

I told him about my visit with Trent Brady. "The guy got demoted to writing obituaries for five years because he dared to ask questions in an article he was assigned to write. It makes me wonder if anyone knew about the play."

Arlo raised his eyebrows. "That's interesting."

"I have no proof, just paranoia." I thought of the reporter's office, how dark and dim it had been, along with the vague scent of old sandwiches. "The guy I met with gave me a ton of research. I plan to sift through at some point soon, but things have been busy."

"I can help," Arlo said. "It sounds fascinating."

"Maybe." I tried to picture him at my grandmother's house, sitting at the table in the backyard. The idea appealed to me more than it should have. "I don't know. You probably shouldn't get involved. The last thing you want is for your picture to appear in the paper, talking about murder."

Arlo shrugged. "I wouldn't be talking about murder. I'd be talking about justice."

Benjamin Hamilton jumped to mind. There'd been so many moments since the beginning of all of this where I'd seen him as a villain, but if any of this was true, he was the victim. He and his family. I was lucky—I could go home and hug my daughter, something that man couldn't do.

Arlo studied my face. It made me feel self-conscious.

"What?" I said. "Why are you staring at me?"

He drummed his fingers against the concrete floor. "Just trying to figure you out. I spend more time thinking about you than I should."

Such a line, but his delivery was perfect.

I glanced over at the actors. They were busy telling ghost stories. The one talking would shine their phone flashlight up into their chin, making their chin turn red. The effect was oddly creepy.

Arlo brushed his thumb over the back of my hand. "You know, this would be the part in the movie where two people trapped in a basement during a tornado would share a sweet, lingering kiss because it might be the end of the world."

"Hmm," I managed to say, even though heat was rushing through me. "How could that even happen? You save the world, every time."

Arlo laughed and leaned back against the wall. Outside, the lightning kept time with the beating of my heart.

∼

The storm passed, and Kaia texted to let me know she was safe. It took everything I had to not drive straight to the school, dodging downed trees and power lines, to get to my daughter. Instead, I settled for letting her spend the last day of the school year in peace. The moment it turned three o'clock, though, I was at the front door of the building with a colorful bouquet of helium balloons.

"Mom!" The word was uttered with equal parts embarrassment and joy. I held on when she hugged me tight.

"Happy last day of school," I said. "Are you excited for the summer?"

Kaia gave me a look indicating my question was the dumbest question in the history of humankind. Balloons bouncing against her wrist, she waved goodbye to her friends, and we headed for the parking lot.

"I would have been leaving for Japan tomorrow," she said suddenly. "I'm kind of . . ." She stopped walking, her backpack dangling from her hand. "Dad didn't want me there. Did he?"

My breath actually stopped. The pavement was wet and shiny from the storm, with little pieces of debris all over the parking lot. Steering Kaia over to a bench in a grassy area, I brushed off the water and laid down my coat, indicating she should sit.

"Kaia, your father was heartbroken this summer didn't work out," I said, thinking about the conversation Arlo and I had shared that first day. The importance of telling her what she needed to hear. "Remember the letter he sent you?"

Thank goodness, Jin had followed through on sending a letter that expressed heartfelt disappointment at the change in plans. She'd read it more than once and had even tucked it into the journal she kept in her room.

Kaia looked up at the balloons. "I know, but . . ."

"Norah got that grant, and it would have been—"

"Hard for him to be a parent?" Her dark eyes looked too wise for her years. The earrings she wore, the small lightning bolts made of diamonds, had been a gift from Jin.

I stared down at the delicate blades of grass next to the bench, wishing I had addressed all this sooner. Kaia had seemed to handle the situation with the canceled trip so well that I'd been much too quick to move on. It was clear that she missed her father, and it made me angry that I hadn't accepted the fact that she was hurting.

"Being a parent can be hard, yes," I said. "He lucked out, though, getting a daughter like you."

Kaia's face had started to soften, so I kept talking. "Did you know that when you were born, your father slept on the floor of your room almost every night?"

It was true. Jin had been so in awe of Kaia that he spent hours on the rug of her room, watching her sleep. It was a shame that dedication hadn't carried over to the present time, past the influence of Norah, but I still hoped the pendulum would swing back in her direction.

"He slept on the floor?" Kaia said. "You mean, in a sleeping bag?"

"No, the floor. He had a pillow, a blanket, and the floor. He just wanted to be with you."

"Until I started to walk and talk and have opinions that were different than his."

It hurt me to hear Kaia talking like this. There had been a point in her life when she'd been so close to her father, but at the same time, I recognized her words for what they were. He'd hurt her, and she didn't want to get hurt again.

"Your dad loves hearing your opinions," I said. "There were nights he'd be working on a project, and he'd say, 'I should wake up Kaia, she'll know the answer.'"

She laughed. "You wouldn't let him, I bet."

There was a hint of accusation in the statement, but I nodded. "No, I wouldn't."

We sat in silence, the air cool and fresh after the storm.

"Will I ever see him again?" Her voice was small.

"He's your father," I said.

"Please answer the question."

"I thought I did." I rubbed the back of my neck, trying not to hate Jin for making her feel this way. "You'll see him. It might not be this summer or even this fall . . ."

Kaia made a small sound, and I took her hands.

"You *will* see him. Many times, for many reasons. He's your father, and he loves you."

"I miss him," she said.

"Then let's call him," I said. "Right now."

It was five or six in the morning in Japan, but what did that matter? I should have started doing this a long time ago, to make sure Kaia felt a connection with her father, in spite of how it made me feel to see him.

The video call rang and rang, but he didn't pick up. She stared down at her hands as I tried again, feeling fury build with each ring. "He might already be at the grant site," I said. "The reception there could be spotty."

Kaia got to her feet. "Let's go home."

"Of course." I hesitated, wanting to say more, but she was already on the move. When I caught up with her, I said, "You're the best thing that ever happened to us, you know."

Much to my relief, she smiled. "Let's go get a pizza or something to bring home for dinner."

"You don't have to ask me twice."

Kaia narrated the adventures of the tornado warning on the drive home. I listened, but inside, I couldn't get past that moment she'd said, *Dad didn't want me there. Did he?*

It was a truth that I'd hoped she'd be too young to figure out on her own. There was only one thing I could do about it: I had to talk to him. I didn't want him to be a part of my life, but Kaia needed him.

I was going to have to put aside my anger in order to make sure that he understood how important it was to be a part of her life and how lucky he was to be her father.

Chapter Twenty-Five

The balloons were bouncing against the ceiling, and the pizza, steaming in the box. Setting a mixed salad onto the table, I called, "It's ready."

Kaia came running in, already dressed in her pajamas and her hair up in a ponytail. We'd planned to have a movie night once dinner was over. My mother showed up next, followed by my father.

He washed his hands, which were covered in some sort of grease. Then, once we were all settled at the table, he gave us a big smile. "I have an announcement to make." He looked pleased as punch. "First, Kaia, congratulations on the last day of school. We're so proud of you, and your grandmother and I are grateful every day that you're here in our home."

His words touched my heart. "That is so sweet. Kaia, what do you say?"

Kaia didn't answer. I realized she was wearing her earbuds and hadn't heard a thing.

"Kaia," I said, irritated.

Looking guilty, she pulled them out. "Sorry. Yes, I'll take some salad. Thank you."

"That's not what we were asking. Grandpa said something nice to you," I told her. "Please don't wear your earbuds to the table."

My mother spooned salad on both her plate and Kaia's, and my father clapped his hands together. "That's not my only announcement," he said, turning to me. "I wanted to say that I've given a lot of thought to the things your mother has said, and I scheduled those dance lessons that she wanted."

My mother clapped her hands together. "That is wonderful!" She rushed over and kissed him, which made me and Kaia roll our eyes. "Thank you. I'm so excited."

He nodded. "It starts next week, Wednesday nights. So, we'll go to the fish fry first and then—"

Her face fell. "I have rehearsals on Wednesday. The only night I'll have off for the next few weeks is Monday."

"You can skip one night to go to dance. It won't hurt anything."

"No, the cast is relying on me."

"Oh, come on," he exploded. "You barely speak! It's not going to impact anything."

My mother's cheeks turned pink. "I am an important part of the ensemble. The director told me that when I picked up the script."

My father grunted. "I bet he did."

My mother gave me a look, and I pressed my lips together. I was not about to get into the middle of this.

"Monday night is the only option," my mother said, dumping some garlic sauce onto the plate next to her pizza. "After that comment, though, I'm not sure that I want to do dance lessons with you at all."

She swept out of the room. Then, she returned and grabbed her plate before sweeping out once again. My father watched her go, chomping on a slice of deep-dish pepperoni.

I didn't know if I could stay quiet about this for much longer. Their fighting made me wonder if there were real problems, ones that I didn't want to see.

"Dad, I think it's really nice that you set that up," I said. "You didn't have to say that about the play, though. She'll have a lot to do backstage and with the chorus. Why don't you just reschedule the dance lessons when the play is over?"

"Because I've spent most of my life working around that theater," he said. "I never thought it would be something that I would have to do as a grown man. This is ridiculous! Your mother said she wanted to take dancing lessons with me. I set it up. She can show up."

"You're being unreasonable," I told him, but he'd already left the room.

Kaia looked at me. "I would have preferred to have my earbuds in for all that, but thanks."

I nodded, focusing on the pizza until I had my emotions under control. Finally, I sighed. "Let's start movie night early. Take our good vibe and our pizza to the couch?"

"Now you're talking."

Kaia and I moved our plates into the living room. Ten minutes into the movie, my mother came in to join us.

"I feel guilty," she told me. "I want to do the play, but I don't want your father to be mad at me."

My mother pulled a throw around her shoulders, still looking wounded. I stared at the television, uncomfortable with the entire situation.

I thought back to the night that they'd closed their fishing shop. It was the ultimate celebration, and when it came time to close the door for the last time, half of Starlight Cove stood outside, solemn. My father had put the key in the lock and looked at my mother. She'd put her hand over his, and they'd locked the door together. Everyone had burst into cheers and applause, and they'd kissed. It was one of the sweetest, most romantic displays of teamwork I'd ever seen, and I was convinced they'd rehearsed it.

My mother had been confused at the idea, and it touched my heart even more to realize that it was completely spontaneous. They were that good of a unit; they worked together in tandem, like two fish in a tank.

Now, they were more like fish out of water. Unsure of what the other was doing or wanted to do, and unsure with what they wanted to do. It was a good decision to close up the shop—they were both ready for it—but I didn't think they had been ready for the blank canvas that came next.

"Mom, can I talk to you a second?" I asked. "In private?"

Kaia let out a hearty sigh. "I sincerely hope you're not going to ask me to pause the movie."

"No, honey," I said. "You go ahead. We'll be right back."

I led my mother out to the back porch and took a seat on the outdoor sofa. It had started to get dark, the fireflies were out, and I could hear cicadas somewhere in the forest. Finally, I turned and looked at her.

"I get it that it's a time of transition for you and Dad. But what on earth is going on with the fighting? You guys never fought when I was growing up, so why are you doing it now?"

The catch in my throat was embarrassing, but I'd had enough.

"Lily." My mother sounded baffled. "Your father and I fought all the time."

"No, you didn't," I told her. "You fought about that turkey that one time, and that was pretty much it."

"Oh." My mother sat in silence for a minute. "You must have thought we had the perfect relationship. When in truth—"

"When in truth what?"

"It was a good relationship, but it was never perfect. No relationship is." My mother smoothed her cardigan, staring out at the trees. "We spent so much time at the store. That's where we did our fighting because that's where we had things to fight about. We were never perfect, but I think we did okay. Everyone fights. You work through it and move on."

That brought the tears. The idea that Jin and I couldn't work through it was so humiliating.

"Lily." My mother's voice was quiet. "I was speaking of my marriage, not yours." She looked down at her hands. "There must be times where you wonder whether or not you and Jin did the right thing, separating. I think you did."

"Really?" I said, fumbling in my pockets for a tissue.

My mother had never given me her opinion about the divorce. She'd kept it vague, saying things like "It's your life, and you have to do what you think is right."

"I thought you were disappointed in me," I said. "That I didn't work it out."

"No." She thought for a minute. "The thing that I'd liked about Jin was the way that he watched out for you. He'd bring the umbrella, the bug spray, an extra sweatshirt. I'll never forget . . ." Her voice trailed off, and I could see she was hesitating.

"Say it," I told her.

"When we visited for Kaia's ninth birthday."

My cheeks heated. I remembered that day well.

"Your dad and I flew in for her party, and since you were both busy, we decided to take a car from the airport. We walked in to find you desperately trying to make gift bags. The dishes weren't done, the cake needed to be picked up, and Kaia wanted you to braid her hair. Jin was right there in the living room, watching a baseball game. Do you remember that?"

I nodded. My father had turned off the television and said something like, *Come on, son. Looks like Lily needs help getting ready for the party.*

Jin had been furious about that.

"His reluctance to participate in the day was obvious," my mother said. "He was happy to celebrate Kaia, but he'd stopped watching out for you."

It hurt, hearing my mother say the truth.

"I kept hoping it was just a season." She glanced at me. "It wasn't."

"No."

There were several times before the text thread between Jin and Norah popped up on my computer that it was obvious he had already checked out.

"You deserve so much more than that, Lily. Forever is a nice idea, but happy has a better ring to it."

I nodded, surprised and a little worried to hear her say that. "What about you, though? You and Dad seem unhappy. I don't like seeing you that way."

"We'll be fine," she said. "I think we're just trying to figure out how to manage retirement. It's not easy."

"Sitting around doing nothing isn't easy?" I said.

She laughed. "It's a lot harder than it looks."

I stared up at the sky, watching as it darkened in slow patches. "I think it's good that Dad made the effort with the dance lessons. Just give him time."

"I will." My mother nodded. "The good news is that we have plenty of that these days."

~

Even though the talk with my mother made me less worried that my parents' relationship was falling apart, I still couldn't get the fighting out of my head. It motivated me to do better at handling my relationship with Jin. I tried to call him again once Kaia went to bed, but he didn't pick up. I found myself worrying about him as I got ready for bed, which was frustrating.

Even though we no longer shared a life, he still had the ability to take up my time and energy. Because he was Kaia's father, he always would.

I'd done my best to push the heartache of the divorce far from my mind, but given the fighting with my parents and the way Jin had disappointed our daughter, the failure of it all was right there at the surface. The idea that I'd made the choice to marry—and have a child with—someone who I'd misread had done a number on me.

I hadn't walked into marriage thinking that one day, it would come to an end. I'd never dreamed my husband would suddenly decide he wanted a completely different life. The fact that he had . . .

I shook my head. There were days I was better at handling it than others.

Those days, I was strong enough to remind myself that I wasn't the one who had decided to fail. I hadn't fallen in love with someone else. I hadn't walked away from my child. The other part of me, the part that loved to consider the other side of things, kept asking what I could have done different.

Should I have been a better listener? A better friend? It was hard to not blame myself for the fallout that now faced my daughter.

Pulling the pillow close, I squeezed it tight. Maybe I could have done something to change the way that it had all played out, but here I was. Living with my parents, raising my daughter alone, and caught up in a ridiculous crush on a movie star who would forget all about me the moment he left town.

It was hard to feel like I mattered at all, but that was just the heartache talking. I had to move past it, to let it go. Letting out a deep breath, I stared out my bedroom window at the expanse of the stars.

Kaia had been the greatest gift of my life. I wouldn't have her if I hadn't walked the path that I did with Jin. In spite of that, I couldn't help but find it unfair that, in order to see the light, I had to sit for these long and lonely moments in the dark.

Chapter Twenty-Six

It took a few cold slices of pizza and a dish of ice cream to pull myself out of my melancholy, but I got it done. That's when I remembered I had other things to think about, like the accordion folder full of information that the reporter had given to me. My parents were asleep, so I spread the paperwork across the kitchen table.

There were several documents. The design plans for the bridge, the dates and permission documents, the inspector notes, and the report following the accident. I flipped through each page, reading every word but not finding anything that wouldn't have been seen before. Drumming my fingers against the pages, I picked up the newspaper article about the ribbon-cutting ceremony.

It seemed that the bridge was rushed because Mayor Matty had planned the ribbon-cutting ceremony around an enormous campaign fundraiser that took place during the Starlight Cove wine festival. The fundraiser was a huge event that brought in the big-ticket summer people—the types that would pay $200 a plate to attend the gala and contribute a great deal of money toward the silent auction.

The records showed that the timeline of the bridge had fallen behind. In the days leading up to the festival, the crew had worked for an accelerated rate to get it done. That was one of the details highlighted in the paper—how rapidly the crew had worked toward the end, and how many hours of overtime had been filed for the workers.

I flipped through to find the paperwork of the final inspection. It was signed with an illegible signature. But if Belinda's play was to be believed, the inspection never happened.

I sat back in the chair, considering the idea. It was hard to believe the construction company would have falsified the paperwork, regardless of who was pressuring them. There was just no need to do that. They could have cut the ribbon, had the ceremony, and still finished up the safety-precaution protocols before opening the bridge.

Back when this happened, Mayor Matty had just been elected. He'd only been in office a year or two. If he had made a mistake that caused the bridge collapse, it should have ended his career. The fact that he remained in office, and the construction company was cleared, indicated that there was no wrongdoing. In spite of the suggestions Belinda had made, there was no way they could have gotten away with all that.

The only wrongdoing I could see was that the bridge was not structurally sound. Like Trent had mentioned in our meeting, the construction company built the bridge and, therefore, should have been responsible when it failed. The part that seemed odd to me was that they were cleared of any wrongdoing and, twenty years later, welcomed back to our town to build another high-profile project.

I flipped through some further pages and studied the photo that had appeared in the paper, taken the day before the bridge collapse. It had several of the city leaders standing at the entrance to the bridge, squinting and smiling in the bright sunlight. I didn't recognize many of them, but it struck me that Mayor Matty and his wife had been so young.

I hesitated, studying another man in the photograph. He was hard to see because the picture was old and a little grainy. I grabbed a pair of my mother's reading glasses and squinted at it under the light.

It took me a moment, but I realized what had pulled me in. The man in the photograph was the same guy who had been in the photo album at the theater, the one the girls had teased Jade about dating. Running my finger along the caption, I found his name: Everett Ferris, owner of Ferris and Illyiad Construction.

I sat back in my chair with a thud.

Jade had been dating the head of the construction company. The one who had built the bridge. The one who had something to lose if people refused to accept the story that they'd been spoon-fed about the bridge collapse.

To be absolutely certain, I looked him up online. Sure enough, his face popped up on an announcement about the Starlight Cove ski project.

Everett Ferris was older and grayer, but I recognized him in an instant. He was the mayor's brother-in-law, the owner of the construction company, and the one on the bridge crew who had a connection to the theater. He was also the one who now held a multimillion-dollar contract to bring a ski resort to Starlight Cove.

~

The next morning, I paid a visit to the costume shop, carrying two cups of coffee. I'd planned to bring Kaia in that day to start as an intern, but she was still asleep when I left, so I wrote a note to my mother asking to bring her over after lunch. I didn't know how much time I'd have for this conversation with Jade, but I wanted to have it in private.

"Good morning," I called, walking in.

The sewing machine was whirring away in the back. I followed the sound to Jade's office to find her with a needle and thread stuck between her lips, busily pulling the seam out of a purple sequined dress. I'd seen her with the same dress up onstage the day before. Under the magic of the lights, it had looked magnificent, but here, it seemed worn out.

"What happened to that dress?" I said, setting the coffee down and taking a seat. "Its color was so pretty yesterday, but you did something to change it on purpose, right?"

"It's the opposite," Jade said. "The gels in the lights changed it to look good onstage. The lighting makes all the difference. The gels affect things like the time of the day—morning looks different than dusk, so we have to have a way to show that. The gels also impact colors, like this dress. By now, I can spot the costumes that might not look great on the surface but will absolutely sing beneath the lights."

"That's pretty impressive."

"It's the magic of theater, isn't it?" The needle flashed like a sword as she attacked the seam of the dress. "We accept what we see, no matter how many times it's been shifted and twisted to suit our purposes." She studied me over the rim of her glasses. "What's on your mind? I know you're not here to talk about light gels."

"Well, it's complicated," I said. "I need it to stay between us."

Jade nodded, stitching away.

"So, I found a play hidden in the theater," I said. "It was written by Belinda Hamilton."

Jade stopped sewing. "Oh." She set down the dress, slid her reading glasses onto her head, and took a sip of coffee.

"Did you know she was a writer?" I asked.

"Belinda was exceptionally talented onstage. I'm surprised to hear . . ."

My heart felt hopeful. "You didn't know?"

If Jade hadn't known about the play, Everett Ferris would not have known either. That would make my theory impossible.

"My son loved writing poetry," Jade mused. "I haven't thought about it in quite some time, but yes, he and Belinda shared a love for writing."

My stomach dropped. "Oh."

"I'm surprised to hear that you found the play here, especially after so much time. You should get it to her father."

"That's not a good idea," I admitted. "It's about the bridge collapse."

Jade raised her eyebrows. "Sorry, what?"

"Belinda's sister died in a bridge collapse a few years before her death. She had some pretty big ideas about who was responsible, and even though the event is disguised as a building collapse, well—"

The door opened, and Arlo walked in. He wore a pair of cargo pants and a tight gray T-shirt that fit him in a way that made me lose my train of thought.

"Hi," I said.

He glanced between me and Jade. "Ladies." He settled into an armchair, his spicy cologne drifting toward me. "What am I walking in on?"

"Sewing," Jade said.

"We were talking about the play," I told him. Turning back to Jade, I said, "He was with me when I found it."

"Yes, it's intense. I've only read a small amount of it," he said, giving me a pointed look. "So much raw emotion."

Jade raised her eyebrows. "Does it say good things about my son?"

"The boyfriend in it was a dream guy, so I imagine that came from somewhere," I said. "You're welcome to read it, but it can't go further than these walls. You mentioned Belinda's father—he once told me that Belinda felt she was in danger. In my opinion, it was because of the play—she was blaming some pretty powerful people. I don't want Benjamin Hamilton to see the play at this point. It will just reinforce his belief that something intentional happened here."

Plus, if he really was the one sending those emails, it might push him to take action.

"What do you mean?" Jade demanded. "Something intentional?"

The words felt stuck in my throat. I'd been so focused on the idea of Belinda that I hadn't considered the fact that Jade's son had been a casualty of the same theory. Now that I'd opened my mouth, I had to explain.

"Benjamin Hamilton showed up on my doorstep the night he heard the Playhouse was reopening," I told her. "He was really upset and told me that Belinda felt like she was in danger the last few weeks of her life. She thought someone wanted her dead. He thinks what happened here at the theater was not an accident."

Jade bowed her head. "I didn't know that."

"Yeah." I ran my fingers over a scrap of fabric. "I didn't take him seriously until we found this play. It's intense—it points some fingers."

"Could you be more specific?" Jade said.

"The mayor, the construction company, the people involved with the bridge collapse."

"I think it should be performed," Arlo said, stretching. "Workshopped, at least. Bring it all to the surface. 'What's past is prologue,' you know?"

The Tempest. It was irritating how he managed to look hot quoting Shakespeare about a topic that got under my skin.

The three of us sat in silence. Finally, Jade pulled a needle out of the pincushion and got back to work.

"Even if it's inflammatory," she said, "I would still like for my son to have a chance to see what she wrote. It might bring back good memories. He never got over her, you know. I wish . . ." Her voice caught, and impatiently, she straightened her shoulders. "I'd like to read it, if I could."

"Of course," I said. "I'll get you a copy."

"From what I understand, copy machines have the capability to create multiple printouts." Arlo challenged me with his ice-blue eyes. "Make me one too."

I shot him a look, and he grinned. "Please."

Jade looked back and forth between him and me. Then, understanding seemed to dawn on her face.

I shook my head. "It's not what you think."

"Don't presume to know what I'm thinking." Her voice was light, but there was a threat behind it. "When will it be ready?"

I'd kept the folder at home in my desk because I didn't want to drag around the original. It had been preserved for years, and I didn't want to risk losing or damaging it.

"I'll have my mother bring it in when she comes here today, and I can make the two of you copies," I said. "She and my daughter will be here after lunch."

Quickly, I sent a text with the request. Then, I added:

Please be super careful. It's irreplaceable.

"Thanks." Jade closed the seam, and I marveled at her skill as, lightning quick, she secured it with a knot. "I didn't plan to revisit all of this, but the past seems to insist on showing its face, doesn't it?"

"I guess so," I said.

"And Arlo, I'm sorry we got sidetracked," Jade said. "You wanted to go over the event, right?" She glanced at me. "I've organized an event at the animal shelter. Something small, but Arlo has agreed to make an appearance. They'll have adoptable animals on site, information about their programs, and a silent auction. It should be a good cause, so if you can make it, please do."

I was surprised I hadn't already heard about it.

As if reading my mind, she added, "There should be something in the paper tomorrow."

"Jade, I love it that you're doing that," I said. The schedule at the theater was somewhat demanding, so I was impressed she'd made the effort in a town that wasn't her own.

"I help where I can," she said, sliding a pair of readers onto her head. "Especially here. I'm happy to give back."

The two of them discussed the details, and I wasn't sure whether to stay or go. When I finally got up to leave, Arlo also stood and stretched. His shirt crept up, showing off his perfect abs.

"I should get back to rehearsal," he said. "Lily, walk with me?"

We headed out together, through the costume shop with so many stunning getups on display, and back out into the hallway.

Once the door clicked shut, Arlo said, "I'm still thinking about the play. I'm a little worried to have Jade read it. If there's any truth behind the idea that the fire was not an accident . . . that's a painful thing to consider. It would mean her son's injuries were preventable, and that the person who caused them could still be out there."

He made a good point. It was one thing to theorize about what had happened to Belinda but another to have someone directly affected by this requestioning all that had happened, especially when she was here for the very purpose of letting go of the past.

"I realized that when I was in there, explaining it all to her." I rubbed my hands against the sudden chill on my arms. "I shouldn't have said anything."

"How did the topic come up?" Arlo asked. We walked down the hallway toward the lobby and my office, the red carpet silent beneath our feet. "I know you feel bad about it, so I'm really not trying to make you feel worse. I'm just curious."

"Because I wanted to find a link between the theater and the bridge collapse. The man she dated back then was the head of the construction company."

Arlo stopped walking. "Oh." He frowned. "You know, I've known Jade for a long time now, and—"

"You have?" I said.

He rested his arm on the wall outside my office door and gave me a curious look. "You really haven't spent much time researching me, have you?"

"Do you want me to?" I asked.

The way he was looking at me made my heart pound. He reached out and smoothed the collar on my shirt in a way that made me flush.

"I'll save you the trouble," he said. "Jade was the costume designer on the only film where I was nominated for an Academy Award. I was nominated because her costumes were so good." He grinned. "Not true. I was brilliant. That said, she did champion my career from the beginning."

"Did you know she was going to be here at the theater this summer?" I asked.

"That's why I signed on," he said. "We're good friends."

I sat with that for a minute. It was a surprise, in some ways.

"We were never together," he said, as if reading my mind. "She's been like my mother. She's always watched out for me, been protective. The thing that no one tells you about fame is that you do it alone. The people who come up with you become your family because you've been through it together."

"You've met her son, I guess." I beckoned Arlo into my office. We both took a seat on the couch, and his gaze searched mine, as if he was deciding how much to say. "You can trust me," I assured him. "I'm not going to talk about it with anyone."

"Thanks for saying that." He sat for a minute, thinking. "One of the things that has caused her a lot of pain is that this all happened when he was at the age where their relationship started to shift, you know? She'd stopped being just his mother, and he started to become a friend. They'd had this amazing summer here, so many adventures out on the water, going to Mackinac, hiking the dunes, all of it. After the fire, things were never the same. He had all those surgeries, got addicted to pain meds. It was hard." He shook his head, sitting back into the cushions. "Ryder's strong. He went through it, but now he's a successful business guy, travels a lot, enjoys his life. He avoids the arts, though, which is Jade's whole world. It's hard on her . . . there's so many levels of loss in that situation, you know?"

"In some ways, she lost him that night."

He nodded. "Yeah. Sharing those moments that summer, back when Ryder had just become a grown-up, meant everything to her. In some ways, I think that's why she came here. To get closer to the memory of all that."

"That breaks my heart," I said.

It was years away from when Kaia would be that age and stage, where we would be on an equal level and she would treat me like a friend. Still, I'd already imagined what it would be like during that time. I could understand how significant it had been for Jade and how much it must have hurt to have that taken away from her.

"She's so strong," I said. "I can tell how much she loves him."

"Yeah." Arlo nodded. "There's no doubt about that."

"I hope that being here is the best thing for her," I said. "I hope it helps her find the good memories, instead of the bad ones."

"Jade fights to find the good," he said. "Really, she never stops. Today, it's animals. Yesterday, she was holding babies."

"What do you mean?" I said.

"She gets up at the crack of dawn two days a week, drives downstate, and holds babies in the NICU. She's been doing it about a month now, here. She does it in LA too."

The news surprised me. "Really?"

Arlo nodded. "One of her main causes back home is helping underprivileged kids get prom dresses. She organizes donation drives and spends hours cleaning the dresses up, sewing them, all of it. She has a heart of gold. It's just been hurt many, many times."

"Wow," I said. "I didn't know any of this about her."

We sat in silence for a moment. Then, he said, "Would you like to go to dinner with me tonight?"

The invitation made my heart pound. "No. That's not a good idea."

"It sounds like a great idea to me."

I wanted to spend more time with him—there was no question about that—but like he'd guessed that night on the stage, I hadn't been on a date since the divorce. I certainly hadn't expected to start easing back into it all with a movie star.

Looking around the office, I tried to find a good excuse hidden somewhere in the small bookshelf, the detailed decorating, or the comfortable couch, but I couldn't come up with a thing.

"I'm not ready for all that," I admitted. "You're bored, so you're looking for some sort of entertainment, and I get that, but I can't be that for you. It would be too hard on my heart."

"It's not like that." Arlo's eyes searched mine. "I look forward to seeing you, Lily. You're one of the few people I've met in the past few years where I have no idea what's going to come out of your mouth. You're also one of the most attractive women I've ever seen, so there's that."

I started laughing. "You had me up until that line."

"I mean it." His eyes dropped to my lips. "There's something about you that's captivating. Your ex-husband is an idiot. Sorry, but he is."

"You're very good at this," I said.

"I *have* been called a heartthrob."

He was so funny, so unassuming. What was the harm in spending some time with him, giving myself a chance to feel good? It didn't have to go further than that.

Our eyes met, and a warm feeling spread all the way down to my toes.

"When do you have rehearsal today?" I asked.

"Not until this afternoon."

I stood up.

"Then, let's get out of here," I said, before I could change my mind. "It's not dinner, but I know a place where we can talk."

"I wouldn't mind something to eat too," he said.

I smiled at him. "Do you like ice cream?"

Chapter Twenty-Seven

Arlo's eyes lit up as I handed him the warm waffle cone, the two scoops of hard ice cream practically steaming with cold. The butter pecan had looked delicious, so I'd gotten the same for myself.

Eyes closed, I licked it, practically melting as a slightly salty pecan crunched against the cold sweetness of the buttery, burnt-caramel flavor.

"This is heaven," I murmured.

Arlo was equally lost, finding creative ways to take bites of the waffle cone.

We were seated on a bench that was blocked from view thanks to an enthusiastic weeping willow and the way Arlo had parked the Range Rover. We ate in blissful silence, surrounded by the scent of vanilla and spun sugar. The families that walked in and out of the shop were so focused on deciding between flavors and whether or not to get a cone or a sundae with chocolate sauce and a dab of fluffy whipped cream that no one was really looking around. That left us to sit in silence and privacy, enjoying every bite.

Once we'd eaten, Arlo leaned back on his hands. "Sometimes, I dream of giving it all up and moving to a small town."

"Where do you live in LA?" I asked.

"Brentwood." He squinted out at the street, watching as kids rode by on bikes. They rang bells and laughed, having the time of their lives. "It actually has an incredible small-town feel, but of course, it's not. It would be such a different experience growing up in a place like this. How did your daughter deal with the weather situation yesterday?"

"Good." I appreciated that he'd asked. "It was her last day of school, so that was the real excitement. She's going to help out at the theater, starting this afternoon. You'll get to meet her but . . ."

"Keep my burning attraction on the down-low?" He chuckled. "I get that."

Even though I knew he was joking, I still liked hearing it. "Look, I feel the same," I said. "It's no secret."

"You're doing a pretty good job keeping it a secret from me."

"Well, you have a girlfriend, you're in town for just a few months, and I have a daughter. Oh, and everyone in the world likes you, so this shouldn't really be a news flash."

Arlo pulled on his ball cap. It drew attention to his eyes, which were sometimes so enchanting that they were hard to look into. "What if I said Tatiana dumped me?"

"I'd feel better, but don't you guys break up a lot?"

"It keeps us honest." Reaching out, he brushed his thumb over my lip. "You had a little drop of ice cream," he said, but I didn't entirely believe him. I just knew that my whole body felt like it was melting because my attraction to him made it difficult to focus on anything else.

"We should head back—" I started to say, but then, he leaned in and kissed me.

A real kiss, much more intense than the sugar rush from the cone. I wrapped my arms around him and felt like I was falling as he pulled me closer, kissing me in a way I hadn't been kissed in years and making me wish to be somewhere other than a public picnic table where anyone could see us or—I drew back—take our picture. Quickly, I looked around. Everything was as it had been, the branches from the weeping willow waving gently in the wind.

Arlo took my hand, his grip firm as if leading me somewhere. He opened the door to the car, and I climbed back up. He leaned in and gave me another kiss. Then, he was in the driver's seat.

"Back to the theater," I said, but he ran his hand up my thigh.

"You sure? The tiny little cottage I'm living in is pretty interesting," he said. "So cozy. Do you want to see it?"

My cheeks flushed. "I . . ."

The clock on the dashboard said it was almost eleven. There was still plenty of time until my daughter would be at the theater. Plus, the smell of his cologne was back on my cheek, and it was all I could think about.

"I like cozy," I managed to say.

His eyes darkened, and deftly, he backed out onto Main Street. Next thing I knew, we were heading up the bluff. He reached over and took my hand, and I squeezed it tight, not knowing what had come over me.

Bravery, maybe? It might also be stupidity. For now, though, I was perfectly okay with both.

Chapter Twenty-Eight

Arlo and I agreed that he should wait out in his car for ten minutes before coming back into the theater. It made it less likely that people would see us arriving together. My cheeks felt flushed, and my body tingled as I walked to the front doors. I didn't know if I'd just made the biggest mistake of my life or the best decision ever, but I did know the last hour of my life had been incredible.

The cast members that had been in rehearsal had just come out for their lunch break, and I said hello, hoping my smile wasn't too bright. Walking toward my office, I jumped a mile when I saw my mother walking down the hallway with Kaia.

"There you are," my mother called. "We're here!"

"Hi!" Instantly, I felt guilty. "I thought you guys were coming after lunch?"

"Kaia was so excited that we decided to come early to surprise you."

"Then, come see my office," I said, quickly steering them down the hall. I did not want the three of us to be standing there when Arlo walked in. "Honey, you look adorable."

My daughter wore a combination of colors that never would have looked right on me but somehow made her look as bright as a flower garden. She had a gift for putting together cute outfits. I wondered if Jade would be interested in having her help in the costume shop.

"Did you bring the play?" I asked my mother. That text seemed like a thousand years ago. My cheeks and neck felt chafed, and my body, exhausted in the best possible way.

"Yes." She pulled it out of her oversize bag and handed it to me.

"Kaia, get ready . . ." I smiled at my daughter, who raised her eyebrows. "I have your first task as an intern. It's time to learn how to use the copy machine."

~

The copy machine had been a challenge for me ever since I started. It felt like I was always having to call on Piper to help, but under my daughter's capable hands, I soon had two collated copies of *The Script Calls for Revenge*. My mother looked on in interest, flipping through a couple of the pages. Quickly, her face changed.

"This is pretty heavy," she said. "Belinda wrote it?"

"Yeah," I said, nodding.

"Who's Belinda?" Kaia asked.

Over her head, my mother and I exchanged a look. "The million-dollar question is, Who's hungry?" I said, keeping my voice bright. "I haven't had lunch yet, and I assume you haven't, either, so let's go grab a bite. I'll introduce you to another important part of the theater, the break room."

My mother glanced at her phone. "I would love to go on that adventure with the two of you, but I have to go to my first rehearsal." She smoothed her hair and gave me a hopeful look. "Do I look okay?"

Once again, my mother had made an extra effort with her appearance. It was so nice to see her out of the house and her bathrobe, finding ways to enjoy her life, that I gave her a spontaneous hug.

"Stunning," I told her. "Ladies, let's go."

We headed out of the copy room, and Kaia stopped short. "Oh, wow."

My heart did a tap dance at the sight of Arlo. I mentally ran through all the reasons I should not think about what he'd looked like an hour ago, his face next to mine on the pillow. Taking a breath, I willed my voice to sound normal.

"Hey, Arlo," I called. "There's someone I want you to meet."

Considering I had spoken to him so many times about my daughter, and after what had just happened between us, my expectations were high for their meeting. I imagined Kaia sharing that same instant connection I had with him, and him showering her with praise and attention. I led her forward, and we stopped next to a pair of baroque wall lamps that provided especially good lighting for his exceptional face.

Full of pride, I said, "This is my daughter, Kaia."

His smile was quick. "Hey, I'm Arlo. I've had a great time working with your mom."

I didn't know what I'd expected, but I felt disappointed, somehow. His smile was the same one I'd seen him give to the members of the ensemble at the theater. Kind but vaguely tolerant. He wasn't rude by any stretch of the imagination; it was just that I'd envisioned something a little more personal.

Kaia stared down at her black Converse sneakers, as if mesmerized by their hot-pink laces. I wanted her to look up, smile back at him or something, but she just nodded, mumbling, "It's nice to meet you."

The three of us stood in silence. I could see Arlo was starting to get fidgety, so I said, "Well, we've got to get some things done, so we'll see you around."

"Sure thing." Arlo reached out and touched Kaia's arm. "Really great to meet you, Kaia."

This time, she smiled up at him. Their eyes met, and I was delighted to see his guard come down. For a split second, they shared a connection.

It was all I'd wanted.

"See ya," I said, and moved on.

∿

I was just getting into bed, about to relive some of the memories with Arlo from earlier that day, when my phone rang. Jin.

"Hello," I said, picking up. "How are you?"

"Busy." He sounded irritated, like returning my call had taken precious moments from his day. "Everything okay with Kaia?"

My shoulders tensed. We'd had such a polite conversation the last time that we spoke. It surprised me that now, he was back to being dismissive. I'd seen him act this way for years toward people he wasn't interested in, like waiters or the guys from the car wash. It was one of the few things I'd disliked about him, and I'd never expected that one day, he'd use that same tone with me.

The purpose of my call, though, was not to pick him apart. It was to figure out how we could come together. I couldn't stand the way I felt when my parents were fighting, and I didn't want to put Kaia through the same thing. The things she'd said, and the misery on her face while she held tight to that colorful bouquet of balloons, made it more important than ever for us to figure out how to work as a united front.

"I need to talk to you about something," I said after closing my bedroom door. "Originally, Kaia seemed fine when you backed out this summer. She got your note, it helped a lot, but on the last day of school, she said some things that concerned me."

"Like what?" Jin said.

I heard a rhythmic scraping sound and realized he was on the rowing machine. If the grant site was so remote, how was that possible? Did he happen to find a piece of exercise equipment perched on the edge of a cliff?

"Um, I'm confused," I said. "I thought you were off doing this big research project in the wilderness. They have workout places there?"

"Turns out, I'm only able to go on the weekends," he said. "The internet connection wasn't reliable enough to work remote, so I have to be here."

The news floored me. "So, you're home? All week? Every week?"

"Yes. That's how it worked out, which is not what I was expecting."

Well, if he was home, there was no reason Kaia couldn't be with him. I wanted her here with me, but I was not about to let my feelings get in the way of what was best for her.

"You told me the reason Kaia couldn't come was because it wasn't a good time. That you'd be at the grant site. If you're not there, I don't see any reason why she can't be there with you."

The pause was long. I could hear him row harder.

"I hear what you're saying," he said. "I've been considering all of that. Trust me, it's a lot more complicated than you think."

"It doesn't seem that complicated. You're there. Kaia would have your full attention for the week, since Norah's not there, so it wouldn't even matter if you two spent weekends at the grant site."

"I know that, but . . . look, we've already canceled the ticket. You told her, I wrote a letter, she's accepted the situation. Why put her through another change? She's young, and I think it would be hard on her if we kept asking her to adapt to what works for us in the moment."

"Jin, she wants to see you," I said. "She doesn't understand why you don't want to see her."

"Did you tell her that?" he demanded.

"*You* told her that when you canceled the trip." I was careful to keep my voice low. Last time I checked, Kaia was asleep in bed, but I didn't want to risk her waking up and hearing this conversation. "I've been doing damage control. The fact that you are available after all and that you didn't make a point to tell me that right away is kind of heartbreaking, to be honest."

"Because it won't work out to have her here right now," he said. "It's not the right time."

"To be a parent?" I cried.

"Lily, please don't make this dramatic."

The words were so filled with disdain that I wanted to throw the phone across the room. So much for having a calm, rational discussion where we could figure out how to work as a united front.

"I am not being dramatic," I said, fighting to keep my voice steady. "I'm telling you what's happening with your daughter, and I'm asking you to step up." Letting out a slow breath, I said, "What if she came to visit for two weeks? Could you handle that?"

"She wouldn't want to come for such a short time."

"I bet she would," I said.

The fact that he was hesitating made me wonder why I was fighting so hard. Maybe Kaia didn't need to have a relationship with him at all at this point. If he couldn't recognize how amazing she was, how important she was, then he didn't deserve to be with her.

It wasn't a fair thought. I'd called with the purpose of trying to plant the seeds for some sort of positive relationship. I needed to push myself in that direction, regardless of how it made me feel.

"I'm sorry," I said. "I'm not trying to cause problems. I'm just trying to do what's best for Kaia."

He paused. "I'm sorry too. These past few months have been complicated, and I'm doing my best to figure out how to navigate it all."

"Let me ask you something, and I need you to be honest." I pulled a pillow close because I was afraid the answer would hurt. "Do you want to be involved? I don't want to fight for this if it's a debate in any sense of the word. She deserves so much more."

"Lily, I love Kaia." The frustration in his voice turned to sorrow. "I hate not seeing her, and I hate putting her through this. I wish you would trust me enough to believe that I'm trying to do what's best for her. I just need to think. I need to talk to Norah."

"Why?" I asked. "I'm genuinely trying to understand. Why does she get so much say in any of this? Kaia is your daughter. She should take priority over everything."

"That's the thing," Jin said. "I wanted to wait to tell you this, Lily, but fine. I'll tell you now."

The realization hit me two seconds before he spoke.

"Norah's pregnant."

Chapter Twenty-Nine

Instead of falling asleep with images of Arlo Majors and our scandalous morning in my head, I had to fall asleep with the knowledge that my ex-husband had managed to add a whole new level of trauma to our lives.

Norah was eight weeks. They planned to share the good news in a month or two. So, basically, when Kaia found out, she'd piece together the truth: her father had canceled her trip to Japan because he was too busy getting ready to be someone else's father.

The situation made me want to scream and cry, but instead, I stared up at the ceiling. I felt the same sense of numbness each one of his betrayals had brought as they chipped away at our foundation. It wasn't like there was much left to chip away at, but I had still believed it was possible for him to be a good father to Kaia.

Now, I wasn't so sure. A good father would have made a point to spend time with his daughter. He would have done everything possible to make her feel that she mattered. He would have made absolutely certain that she knew that she was loved. So far, he had done none of those things. Once again, I was stuck figuring out how to limit the emotional damage Kaia would have to face. That included deciding whether or not she should go there for two weeks—assuming Norah even gave it the green light.

The conversation with Jin had not ended on a friendly note.

"Do you still want me to check with Norah to see if she can come?" he'd asked.

"I don't know. I don't know what to say to any of this," I told him and hung up.

So much for my resolution to develop a mature relationship.

I'd failed at that one, straight out of the gate.

∿

The next morning, Kaia burst into my room, her hair flying. "Gigi said yes!"

I was still in bed, trying to find the energy to get up and face the day.

"What did she say yes about?" I asked, fighting off the image of that smile changing to heartache when she heard the news about Jin.

"I told her that she needed to set up a social media account and that I'd teach her how to do videos, pictures, all of it. She thought about it for a few days, and she just sent me a message."

I propped myself up on one elbow. "What does it say?"

Kaia showed me her phone. It said:

I'd be happy to taint my legacy for you.

I laughed. "Please don't let her do that."

"Oh, I've got it all under control." Kaia hopped onto the bed and showed me her phone, where she'd written out a detailed plan of the type of pictures and videos they could do. Most of them involved my grandmother talking about her history as an actress, but it also included specific moments like the first time she was on set.

"These are really good," I said, surprised that Kaia had come up with such a clear plan. "How did you decide on these?"

"I just thought about what I'd want to know about someone who's lived a life so different from mine."

Reaching over, I pulled her in tight for a hug. She smelled like peach-scented bodywash. "You are amazing. I am so proud to be your mom."

She gave me a hopeful look. "Would this be a good time to tell you I got a C in Spanish?"

"Still proud," I said. "But next year, we might want to get a tutor."

"Deal." She leaned against me for a minute, then hopped out of bed. "Can you drop me off at Morning Lark on your way to the theater? Grandma said she'd pick me up and bring me over when it was time for her to go to rehearsal."

"Sure," I said. "Give me twenty minutes."

In the shower, I couldn't help but be grateful that Kaia was taking advantage of the opportunity to get to know her great-grandmother. Even though she was missing out on being with her father, she had three new family members at her fingertips. I could be mad at her father all day, but in the end, I had to trust that we were exactly where we were meant to be.

Chapter Thirty

Since my mother had started at the theater, she'd managed to make herself indispensable. She helped out in the box office, answered phones and managed tickets, painted sets, helped Piper call cues, and even helped wipe down everything in the bar area.

"It's easy to tell you've run a business before," I told her, as we packed up for the day.

"What do you mean?" she said.

"Because you know what needs to be done. You jump in and take care of things."

"That's also called being a mom," she said. "Kaia seems to be enjoying herself. She spent at least an hour making up dance routines on the stage."

"She told me that's where she plans to spend the summer," I said. "You ready to go?"

My mother nodded, and we headed outside, where Kaia was waiting. It was already hot, the air thick and muggy. Kaia had caught a dragonfly and was watching it sit on her finger.

"Hey, do you think . . . ," I started to say.

"What?" my mom asked when my voice trailed off.

"I'm wondering if you could talk to Dad. Get him interested in coming over to the theater too."

Now that the three of us weren't around much, my father was the one I was worried about. He had plenty of activities, and he was often out and about with his friends fishing on the lake, but he didn't look happy. Not the way that my mother did.

"He's not interested," she said, with a sniff. "I'm not about to let him rain on my parade."

"That's fair," I said. "But I might talk to him about it myself."

~

When I got home that night, I found my father reading in his office. I walked in without knocking, giving the door a firm shut behind me, and set down a plate of cookies. Oatmeal raisin, from his favorite bakery on Main Street.

"We need to talk," I said.

The statement was starting to feel like my own personal catchphrase.

My father peered at me over his reading glasses. "Can't a person delve into the written word around here without interruption?" he said but laid his leather bookmark between the pages. The bookmark had a fish on it; my mother had given it to him years ago. "What do we need to talk about?"

"Well . . . I'm worried." I offered him the plate of cookies, and he took two. "It seems like me, mom, and Kaia have started living this separate existence. It's only been a few days, but we miss you."

He grunted. "Well, then you shouldn't have gotten your mother mixed up in that theater."

"Dad," I said. "Mom was sitting around here, bored out of her mind. This has made her happy."

"I never see her anymore." He bit into a cookie with fury. "She doesn't want to do anything that I want to do, and that's not like her. She doesn't seem to remember a thing about how we used to be."

I handed him another cookie. "Have you considered the idea that maybe Mom has spent a good portion of her life doing only the things that you want to do?"

"What are you talking about?" he demanded. "She had a good life. We both did, until we sold the shop. I'm thinking I might buy it back."

"You were done with it. Over it," I reminded him. "Don't go back because you don't know how to move forward."

"Speak for yourself." He brushed crumbs off his T-shirt. "Retirement is not all that it's cracked up to be. I'm supposed to sit here like some bull put out to pasture? Your mother's mad at me all the time? Things were a lot better when we had the shop."

"You sold it because you were ready." They'd complained about the grind for the past few years. "Now, you guys have to figure out what you want to do in the next chapter of your life. Together."

It made me uncomfortable to be in the middle of this, but I'd managed to pull my mother out of her funk. I didn't want my father sitting around looking sad all the time either.

"Could you talk to Mom?" I asked. "Please? I bet if you sat down and discussed the things that you want to do, instead of being angry that you're not doing all of the same things together, you could figure out a way to be happy on your own and as a couple." I held up my hands. "By the way, I am not making any claims about knowing how to make a marriage work. But I love you and Mom, and I think it would be easy to figure things out if you two would sit down and talk to each other."

"I've tried, and she just walks away," he grumbled.

I chewed on a cookie for a moment. "Then maybe . . . talk where it's not so easy to walk away."

My father brightened. "The fishing boat?"

"No, she'd jump overboard," I said. "What about the Harringtons' winery? I can get a car to take you there for dinner. I'll have Abby get you guys a secluded table, and you can hash it all out."

I felt certain my father was going to say no. To my surprise, he nodded.

"Find out a time she doesn't have rehearsal," he said. "Heads would roll if we planned it then."

I hid a smile. "I think this is going to work out, Dad," I told him. "You're already listening."

He slid his reading glasses back on and picked up his book. Even though his lips were pinched, he looked more hopeful than he had in days.

~

I was just climbing into bed when my cell phone rang. My heart gave a little leap.

It was Arlo.

Our ice cream date had been three days ago, and I'd been avoiding him ever since. It was so busy at the theater with Kaia and my mother there, and the production was right around the corner, so there was plenty of opportunity to focus on other things. Like sorting through my feelings.

That time with him had been one of the most perfect hours of my life. There was a big part of me that wasn't ready to move past the memory and into the real world, where it was more than possible to mess things up. Still, I was happy to hear from him and picked up the phone.

"Hey." Arlo's voice was melancholy, which surprised me. I'd expected smooth talk or, worst case, a perfunctory *That was fun but let's move on* tone.

"What's going on?" I said. "You sound sad."

"I am," he said. "I read the play and . . . man. There's really something there, Lily. It's heartbreaking. I mean, the characters that she's drawn are clearly her father and her sister, and her feelings about the whole situation are so painful. The mayor . . . That scene where he threatens her? It was tense. The whole thing was tense. It's great, man."

"I know." I held the phone for a moment, imagining what it would be like to have my head on his chest, talking about this.

"Where are you?" he asked.

"In bed," I said. "What about you?"

"Walking the beach down by the lighthouse. I've been out here just pacing, listening to the waves crash, thinking about diving in."

"Don't do that," I said quickly. "We don't need you getting swept away in a fit of passion."

"Yeah, that already happened. It was a few days ago, with you." His voice was low and intimate and warmed me from head to toe.

"You know," I said, "if I didn't live with my parents—which basically means this entire house is surrounded with barbed wire and alarms—I would head your way right now."

"Fake an emergency at the theater."

I laughed. "They'd follow me! They wouldn't want me to go there at night."

"That is ridiculous," he said, and we both started laughing. "Well, then get some sleep. I just wanted to say hi. Let you know that I've been thinking about you."

"Me too," I said. "Good night."

We both stayed on the phone, waiting to hang up. I closed my eyes, grateful to remember what this felt like. To fall for someone and to have the other person feel the same. Forget the fact that he was Arlo Majors; he was the first guy I'd connected with in years.

"You didn't hang up," he said after a long pause.

"Neither did you."

"Then I'll put you on speaker," he said. "Lie down, pull up your blanket, and listen to the waves. I'm going to lie down in the sand and pretend you're here with me. Good night, Lily."

My heart swelled. For a minute, I felt the impulse to keep talking, but instead, I pictured him sitting on the cold sand, under the expanse of stars, with the sound of the waves crashing on the shore next to him. The breeze catching the small droplets of water and sending them his way, brushing up against his cheek like a kiss.

My eyes started to close, and I listened as he sang softly to me, as the waves crashed all around.

Chapter Thirty-One

"I have an incredibly important task for the two of you today," I said to my mother and Kaia once we arrived at the theater. "It should be fascinating, but it might be a little messy."

My mother cocked her head. "The sets are all painted and ready to go."

"It's not that. It's . . ." I led them to the trapdoor to the basement and opened it with a flourish. "The basement! Consider it an exotic journey through years of history, mystery, and excitement."

Kaia held up her hands. "I'm out."

"Why?" I said.

"Because it's a basement. With spiders."

We were definitely related.

"I was down there for the entirety of the tornado warning, and I did not see one spider."

"They're down there," Kaia said, biting her nail. "I'm also confident that they're big."

"Nothing worth doing is easy," I told her. "I promise—sorting through those boxes is going to be worth it."

"Spiritually? Emotionally? Oh, right . . . *financially*." Kaia stretched. "It will cost you fifteen dollars an hour, cash, for each second that I'm in the basement."

"That's going to add up," I said.

"Well, maybe I'll just have to get a job at the ice cream shop instead. They do pretty good I hear, with tips."

"Free ice cream too," my mother pointed out.

I looked back and forth between the two of them. The basement door was open, leading to a dark cavern that could be full of exciting secrets waiting to be discovered. Personally, I was interested in finding out what might be packed away down there.

I held out my hand to Kaia and shook on it.

"You've got yourself a deal."

~

The mountain of boxes and storage bins stacked up in the basement made me tired just looking at them. It was a massive section by the back wall, and there was not an ounce of organization to what had been put where. At least, not that I could tell from looking at it.

"Look at all that," Kaia said cheerfully. "But I did just make fifty cents for walking down the stairs, so let's keep this money train rolling."

My mother considered the boxes, clucking her tongue. "I imagine you'd like for us to sort through them all, catalog what's there, and then figure out what to do with it?"

"Yes," I said. "I bet there are tons of props and old costumes, or it would have been thrown away back in the day."

If there were clothes, they would be old and musty, but it was worth a look. Besides, Jade would know how to freshen them up.

"This is great," Kaia said, rubbing her hands together. "I think I'm already at a dollar, and we're just talking." She took in a deep breath. "Why does it smell good down here? I thought it would be gross."

The basement did have the aroma of vanilla coffee, and I wondered if someone had spilled some or left a cup down here that day we were here for the tornado. I didn't know whether or not mice would be interested in that, but I'd have to find where it was and clean it up before they developed an interest.

"We should get Cody down here," my mother said, once she'd considered the stack of boxes. "He's in rehearsal, but I don't like the way these are set up. They could topple over pretty easily."

It was a good point. I didn't want to risk a mountain of boxes and bins landsliding onto Kaia or my mother.

"It might require two Hendersons," I said. "Let me give Carter a call, and we'll plan it for when Cody's out of rehearsal."

"Is there anything else we can do down here while we wait?" My mother set off with her flashlight to explore. "I'm thinking we could . . ." Her voice trailed off. Then, she walked back toward me, her eyes wide. "Upstairs," she hissed. "Now."

Her expression was enough to make me grab Kaia's arm and pull her to the stairs as quickly as possible. For once, my daughter didn't waste time debating me, and she scampered up the steps. My mother was right at our heels, and she didn't stop there. She clipped at the world's fastest pace into my office, then shut and locked the door.

"Mom, what is it?" I said.

"You're acting like you saw a bear," Kaia said. "Did you see a bear?"

My mother held up a hand. "I think we need to call the police."

Kaia's mouth dropped open. "Did you see a dead body?"

My mind went straight to the emails, and immediately, I tried to find any excuse other than what could actually be happening.

"The actors joke around sometimes." I thought of Millie that one day. "Maybe we walked in on the setup for a practical—"

"It wasn't a body," my mother said. "It looked like someone is living in the basement."

"Living," Kaia repeated. "That's the opposite of dead."

"What do you mean?" I said to my mother, pulling out my cell phone.

"I saw a roll-up bed, blankets, and a coffee maker. It had fresh coffee in it."

I hesitated. One of the actors could have set up a place to rest between rehearsals or maybe even as a rendezvous point. It sounded like an Arlo thing, actually. Quickly, I texted to see if he'd made himself a quiet space.

He texted back right away:

No. Why?

I called Piper. "Hey, will you check and see if anyone was brewing coffee in the basement?"

Moments later, she came back on the line. "No, but now they all want coffee."

"Great." I let out a breath. "Ask if anyone had a sleeping bag in the basement?"

"Hold on." Piper came back on the line, sounding a bit more worried. "No. What's going on?"

"Tell them to stay calm," I said. "I need you to get everyone to lock down in the rehearsal room. Please tell them there is no active danger, as far as we know, but we do have to get to the bottom of this."

"On it," she said.

I sent out messages to the whole theater. Within moments, I heard footsteps headed toward the rehearsal room, along with lots of chatter.

"We really should call the police," my mother said. "They need to check it out, make sure no one's hiding here."

"I am," I said. "I just can't believe this is happening right now."

The theater was designed for drama, but did that mean we had to live in the thick of it? I picked up the phone and called Dean.

"Get everyone out." The siren started to blare in the background. "I'm on my way."

Kaia rubbed her hands together. "Well, this is excitement we weren't expecting."

There was nothing exciting about it. The day Millie had done that stunt with the fake blood, one of the cast members suggested we had a vagrant. It made sense, given all the comments about having a ghost. People had been hearing and seeing things, but maybe there was a reason—like that day in my office when the Post-it Note drifted to the floor. I was certain I'd seen someone but had convinced myself I was imagining things.

Apparently not.

"Piper," I said, once she'd picked up. I could hear the actors talking in the background. "The police want us to get everyone out. Take everyone to the park in town. There's a big covered area where you should be able to rehearse. I'll let you know what they find out."

Five minutes later, the cast and crew had vacated the building, and Dean pulled in. He had his lights and siren off now, and another cop was right behind him. They stepped out, looking grim.

We met them outside the front door.

Dean greeted my mother, then smiled at my daughter. "I knew your mother when she was your age. She was always eating Fun Dip. Purple, red, green . . . her tongue was always some alien color."

Kaia laughed. "Ew."

I was surprised Dean remembered my obsession with Fun Dip. It had been years since I'd even thought about it.

He pulled out a small notebook. "Tell me what's going on." He took notes as my mother described what she'd seen. The other officer listened closely.

"Everyone's out?" he confirmed.

"Yes." I indicated Kaia and my mother. "These two were just leaving."

"No way." Kaia's eyes were bright with excitement. "I want to stay and see who it is."

Dean and I shared a quick glance.

"It's time to head home," I told her. "It's good that we figured this out before someone got hurt."

The seriousness of it all started to weigh on me, as Dean and the other guy set up a plan to sweep the perimeter.

The idea that someone could be hiding out in there gave me the creeps. When I let my mind go deeper with it, thinking of all the times I'd stayed late or the moments Kaia had been off by herself, I actually started to sweat.

"You okay?" Dean asked. "You look like you saw a ghost."

"Yeah." I nodded. "That's kind of how it goes around here."

~

Twenty minutes later, Dean met with me in the lobby.

"We can't find anyone," he said. "There is evidence that someone has been living here, so we do need to have a little chat with your people and make sure it's not one of them. Have you been monitoring the cameras?"

"Yes," I said. "I fast-forward the night footage when no one's here and before people start to arrive in the morning. The key fob has to be swiped to enter or exit, so no one's been coming or going either."

"Well, at least not using a door," he said, his eyes sweeping the lobby. "Let's get some cameras into the basement and the lobby if this doesn't end up being a member of the theater company. We'll get you a security guard around the clock and periodically sweep the building, particularly in the middle of the night, to see if we can catch anyone staying here. It won't take long to send the message that they're not welcome to live rent-free at our theater."

"When will you talk to the cast?" I asked.

"Right now," he said. "If it's someone who's made up a resting spot, good deal. False alarm, and we'll all feel a little annoyed. If it's not, though, we can't let an existing threat remain without support. We'll get someone here in the morning."

I nodded. "Okay."

"You said they're at the park?" Dean confirmed, and I nodded. "Great. Let's go find out if someone was sleeping on the job."

~

I met Dean at the small but cozy park located off Main Street. It was bustling with all sorts of people, some grilling hamburgers at the public grills, some riding bikes, and some playing volleyball in the sand over by the water. Our cast was rehearsing beneath the shaded awning of the lunch area, not phased at all by the change in location.

"You guys are troopers," I said, walking up to them. "Thank you so much for keeping our day productive. If you don't mind having a quick seat, Officer Harrington has a few questions for you."

The group fell silent and filed into the green-painted picnic tables. The day was muggy, and several of them fanned themselves with their phones.

"Let me tell you what's going on," Dean said, once everyone was seated. "I'm hoping we can work together to get to the bottom of this."

Dean explained the situation and then asked five different times in five different ways if the sleeping bag in the basement belonged to anyone. The other officer stood in the back, keeping a general eye on the group. The actors started to look hot and frustrated, and I sent a text to my friend at the ice cream shop down the street to send over Popsicles.

"We're going to pass around some papers," Dean said, holding them up. "They say yes and no. If you've been camping out here and don't want to tell us, fine. Check 'Yes,' and we'll be done with it." His dark eyes surveyed the group. "It's important to emphasize that no one's in trouble here. We just need to know if you actually do need one of us at the theater to keep you safe."

His backup guy passed around the papers, followed by a box, and Dean went out to the lawn area to make a call. I stood at the edge of the lunch area, watching in silence as the box was passed around the group.

It occurred to me that the squatter had not stolen a thing. So, what were they doing there?

The last actor put his paper in and handed the box to the officer.

I jumped up to help sift through. Every single paper said "No."

"Well, that's that," he said.

I addressed the cast as he headed over to tell Dean.

"It looks like it's not one of us," I said. "So, let's keep rehearsing here today—I have Popsicles on the way—but starting tomorrow, we'll be back at the theater with police protection."

"Is it going to be the hot one?" Millie said, with a giggle. "I wouldn't mind answering a few more questions from him."

It took me a second to realize she was talking about Dean. I didn't know why I felt a pang of irritation at the comment, but I did.

"I don't know who it will be yet, Millie," I said. "But whoever it is, we'll treat them with kindness and respect."

"Oh, I plan on it," she said with a grin.

The Popsicles arrived then, and eagerly, the cast leapt on the frosty treats. Piper approached with her clipboard and a worry line between her eyes.

"Is this okay for now?" I said. "I know it's hot."

"There's water fountains and shade," she said. "We should be fine. The only chink in the chain is Arlo."

He'd left a few hours ago since he wasn't a part of this afternoon's rehearsal.

"What do you mean?" I said. "What's wrong?"

"Well, he's afraid it's a stalker," she said. "He's threatening to go back to LA."

Chapter Thirty-Two

"Arlo, it's me." I sat outside the security box on the fence at his bungalow. "Please, let me in."

Silence.

I hit the buzzer again. "Arlo, come on. I know what you're worried about, and we need to talk."

There was a click, and the gate swung open. It closed the moment I drove through, practically bumping into my car.

The paved driveway led down and around a gigantic fortress of a house with massive glass windows and two tennis courts. In the back, Arlo's cottage was nestled in a nook surrounded by rosebushes. Bees buzzed lazily around the flowers.

The door opened as I walked up, and Arlo stood there, holding a spatula and a pan of scrambled eggs, looking as inviting as ever. He wore a pair of gray sweatpants, a rumpled black T-shirt, and the faded scent of alcohol. It was hard to tell if he'd been drinking all night or had just started.

"Morning," he said. "Care for some breakfast?"

I held up my wrist, showing him my watch. "It's one in the afternoon."

"I was out late on the beach last night."

That moment on the phone felt like a thousand years ago now.

"Can I come in?" I said.

"Sure." He stepped away from the door, and my mind instantly shifted to the last time I was here.

"Piper told me you have some concerns," I said, taking a seat at the kitchen table. He served me some eggs even though I'd waved him away, and once he was seated, I tried them. Surprisingly good, with a fluffy texture and lots of salt.

"Milk's the trick," he told me. "You've got to add a dash of milk."

"They're delicious. I didn't know you were a chef." I took a few bites, then set down my fork. "Listen, I need to know what you're going to do. The show's in a week and a half. This whole situation is strange, but why do you think it's a stalker?"

He frowned. "Well, this person has been living in the theater. Can you think of a good reason a person would choose to live in a theater?"

I tried for levity. "Ticket prices are too high?"

"No. There's not one good reason a person would live in a theater," Arlo said. "There's no unhoused population. It's not that cold outside. It has to be someone trying to get at me, and I'm not going to let that happen."

"I understand."

"No, you don't." The pupils on his eyes were small as he shoveled in the eggs. "Do you know what it feels like, Lily? To think that people are watching you all of the time? To know it's not just paranoia—that they're actually watching you?"

The pain in his voice hurt me too. "No."

"Well, it's uncomfortable." He took a sip out of a coffee mug, and I realized that, yes, he was drinking.

"I might not know how it would feel," I said, "but I know that it's hard on you."

For the first time, it occurred to me that it had taken a lot of trust for him to bring me here and into his bed. It had taken a lot for me, too, but for him, it was a different type of trust entirely.

"The police will be at the theater," I said. "Every second from this point forward. If there's any type of threat—"

"Yeah, they might be able to help." He took another bite of eggs. "Or they might not. It's the way that it is, and I get it but . . ." He slammed his fist down on the table, and I jumped. "Sorry." He looked worried and touched my hand. "I was just having so much fun here, you know? For once, everything felt free. Last night I was alone on the beach, thinking I was king of the world."

"It can still be like that." My heart raced as I tried to put myself in his shoes. "We'll figure it out."

The pain behind his eyes made me reach for his hands. He left his chair, came over, and crawled into my lap. I held him tight, resting my head against his. Every time he blinked, I felt the soft flutter of his eyelashes against my cheek. Finally, his body relaxed.

"You haven't slept at all," I said.

He didn't answer.

"Okay," I said. "Come with me."

I helped him to his feet and guided him up the staircase and into the bedroom. After leading him to the king-size bed that took up much of the small space, I pulled back the blue checkered quilt and ushered him in.

"You need sleep," I told him.

He reached as if to pull me in with him. It was so incredibly tempting, but not like this.

"I'll sit here," I said. "Do you want me to stick around or lock the door when I leave?"

His eyes were nearly closed. "Stay," he mumbled.

Gently, I kissed his forehead. It was damp with sweat and smelled sour. He needed some rest and some time to think about this with a clear head.

"I love having you around," he told me, then turned his head into the downy pillow and went to sleep.

I sat there until his breathing steadied and slowed; then I sat in a chair in the corner of the room. I had a ton of work to do, and I needed to figure out how to do it from here.

The opening night of *Chicago* was not that far away. If someone was coming for him, we'd have to cancel. The only way to move forward was to have a strong enough strategy to keep him safe. I had no idea how to do that, but if I wanted the theater to stay open, I needed to figure it out.

Chapter Thirty-Three

The rays of sun grew long across the floor, and outside, insects droned with the sound of the evening. I'd spent half of the day downstairs, on the phone, talking with everyone from the lawyer to Piper to Arlo's agent.

In the end, it came down to Arlo. There was a clause in his contract that gave him the right to pull out at any time for any reason. That was vaguely concerning, even if we did figure this out.

"It's a formality," his agent assured me. "Arlo doesn't have to do a thing other than sit back and collect residuals for the rest of his life. He wants to do small-town theater, which is why he's there."

Late in the afternoon, Jade called. It was good to hear from her, given what Arlo had told me about their history together in Los Angeles.

"Is he doing okay?" She sounded worried. "Do you need me to talk to him? We go way back."

"He's sleeping now." I rested my hand on the grainy wood of the kitchen table, thinking. "Let me ask you this—do you think it's safe for him to continue on? You know the world the two of you live in better than I do. I don't want to do anything that would actually put him at risk."

"It's hard to tell, Lily." There was a weight to her voice. "He'll have to bring in security. He's got a guy he works with in LA. It's going to frustrate him, though, so be prepared for that. For him, the purpose of doing theater is the opportunity to step into a simpler time. If I were you, I'd encourage him to focus on the reason that he's here because otherwise, he could cut and run."

I hung up and stood in the living room, staring blankly at the kitchen. The dishes from the eggs were piled in the sink, so I walked over and washed them. Folding the dish towel, I considered the cozy space he'd been living in. There were books everywhere, dog-eared plays, and a guitar leaning against the couch. The fireplace had ashes in it.

It was clear that Arlo spent his time off relaxing, learning, and enjoying his life. It was peaceful here. He deserved to have that time, to feel safe, and to feel free to do the things that he enjoyed, without looking over his shoulder. Since he couldn't do that alone, he'd have to bring in protection.

I headed back up to the bedroom. The moment I stepped into the room and the floorboard creaked, his eyes shot open. There was a split second of worry, and then he gave a slow smile, holding out his hand. This time, I let him pull me into the bed with him, the warm scent of sleep and spice radiating from his body.

"Did you get some sleep?" I asked.

It was a silly question, considering I'd been there for the past six hours, but it was hard to focus on quality conversation with his body so close to mine.

"Yeah." He played with a strand of my hair. "Thanks for sticking around."

"I couldn't leave you feeling like that."

"How do you want me to feel?" He ran his hands up my torso. My mind went blank, and he smiled. "I was thinking the same thing."

~

It was tempting to stay in bed for the rest of the night, but I had to get back home. My mother had texted earlier to get permission for Kaia to sleep over with a friend, but there was no chance I'd be able to get away with an overnight of my own without explaining where I'd been.

Arlo took a drink out of a water bottle on the nightstand and yawned. After stepping out of bed in a pair of jogging pants that showed off his incredible abs, he opened a window.

"What a gorgeous night." He pressed his palms against the windowsill. "Lily, I'd love to take you on an actual date. Grab dinner somewhere that's safe and won't create a circus. Is that possible around here?"

"Let me check." I sent a text, and when I heard back, I nodded. "Let's go."

Arlo grabbed his keys. Outside, the night was balmy and peaceful—a mood that was a far cry from the drama from earlier that day. Still, I noticed him stop to consider the dark driveway and the yard before walking to his car.

He opened my door, and I climbed in, pulling directions up on my phone for him. We chatted for the first few minutes and then settled into a somewhat exhausted but comfortable silence. We held hands as he drove, and I stared out the window, reliving the finer points of the last hour in my mind.

Starlight Cove faded into the distance, and the hills led us out on the peninsula, where we wound through the back roads of huge houses up against the backdrop of the lake. I'd noticed that Arlo had been checking the rearview mirror at the beginning of the drive but had finally relaxed.

"Wine?" he said as the Starlight Cove Wine Trail sign came into view. "I didn't know that existed here."

"My good friend Abby, her family owns a winery. I just recommended this to my dad for a date with my mom, which is why it jumped to mind."

Even though Abby was one of my best friends, I rarely made the trip out to the vineyard. I'd texted her right before we'd left the cottage, and she promised to make the experience comfortable for Arlo. He drove up the long drive, while I admired the orderly rows of the vines, already ripe with fruit.

"Here's the plan," I said. "She's going to put us at a private table with a good view of the water and the grounds. It should take a while for anyone to figure out that you're here, if they notice at all."

Arlo gave me an appreciative look. "Thank you."

There were dark circles under his eyes. He was clearly exhausted but turned on the charm when Abby came out to the parking lot to greet us.

"You must be the world-famous Abby," he said, flashing his best grin.

Abby smiled back. "And you must be the world-famous Arlo. I am so honored to have you here."

"Would you like me to sign a menu?" he asked. "Some places like me to do that."

Abby looked horrified. "No! You sit back, relax, and enjoy your night with my beautiful friend. Follow me."

We followed Abby across a gravel drive to a door that led in through the kitchen. Her kitchen staff had their backs to us, so we walked right by, and no one even noticed.

"There." Abby led us to a table beneath a trellis draped in vines. "The view's pretty good out there, isn't it?"

Rolling green hills, rows of vines, and the lake seemed to stretch on for miles. There were several boats on the water, and the lighthouse looked pretty in the evening light.

"Thank you, Abby." He nodded, taking it all in. "This is impressive."

Abby winked at me and poured some Pellegrino before scampering away. Sauvignon blanc and a charcuterie tray soon followed. The tray had a wide array of thin meats, cheeses, and olives.

Arlo clinked his glass to mine. "To you," he said. "Thanks for making this rotten day one to remember in a good way."

I drank to that. The sauvignon blanc was light with hints of grapefruit, which made it refreshing in the heat.

"How are you feeling about all of this?" I asked.

Arlo constructed a sandwich out of fresh bread, smoked cheese, and prosciutto. "Mad. It's an unnecessary distraction when I want to focus on what I came here to do."

"You need to bring in private security," I said. "That's what your agent said should happen."

He gave a slight smile. "You talked to Elijah?"

"He was great. Probably the most intense person I talked to today, and I talked to a lot of people."

"Because you want a summer season starring the amazing Arlo Majors." He took a hearty drink of wine, irritation on his face.

"I'm not going to apologize for wanting to see you up onstage," I said. "You're brilliant. But if you're saying I would want that at the expense of your safety, that's not true. I don't think you should stay if it could put you at risk."

"Do you think I'm at risk?" he asked, taking a bite of cheese. "Or do you think I'm being paranoid?"

"I think it's all pretty strange." He started to speak, but I held up my hand. "I mean the whole sleeping bag in the basement thing, not your reaction to it."

Before we'd closed up the theater for the day, I'd had Dean take me down to the basement so I could see firsthand the sleeping bag setup. It was rudimentary but so deliberate that it gave me chills.

"The idea of someone being in the theater is scary," I said. "I was there by myself so many times late at night, and my daughter, she was there . . ." It took a minute to be able to speak again. "Look, no one has been attacked or robbed. Unfortunately, if those things had happened, this would make sense. The fact that they haven't is what makes me worry that it could be someone trying to get close to you."

Arlo took a drink of wine. "I know."

"It's tough because I want the theater to run its full season but also . . ." My cheeks heated, and I reached for the Pellegrino. "This thing with you has been unexpected, and I don't want it to end. It will end, but I don't want it to end like this."

This flirtation with Arlo had never been sustainable, not by any means. That's probably why I'd allowed myself to be a part of it. The outcome was clear from the start—it would end—and that was fine because the outcome had nothing to do with me.

It wasn't like with Jin, where I had to live with the regret and heartache of a failed marriage, wondering what I could have done to make it work. The thing with Arlo might last days or months, but I had known from the start that his life was so different from mine that we could never last. Still, I hadn't expected it to be over so quickly.

Abby returned to the table with a big smile. "Do you know what you'd like?"

"To kiss your beautiful friend," Arlo said. "We can order instead."

Abby gave me her best *You better tell me everything later* look.

Once our orders were in and Abby had left, Arlo leaned across the table to give me the sweetest kiss. It was so easy to forget he was a movie star until he sat back in his chair, the sleeve of his pullover falling back to reveal his ridiculously expensive watch, one that I'd actually seen him wear in a movie.

"I don't want to leave," he said. "I've wanted to do small-town theater for years. Take a few months and let life be simple."

"Well, we've failed you on simple."

He grinned. "Like, really bad. But I'm not going to let some threat decide my future."

"Really?" I said.

"I'll bring in security. Look over my shoulder. It's not enough to make me run away."

I was surprised at how incredibly glad I felt at the decision.

"I will do everything possible at the theater to make sure that you feel comfortable and protected at all times," I said. "I also understand that feelings change. Plans change. If you wake up tomorrow with a different decision, that's fine. You need to be safe. It's that simple."

"Thank you," he said, looking back out at the view.

I took a drink of wine, fighting waves of emotion. I meant what I'd said, but losing him would be hard, personally and professionally. If he bowed out of the shows, it could end the theater altogether, and lately, I'd started to wonder whether the theater was something I might want to keep as a part of my life, long term.

"I have a strange confession," I said as Arlo poured us both more wine.

"It was your sleeping bag in the basement?"

I laughed. "No, mine has Disney princesses on it. I've been thinking I might want to leave my old job permanently and try to keep the theater alive."

Arlo nodded. "You feel passionate about it?"

These actors went straight for emotion words.

"I mean . . . I grew up in the Playhouse. The idea of keeping it going appeals to me. I can't stand the thought of doing one season and closing the doors."

"Then do it." He lifted his glass. "Change the world."

"Would you be a part of it?" I asked.

"I wish. I have projects lined up back to back for the next three years of my life, but you could call anytime to ask for my input."

It made me sad, a little, to have my thoughts about the timeline on our relationship confirmed, but I'd known that from the start. He wouldn't be around, so there was no point in looking forward.

Arlo rested his hands on the table. "Do you think there's a bathroom around here that would be safe to use?"

"Hold on." I texted Abby. She unlocked the tasting room and sent him there. While he was gone, she pulled up a chair and gave me a big grin. "So . . . how's it going?"

"Great," I said. "This has been so special to have the space and privacy to have a dinner with him. Thank you. It's been a day."

"Dean told me," she said. "I can't believe that someone's been living at the theater. That's so scary."

I thought of Dean talking to the actors before we'd passed around the yes-or-no box. His expression had been so intense. "It's fun to see your brother in action."

"I hoped he'd stop by tonight. He's typically home by now."

The thought made me nervous, somehow.

"Does he know that I'm on a date?" I asked.

"No," Abby said. "Why?"

It was hard to explain. I'd known Dean forever, but before all this, I'd barely spoken two words to him in my life. Now that I'd actually spent time with him at the theater, it felt like we'd become friends. I didn't know what he'd think about me getting involved with a movie star—maybe he'd think it was unprofessional.

"I don't know," I said. "Dean might get all protective or something."

Abby rolled her eyes. "Right? He successfully scared men away from me for years, until Braden came along. Either way, he's much more interested in protecting the Playhouse at the moment. Sorry, but I'm thrilled there's finally some crime. He's been such a grump since he and Kelcee broke up."

"They broke up?" I said. He'd been dating Kelcee Whittaker for a while, and I thought it was getting serious.

"Yeah." She shrugged. "Dean loves her like a sister, which was the problem. I'm glad he ended it."

Dean was single. That was news. I felt almost happy about it, which was a surprise. Maybe it shouldn't be, since I'd always had a thing for him, but it was more about the fact that I was even thinking these thoughts.

The day that I signed the divorce papers, it felt like everything had come to an end. That I would be alone forever. Now, I was on a date with one of the most attractive people in the entire world and thinking about a guy I'd been attracted to for years.

Such a strange feeling, considering I'd assumed I'd never get over the hurt, heartache, and complete sense of failure that had come with the divorce. Yet here I was, wondering if those looks Dean had been giving me meant something more.

"There he is," Abby said.

I looked up, surprised to see that she meant Arlo. He was headed back to the table, waving at me.

Abby got to her feet and dropped a quick kiss on the top of my head. "Have fun, you lucky girl. Your food should be ready in a second."

Moments later, she returned with our entrées. Arlo had ordered the veal chop, and it smelled delicious, wafting sage, garlic, and rosemary my way. I'd ordered the Dover sole on a bed of garlic capellini, with braised cherry tomatoes.

He pulled out his phone and took a picture, which made me laugh.

"You're a 'take a picture of food at restaurants' type of guy? I never would have guessed that about you."

"I can remember every meal if I see a picture. It's how I keep good memories." He grinned. "If you ever want a spellbinding night, I can do a slideshow."

He cut into his meat. It was a relief to see him less stressed, and I took a bite of my fish. It was delicious.

"You know, if you do continue on with the theater next year," he said, "it should be easy to get a celebrity now that I've done it. That sounds obnoxious, but it's true. Let me know who you're interested in, and I can put in a word. It would all depend on scheduling, though."

"You would do that for me?" I said.

He gave me a funny look. "Of course."

"Thank you." I wound some capellini around my fork. "It feels risky to even consider keeping the Playhouse alive, but ever since I first walked in the front door, it felt like coming home. That sounds cheesy but—"

"It sounds honest." Arlo's eyes were as clear as the sky. "Never apologize for speaking the truth. Life only gets authentic when we trust our feelings."

"Then, it feels like I belong there," I admitted. "Like it's in my blood. That expression didn't make much sense to me until this summer, but now, I get it."

The idea that my grandmother had started the whole thing was significant for me. I admired and respected her, and the Playhouse had been such a huge part of her life. It hadn't seemed like she'd be able to pass on that legacy, but now that it had all come around, there might be the chance to run with it.

"I'd have to figure out who owns it," I said. "They'd also have to be willing to sell it, and I'd have to figure out a way to come up with the money. I'm thinking there should be a ton of grants that would help, and the locals here would definitely get behind it. It could be a big part of our town, for years to come."

"It's a great space," Arlo agreed, swiping a cherry tomato from my plate. "You could set up classes there, school programs. Everyone would come out to see a Christmas show. You could even rent out the theater for special events. It could be a big thing. You could make it a big thing."

One of the many things I liked about Arlo was how quick he was to support big ideas. In my head, the idea of trying to keep the theater going felt embarrassing, like it was too bold to even suggest. But like my grandmother, Arlo made me feel life was there for the taking.

"Now *that's* a sunset," he said suddenly.

I looked out over the vineyard. The sky had changed from light blue into a fiery combination of pink, gold, and yellow.

He reached over to take my hand. "I'm sorry I can't give you more in all of this. I wish I could."

"It's perfect," I said. "Just the way it is."

Chapter Thirty-Four

The next morning, I arrived at the theater to find Dean as the policeman on duty. He sat in a chair in the lobby, looking bored out of his mind.

"You're the one standing guard?" I slid off my sunglasses, surprised to see him. "Or should I say sitting?"

"This chair is more comfortable than one would expect."

"I didn't think it would be you," I said, fiddling with my sunglasses. "I thought it would be one of the other guys."

"I lost a bet. The police chief knows I can't stand sitting around, so he thinks it's hilarious."

I couldn't imagine the police chief finding anything hilarious.

"What was the bet?" I asked.

Dean mumbled something.

"Huh?" I said, leaning in.

"Doughnut eating competition." When I laughed, he said, "The police chief has something against doughnuts. Barely eats them, unless he's in a mood. I started shoveling in the glazed, and I had no doubt that I'd win."

My mind flashed back to that first day in the parking lot with Arlo, when he nabbed the box of doughnuts.

"The next thing I know," Dean said, "I've eaten five, I'm practically drunk with the sugar rush, and about to throw up. He starts chowing away, like he could do it all day."

"How many—?"

Dean grimaced. "Fifteen." He ran his hand through his hair, looking grumpier by the minute. "He could have stopped at six. Instead, he decided to—how did he put it?—assert his finely tuned male dominance and wipe the floor with my face."

"The floor has never been so clean," I said.

Dean shot me a look.

I grinned. "Are you stuck here for today or—"

"I'm at your service for the remainder of this debacle. There's a separate night-duty guy, but the rest of the time, it's me. I'll be here during the performances too."

"Really?" I said.

He gave a grim nod, and I couldn't help but think about how happy I was at the prospect of seeing him every day.

"Do I have something on my face?" he said.

"No, why?" I asked.

"You're staring at me."

"Oh," I said, voice bright. "No, I was just thinking I'm glad you'll be around."

He held my gaze. "Oh, yeah?"

"You betcha. To protect the theater." I inched toward my office. "It's nice to know that you, as Starlight Cove's finest, have your sights set on keeping this theater safe, happy, and full of good cheer."

"Yeah." Dean crossed his arms, watching me. "Good cheer's my middle name."

~

The entire cast and crew met at the theater that morning for a security briefing. Even though Arlo had made the decision to stay, I was still worried he'd change his mind, and I watched him closely while Dean spoke.

"To wrap up," Dean said, once he'd covered their strategy, "we'll keep watch over everything, but it's the same as everywhere: if you see something, say something. You're welcome to reach out with any concerns, as long as you don't waste my time talking about the weather."

Everyone chuckled. Dean started to head for the door, but Arlo raised his hand.

"Sir, would it be possible for me to speak?" When Dean nodded, he said, "First of all, thank you for doing what you can to keep us safe. I wanted to let everyone know that I'm sorry for this extra step, but I appreciate each and every one of you. I've wanted to do live theater like this for years and never dreamed I could do it in such an incredible setting or with such a brilliant cast. You know, when something like this happens, it's tempting to walk away. That's where I was yesterday." His eyes settled on mine, and he gave me a slow, lazy look that I felt all the way down to my toes.

"The thing about it is, though," he said, surveying the room, "is that I don't want to miss out on this summer. I don't want to miss out on the laughs we'll share, the breakthroughs we'll have, and the incredible opportunity we, as actors, have to brighten someone's day from up on that stage. So, I wanted to promise each and every one of you that I'm not going anywhere. I'm going to ride this thing out until the end. I'm grateful to all of you for doing the same."

The actors and crew applauded, their faces full of inspiration. Arlo clapped right along with them, slapping the guys on the back and hugging a few of the girls.

"Rehearsal onstage in five," Piper called.

My mother was in the back, chatting with some of the locals. I wanted to hear her take on everything, so as I waited for her to head out, I pulled Arlo aside.

"Did you call your bodyguard guy?" I asked.

"Yeah." Arlo put on his baseball cap. "He'll be here in two hours."

"Good." I hesitated. "For what it's worth, I'm glad you're staying."

I was careful to sound as casual as possible because there were still actors trickling out of the room, probably trying to coordinate their exit with his. I also didn't want my mother to pick up on this thing with Arlo because I'd already seen her roll her eyes a few times at the way the actresses fawned over him.

"Me too," he said quietly. "There's no question about that." He brushed his hand against mine and then headed out. Of course, he was instantly surrounded by the other actors.

It occurred to me that if someone was actually stalking him, it could be one of the cast members. Knowing Arlo, the thought had already crossed his mind, but it was still something to bring up with Dean.

My mother picked up a few candy wrappers the cast had left lying around and dropped them in the bin. Walking up, she gave me a questioning look. "You okay?"

"Just thinking about it all."

"Do you think it's safe for Kaia to come back to the theater?"

That morning, my parents and I had discussed whether or not I should allow Kaia to continue on. We'd agreed that she could if the plan put into place felt strong. If it didn't, she'd have to find other things to do for the summer.

"I like it that Dean's the one standing guard," I said. "That makes me feel more than safe. The odds that something would get by him seem minimal."

"I agree with that." My mother turned out the lights in the room as we headed for the hallway. "He's single, isn't he?"

"Yes, why?" I said.

My mother gave me a meaningful look. "Oh, no reason."

"Mom," I said, horrified that she was talking about this here. "He's Abby's older brother."

"Yes, so you already like his family." Giving an eager wave, she called, "Hi, Dean. Thanks for being here."

My cheeks went hot to find he was still in the hallway, keeping a close eye on the actors as they headed backstage and to the front door. I hoped he hadn't overheard.

"No problem, Mrs. Candella. Let me know if you need me for anything."

"Okay," she called. Then, she whispered, "How about you take my daughter on a date?"

Dean's forehead furrowed, and even though he was at least thirty feet away, I could swear he'd caught that one.

I clenched my teeth. "Mom, go to rehearsal, and please, trust me when I say this—I really am doing just fine."

My mother flounced off down the hallway. I dared to look at Dean as I headed to my office. He shrugged.

"Mothers are the wild card," he said. "You never know what they're going to do next."

With a shake of my head, I shut my office door.

Chapter Thirty-Five

The next morning, Arlo had a late call time, so he invited me over for an early coffee. I pulled into the drive already anticipating time with him and stopped short. A man about the size of a pillar stood at the front of the house, arms crossed, staring straight ahead. He had a cut jaw, a cleft chin, and an expression that could have wilted the hydrangeas on the bush.

"Hi," I called once I'd gotten out of the car. "I'm here to see Arlo?"

His eyes scanned me; then he waved me through. I was tempted to ask if he needed to check my bag but kept my mouth shut.

"I'm here," I called, walking into the cottage. I felt uncomfortable, knowing the bodyguard could hear every word from the open kitchen window. "Arlo?"

Coffee was brewing, and the shower was running. Instead of going to say hello, I grabbed a cup of coffee and stood at the counter looking at my phone. The water from the shower nozzle turned off, and moments later, Arlo headed into the kitchen with just a towel wrapped around his waist. He looked damp and sexy, his hair sticking up in all directions.

"Morning," he said, pulling me in for a kiss.

My hands ran up his abs, and just as quickly, I lowered them.

"I met your friend," I said, pointing at the door.

"Phillipe." Arlo poured some coffee. "I've known him for years. Good guy."

"Wasn't he in an alligator wrestling video?" I asked.

"Nah, I think it was snakebites. He had to survive the venom of a black mamba?"

We grinned.

"Have a seat," he said.

The kitchen table was cluttered but cozy. There was a stack of film scripts with the big agency names on the front, a few paperback best-sellers, and an open folder that held Belinda's play. With a flourish, Arlo pulled two yogurt parfaits out of the fridge and set them on the table, complete with long and skinny spoons.

"Greek yogurt, chia seeds, blueberries, strawberries, and granola. Breakfast of champions."

"Thank you," I said, touched he'd made one for me. "You sure this wasn't for Phillipe?"

"He only eats wild rabbit."

I took a few bites, impressed at how good it was. "So, how are you feeling about everything today? And are you planning on wearing that towel all through breakfast because it's very distracting."

"I can take it off," he said, starting to get up.

I gestured wildly at the front porch.

"I'll go change." He left the room and returned in a pair of loose gray jogging pants and a big grin. "Better?"

"So much less distracting." I focused on the parfait because there was not a chance I was going to let anything happen between us with that meaty man standing out front. "Do you feel more comfortable now?"

"Unfortunately, yes." Arlo sat back in his chair, drinking his coffee. "Phillipe isn't going to let a thing happen to me."

"No kidding," I said. "Trust me when I say I'm not coming near you."

"Do you want to come over tonight, instead?" he asked. "I can send him out to scale small buildings or something."

I thought for a minute. Kaia was coming to the theater to work today, but she'd said something about going waterskiing with a friend and her family later, followed by a bonfire on the beach.

"Yes, that sounds perfect," I said, finishing up the parfait.

"Can I cook you dinner?" he asked.

"Only if you take a picture of it."

He laughed. "Deal."

I put my dish in the dishwasher and considered the small space. It was perfect for one person, but it had to be crowded with Phillipe around. His muscles alone could take up the whole couch.

"Where will he sleep?" I asked, trying to picture it all. "Is there a bedroom for him?"

"He sleeps on a roll-out mattress in here." Arlo gestured at the kitchen floor. "I offered him the couch, but the dude's too big to fit. I know it's weird, but he won't be hanging around all the time. Just . . . most of the time."

"I'm all for it if it keeps you safe," I said. "What time for dinner?"

"Eight," he said. "I have rehearsal until seven thirty."

Arlo picked up the folder with Belinda's play and pulled out some pages and a pen. We hadn't talked about the play much, considering all that had been going on.

"Are you taking notes?" I asked.

"It helps me to pick up on things when I'm reading. This play really is brilliant." He studied the pages for a moment. "You know, the thing I love about the theater is that it has the power to change people. This is the type of story that will get under people's skin, that will make them think. I know you have some reservations, but for real, Lily, we have to figure out a way to let this be seen."

This again?

"There are thousands of good, professional plays up for the taking," I said lightly. "Let it go."

"This one is different, though." He had a bowl of loose pepitas on the table and popped a handful into his mouth. "It's painful. It's passionate. It's incredible. This is a play that should be seen."

"Not going to happen."

He got up and refilled his water. Looking at his watch, he said, "I should get to my workout."

It was pretty clear he didn't like hearing the word no. Slinging my bag over my shoulder, I said, "Still want me to come for dinner tonight?"

His face softened. "Of course. Do you like kale?"

"Who doesn't?" I said, trying to remember which leafy green classified as kale and whether or not I liked it.

I let myself out, giving Phillipe an awkward smile. He had his arms crossed and was staring out at the lawn, as if challenging so much as a sugar ant to approach.

"Thanks," I said, for lack of anything better.

"See ya," he growled, in a voice that perfectly matched his appearance.

I looked forward to spending time with Arlo tonight but had to admit, I was relieved Phillipe wouldn't be there. The whole bodyguard thing was a little intimidating.

It served as a clear reminder that Arlo Majors was living a different life from me. I could laugh and joke with him all day, but I had no concept of what he went through. It was important for me to remember that, in the moments that we were on a separate page, it was because we weren't even reading the same book.

Chapter Thirty-Six

Having police protection at the theater complicated things as much as Arlo's bodyguard did. Each bag that came into the building had to be checked, no one was allowed to post photos on social media without getting it approved through me first, and the doors had to remain closed, no exceptions. That got some grumbles from the set crew because everyone had gotten a little more casual about propping the doors open back in the area where they built the sets. The space was so large that the air-conditioning didn't keep it cool, so as the days got hotter, the door had been wide open. Not anymore.

It was constricting to say the least, but the days passed without incident, and everyone started to take the rules more seriously. I was concerned about how it would affect morale, but at the same time, I quickly figured out that no one wanted anything to interrupt the show. On my end, I was willing to deal with an extra headache or two to make sure the show could go on.

Once tech week started, it added a whole new level of pressure. It put us less than a week away from the show, and it meant it was time to add in the lights, sound cues, and props. It was a lot of stopping and starting during rehearsal and a lot of extra steps.

There had been individual moments when the production manager, the director, and once, even Piper had a meltdown, and I did my best to help them calm down and keep going.

The days were long, and I spent so much time inside the theater that I forgot it was summer until I managed to get to the fire escape for a minute alone. Then, I stood blinking in the bright sunlight like a mole, the warm breeze and the sun lessening the chill from too much indoor air-conditioning.

I watched the sailboats skim the water, the depth of the blues always changing on the lake, and the white sand of the beach below the bluff. It was so peaceful it was hard to believe that we needed any form of protection at all.

Inevitably, the moment the thought crossed my mind, a stick would snap in the forest, and I'd think about the emails and the fresh pot of coffee that had just been sitting there in the basement of the theater. Then, I'd head back inside, grateful that Dean, Phillipe, and anyone else willing was watching our backs.

~

The night before dress rehearsal, I got home late to discover the living room in our house had been turned into a stage. Kaia darted around, arranging furniture and turning lamps to shine on my grandmother.

"I think that's perfect," she was saying. "Mom, what do you think?"

My grandmother sat in the middle of the room, decked out in a black designer dress and a flowing sequined cardigan. Her hair was perfectly sprayed and her makeup, flawless.

"It all looks great." I kissed my grandmother on the head. "Especially you, Gigi. What are you, thirty-five?"

"Keep telling me lies." My grandmother smoothed her onyx-and-gold necklace. "I need to feel beautiful. We're about to go live."

"Live?" I said. "What do you mean?"

Kaia pulled up the time on her phone. "Gigi is going to do a question and answer session."

"Oh, wow," I said. "Can I see her account?"

I'd been so busy with the theater that I hadn't paid much attention to the social media Kaia had been putting together with my grandmother. I was surprised and impressed to see that they had already built up an impressive number of followers. My grandmother had even chatted with a lot of people in the comments, her typical humor shining through.

"I need my phone," Kaia said, holding out her hand.

My parents came into the room just then and pulled up chairs.

"We're here to watch," my father said cheerfully.

"Kaia said there would be a performance," my mother added.

"Live stream," Kaia corrected. "We're starting in ten minutes."

My father exchanged a look with my mother. Then, he nodded and got to his feet. "Lily," he said, beckoning at me. "Come here for a sec."

Confused, I followed him into the office. I wondered if he had concerns about Gigi doing something like this, and if he was about to pace and worry. Instead, he sat down in his favorite chair and indicated I should take a seat as well.

"So, your mother said that you're seeing Arlo Majors."

I was completely at a loss. "Why does she think that?"

My father cleared his throat. "If it's true, I want to say a few things. First of all, congratulations. I enjoy his films. Second, I'm worried. I know I don't usually talk to you about your relationships, but this is different. I don't want to see you get hurt."

My father had never offered his two cents on my relationships before. He'd been kind and cordial back when I'd brought someone home from college and was equally kind and cordial when Jin asked permission to marry me. That was as far as it went.

I started to speak, but he held up his hand. "Hear me out. Dating theater people is not like dating regular people. Theater people feel things so deeply in the moment, it can be easy to get caught up and swept away. The thing that people on the outside don't understand is that moments pass. Productions end. Seasons end. Theater people are used to that and comfortable with the fact that intense emotion comes and goes. Regular people are not."

"I appreciate your concern." The fact that my parents had staged an Arlo Majors intervention was straight-up embarrassing. "I'm under no illusions that this is a forever thing. How could it be? Even my marriage wasn't a forever thing."

"That's why I'm worried, Lily," he said. "You're having a hard time with all that. Theater people can be heartless. They're all in. Until they're not."

The words stung. It wasn't as if I believed that Arlo Majors would continue to care about me once he left town, but I didn't need to be reminded of that. The past few weeks had felt so good, and even if it was only a moment in time, it was one I was happy to be stuck in, at least for now.

Something Arlo had said came back to me, something about putting your fears or emotions onto someone else. I studied my father for a second, then said, "Dad, why are you telling me this? Did something like that happen to you?"

He looked surprised, then nodded. "Many times. It took me a while to learn, but when I did, I stopped looking for the brightest star in the room. Instead, I found the one with a steady burn."

"Mom."

He glanced over at her picture on his desk. "The thing that drew me in about your mother was how solid she was. She did what she said she was going to do, even if she didn't feel like it. Even if she wasn't caught up in the moment."

"Is that why it bothered you when she expressed an interest in being a part of the theater?"

My father frowned. "This is not about me. Why are we talking about me?"

How interesting. Even years into a relationship, there were still so many hidden heartaches, so many pieces of the past that could affect the present. What was it that Arlo had said? "The past was the prologue"? In some ways, that was starting to make sense.

"Dad, I know you're worried I'm going to get hurt," I told him. "But the end of whatever this is won't hurt me. The only thing that would hurt me would be to look back and think that I let my path be guided by fear and that I missed out because of it. This is one of the best things that's ever happened to me. Let me enjoy it."

My father nodded. "Okay. Just be careful." Getting to his feet, he said, "Because as much as I'd like to say I'd crush him with my bare hands if he hurt you . . ."

"You like his movies too much to do that?" I said.

"No, I'm scared of the guy. He's fit. He'd kill me."

Laughing, I linked my arm with his. We headed back out to the living room to see what my grandmother had up her sleeve.

~

"Five . . . four . . . three . . ." Kaia did a countdown, and then my somewhat shy daughter turned into a reporter right in front of my eyes.

"Welcome, everyone," she said, smiling into her phone. "We are here tonight to talk with my great-grandmother, esteemed actress Maxine Candella. Please send in your questions, and in a few minutes, we'll dive in. Gigi, how are you tonight?"

The two launched into a witty back-and-forth. I couldn't tell if it was rehearsed or if their natural chemistry was shining through.

The questions began, and I couldn't believe the number of people who sent them in. My grandmother started talking, answering what was asked but also saying whatever came to mind. At one point, a tear trickled down her cheek as she talked about a good friend she'd once worked with who recently died. She burst into spontaneous giggles like a young girl as she talked about tricking the studio head into thinking she was telepathic. Then, my grandmother threw her head back and gave a grand speech about how all women are capable of taking on the world if they are willing to step out of their comfort zone.

I held on to her every word. When the time was up and we clicked off, I stared at her in disbelief. Then, my parents, Kaia, and I broke into applause.

"That was extraordinary," I told her. "How on earth did you know how to do that?"

My grandmother tilted her chin and gave me one of the looks that had made her famous. "Oh, my darling, it's simple. I was born for this type of party. Turns out, it's quite good to show up fashionably late."

Chapter Thirty-Seven

The morning of opening night, there was a sense of excitement in the air. I arrived at the theater early to get a head start on things, and instantly, Dean appeared from the shadows. I'd gotten used to seeing him early in the day, so I barely blinked.

"It's the big day," I said with a smile. "Do you think we have any reason to be worried?"

"You mean about the emails?" he asked. "Or our friend in the basement?"

"The emails."

Even though I'd never seen the one with the date of our opening performance, the idea alone was enough to make me nervous.

He shrugged. "I'm not going to worry; I'm just going to be prepared. We'll check everyone at the door, have officers throughout the lobby, and make sure everything's safe and secure. That's all we can do, other than call it. Do you want to call it?"

"Absolutely not," I said, thinking of the show. It was so bright and so fun, and this town would love it.

If there had been any other indication that there would be trouble, I might have considered it, but ever since the police had been here around the clock, the threats had stopped. There would be so much security now that it seemed extremely unlikely anyone would dare to make a move.

"I think the person who sent the emails was expecting it to become this big news story because of Arlo Majors," I said. "When it didn't, they got bored and moved on."

"It's hard to guess why people do what they do," Dean said. "Best we can do is be prepared for all of it."

I held out a coffee and a breakfast sandwich. "For you."

"What's this for?" He set the coffee on the lobby table and peered into the bag. It was sausage and egg on a sea salt croissant, one of my favorites.

"To say thank you for all that you do."

"This is great," he said. "Thanks."

"Sorry there's only one."

He gave me a confused look. "One what?"

"Breakfast sandwich. I imagine you would have preferred five. Or maybe that's just doughnuts?"

He crossed his arms. "Must be nice to be a comedian at seven o'clock in the morning. Hopped up on coffee and Irish creamer, folks, she's ready for the main stage."

"Look at you, throwing compliments like kisses."

Dean cracked a smile. "It's too early for this," he said and headed off down the hall with his treats.

~

The actors had a final meeting at ten o'clock with Sebastian, followed by any last-minute costume issues with Jade.

Once they'd been dismissed until call time, I went out to the lobby to find Arlo. He and Millie were walking to the front door together. Her hand was on his arm, and they were deep in conversation.

"Hey, guys," I called. "Where are you headed?"

They both looked back. The moment Arlo saw me, guilt crossed his face, and the feeling I'd felt so often with Jin cut right through me. The suspicion, the realization, and the heartbreak that our relationship was not what I'd thought. Still, I was baffled that Arlo had taken up with Millie, of all people.

My stunned expression must have made an impact because he said, "Hey, Millie, hold on. I'll be right there."

Arlo took my hands and led me to a corner of the lobby. Millie stood at the front door and pretended to be fascinated with her phone.

"You sure she isn't recording you?" I said.

It was a weak attempt at a joke, but it fell flat.

"It's not what you think," Arlo said. "We were just going to—"

"Oh, it doesn't matter," I told him. "We are not a couple by any definition of the word."

"Ouch." He tapped his heart. "Well, that's a shame because I'm only interested in you." When I didn't respond, he said, "Lily, we're headed to the park to perform some pop-up theater. To build buzz for tonight."

"Oh." Relief swept through me, followed by confusion. "I wish you would have said something. I could have gotten the news crews there, helped make it a thing."

"We just decided to head over there. Planning kind of defeats the purpose of a pop-up."

I smiled at him. "Good point."

The way I'd reacted to it all made me feel embarrassed. Maybe I was letting my heart get involved a little more than I'd planned.

"You okay?" he asked.

"Yes," I lied. "Just a little stressed about tonight. Security, all of it."

To Millie, he called, "Hey, will you check and make sure it doesn't look like rain?"

The moment she turned her back, he kissed me. Squeezing my hands, he said, "See ya." He headed out the door, looking back once to wink.

Even though he was acting like everything was fine, the whole situation felt off somehow. I couldn't figure out why. It was probably my nerves about tonight.

I headed back to my office and checked my email, followed by the main inbox where the original emails had originally arrived. Nothing—so that was a relief, at least. There was a ton to do, and I started by tackling a list of last-minute issues the box office had sent me. Something kept nagging at me, though, and it finally hit.

Arlo seemed perfectly fine with doing this random pop-up performance in the park, but we'd spent the last two weeks bending over backward to keep him safe. I had no doubt his bodyguard would be with him, but since this was something for the theater, he should have asked for extra protection. It was almost as if he didn't want me to . . .

I stood up, practically knocking over my chair. Picking up my phone, I called him. It went straight to voice mail.

I dialed Brad. The Tourism Council was downtown, right next to the park.

"Hey, it's me," I said. "I need you to check and see if Arlo Majors is out there performing."

"Yes, I'm here, and there's a huge crowd." Brad sounded excited. "I'm going to try to get close enough for a selfie."

"What's he doing?" I said, grabbing my keys and practically running to the parking lot. "Is it show tunes and stuff?"

"Yes," Brad said. "It's from the musical tonight."

I stopped at my car door and let out a breath. "Thank goodness."

I really must have been on edge because for a minute, I'd thought the worst. I took a few more breaths, noticing the sun in the leaves in the trees, trying to slow the beating of my heart.

There was a roar of approval in the background, and Brad said, "Are you coming? They're getting ready to do a scene now. It looks serious. The girl actress is getting all emotional."

"Put me on FaceTime."

Arlo and Millie stood in the center of the park. There was a crowd around them. Arlo's bodyguard stood right at the edge, but everyone stayed back, watching with their phones out.

"You're in for a treat," Arlo told the crowd. "This particular piece was written by Belinda Hamilton, an actress and incredible playwright who lost her life too soon. I hope that this short performance demonstrates the power of her work and her legacy." He shook his head. "This scene will break your heart."

I must have made some sort of sound because Brad said, "Hey, you okay?"

"I'll be there soon," I said and hung up.

This scene will break your heart.

For me, it wasn't the scene. It was the fact that Arlo was going to perform it, in spite of all that I'd said. The fact that he'd looked me in the face and tried to pretend that this was some performance he was doing on a whim. The scene didn't break my heart—he did.

◇

I pulled up right next to the park and ran across the grass. Arlo and Millie were at the part where the girl discovers that no one will be held accountable for the collapse of the building that killed her sister. Everyone watching was silent and riveted.

I pushed through the warm bodies. I was just about to call out to Arlo to stop the performance when Mayor Matty Brown beat me to it. He stepped in front of Arlo and Millie, his face red against the bright yellow of his suit.

"This performance is over," he called, holding up his hands. "Sorry for the disruption, folks, but our town requires a permit for public performances."

Arlo looked personally offended. "Come on, man. It's almost over. Let us finish."

"I wish I could, son." Mayor Matty laid a heavy hand on Arlo's shoulder. "We need security and protocol measures for this sort of thing. We're going to have to end this now, but . . ." He turned to the crowd and gave a big smile. "I do hope to see you at a performance at the Playhouse soon."

The disappointed crowd applauded. Then, someone stepped forward and asked for Arlo's autograph. Arlo signed the guy's shirt right before his bodyguard cut in, ushering him and Millie away.

Mayor Matty stepped into my line of vision, his expression straight-up threatening. He signaled that I needed to join him. He guided me by the elbow away from the crowd, and we stood under a tall oak tree.

"Now, I'm not an actor," Mayor Matty told me, a smile still plastered on his face. "I'm not going to make a scene here in this public park. I'll tell you this, though. That little performance was a very bad idea."

"Sir, I didn't have anything to do with it."

"You're the manager of the Playhouse." His tone was menacing. "So, yes, you did. Expect a fine from the city for not obtaining a permit to perform in the park." He lowered his voice. "You can also expect to hear from my lawyers."

My heart sank. "Mayor, sir, I did not—"

Without a word, he turned and walked away.

I leaned against the tree, the bark rough against my back. The scene Arlo and Millie performed didn't make it obvious that the play was about the bridge collapse, but Mayor Matty knew. Once people started talking and put the pieces together, they would figure it out too.

The timing was terrible. It was opening night, and we didn't need any more trouble. It seemed that Benjamin Hamilton's prediction about getting involved in the Playhouse had been correct, because no matter what I did, trouble seemed determined to show up.

∽

Back at the theater, I found Millie in the greenroom, telling her fellow actors all about the performance. The moment I walked in, she stopped talking.

"Where's Arlo?" I said.

She fiddled with her gold necklace. "He went home."

"Well, it is opening night," I said, looking around the room. "If you don't have a costume issue, it might be a good idea to do the same. Get some rest. It's a big night tonight."

The small group gathered their things and headed for the door, but Millie stayed seated, her cat eyes trained on me. Once everyone had left, she said, "Please don't be mad. I didn't know . . ."

"It's not your fault." I rested my hand on the doorframe. "I can't imagine what a great experience it must have been to perform with Arlo Majors. How long have you been working on that? You were incredible."

Millie flushed prettily. "You really think so? We've been rehearsing for a week. It's a shame that guy cut us off before we could get to some of the bigger scenes because they were really good."

"Well, you should be proud. Get some rest, and we'll have a great show tonight, okay?"

Her face lit up with a big smile. "Definitely."

Once the actors had left, I headed straight for Arlo's house. The gate swung open the moment I arrived, and Phillipe looked out the front window.

Arlo came to the door in jeans and bare feet, pushing his hair back with one hand. "Now, *that* was a performance," he said. "I saw you were there right before it got shut down. Did you see their faces? The way that scene made them feel? It was mind blowing."

"That's one way to describe it," I said, coming to a stop on the front lawn.

"People deserve the truth, Lily. Life shouldn't be about hiding things below the surface. Don't be afraid of your feelings. Bring them out, let them breathe."

"Okay," I said. "Then, how about this? You set me up. Millie said you've been rehearsing that for a week. You knew how I felt, and you hid that from me. You know, you pretend to be this great guy—"

"Hey." His eyes flashed. "I never pretended to be anything. You made assumptions based on who you wanted me to be. That's what everyone does—they shape me into their fantasy. Well, that's not who I am. That's not me."

The hurt behind his eyes was real. I understood how hard it had been for him to trust people, but I felt the same, and he'd lied to me in spite of that. I was not about to let him flip the script.

"I've never done that to you," I said. "I liked *you*—the part you were willing to show me—and a big part of that was how honest you were with me. But sneaking this past me . . ."

"The show needs to be onstage."

"You don't have the right to decide that."

"I do, actually." He squinted at me in the sun. "Belinda's father gave me the right. He gave me his blessing."

The world faded around me for a brief second before I took in a deep breath. "You showed it to Benjamin Hamilton?"

Arlo sat on the front steps, gesturing for me to join him. I stood where I was, in the grass.

"Lily, his daughter wrote it," he said. "He deserves to know. You can agree with that, right?"

"Did you ever think about the pain that it might cause him?"

"See, there's the honesty that you lack," Arlo said. "You lie to your kid because you don't want her to feel bad, you wanted to hide this from a man who was overjoyed to have a piece of his daughter back, and you're telling me I'm the one who's dishonest?"

My eyes filled with tears. "No, you're honest. The truth is bursting out of you. My mistake."

"I haven't done anything wrong here," he insisted, getting to his feet. "I want to do what's right. Benjamin Hamilton was grateful for the performance that we gave today—"

"He was there?" I said.

"Of course! I . . ." He faltered, and for a brief second, I saw his confidence slip. "I invited him to speak tonight. Before tonight's show."

"You did *what*?" I cried.

"The man deserves to be honored. His daughter died in that theater. You all have gone on like nothing happened—"

"It was twenty years ago," I insisted.

"To him, it was yesterday. I told him that we were going to give a tribute to Belinda tonight. He's going to come onstage; we're going to have a moment of silence to honor him and his family. He deserves that much, don't you think?"

In some ways, Arlo was right. I couldn't believe I hadn't thought to plan something like that, but after the stunt in the park, it would look like the Playhouse endorsed the theories written in that play.

"I'm sorry," I said. "I can't say yes to that. Not after today."

His eyes went cold. "I knew you would act like this."

"Look at the logic behind it," I said. "Think of the long-term—"

"Think of the hurt and the heartache that man has endured for the last twenty years of his life," Arlo insisted. "Why can't anyone seem to think of that?"

I didn't know what was right, but I did know that if we put Benjamin Hamilton on that stage, the conversation Arlo had started in the park would continue at a fever pitch. This was more than one man's pain. It was the town, the commerce, and the ski resort, and all the implications behind it. I didn't have it in me to fight that battle.

"I just wanted to be a part of the theater," I said. "I didn't sign up for this."

"Well, I did," Arlo shot back. "I came here because I want to use my voice, to make a change. Even if it only affects one man, I'm going to do what's right."

"That one man meaning . . . you?"

He glared at me.

I let out a breath. "I can't put Benjamin Hamilton up on the stage."

"Oh, but you have to," Arlo said. "Because if you don't, you won't see me up there either."

My stomach dropped. Feeling numb, I turned and headed back to my car.

It would have felt great to slam the door and race out of the driveway, but I was not about to make some grand exit—I was not an actress, and there was nothing in me that wanted to be.

Chapter Thirty-Eight

My grandmother closed the folder that held the play. She sat in silence, her lips pressed together.

"Would you like some tea?" I asked.

I could tell she was upset, and I wanted to give her time to think.

"That would be nice."

When I returned to the room with two mugs of Earl Grey and a plate of cookies, the color had returned to her cheeks, but her eyes still looked sad.

"What a wasted gift." She nibbled at a cookie. "Arlo is right—it's a stunning play. You shouldn't be mad at him for showing it to her father. It was something he needed to see."

"What should I do about tonight?" I asked.

"Let him speak. Arlo has left you with little choice. If you say no, he won't perform. You need him to. Look at the bigger picture."

"The bigger picture is our town," I said. "The price that will come with these accusations."

"If they're not true, they'll fade away."

"You're saying 'if'?" I said, surprised.

My grandmother hesitated, her fingers brushing up against the first few pages of the play. "It's interesting how our minds only see what they can believe. Benjamin Hamilton as the town drunk—that's easy to see. But a young girl's life cut short because she planned to speak out about the people in power doing wrong? It's hard to accept that one. We don't like hard." She took a sip of tea. "Time has a way of helping our minds see, though. Even if it's been right in front of us the whole time." She gazed out at the rose garden. "I've always wondered if something happened at that theater that shouldn't have. Reading this, I have a lot of questions. Hopefully, with time, people will demand answers."

I sat in silence, staring down at the pages.

"Put Benjamin Hamilton on that stage tonight," my grandmother said. "He deserves to be seen for what he is."

"Which is what?" I asked.

She looked at me. "A good father."

~

Benjamin Hamilton arrived at the theater dressed in a white button-down shirt and a brown blazer that fit, with his hair neatly combed into place. I'd instructed security to find me when he arrived. I was not about to let the man go onstage drunk. Dean had assured me that if that ended up being the case, he would handle it, but when Benjamin Hamilton arrived, he looked clean cut, freshly showered, and sober.

"Hello," I said, walking toward him with my hand outstretched. My plan was to keep this as professional as possible and to not say a word about the time he almost ran me off the road or the night on my parents' front porch. "I'm pleased that you could make it this evening."

The words that left my lips felt scripted. The theater was bustling all around as the ticket holders began to arrive, security waving them down with wands and checking their bags. We could have been in a big city, but it was so clear we were in a small town because everyone was looking over at us.

My father, who had spent the afternoon with his fishing buddies, confirmed the rumors had started. People were talking about the performance at the park and had started to question if there was any truth to the things Belinda had said in the play.

Benjamin Hamilton's eyes were pale and watery, his nose bulbous at the tip. "Thank you, Lily," he said. "It means so much that you invited me."

Before I could answer, Arlo's bodyguard walked up.

Benjamin Hamilton brightened. "Good evening, Phillipe."

"Hey, man." He put his thick hand out for a fist bump. "Come on back with me. Arlo wants to see you before the show."

Benjamin Hamilton gave me a questioning look, and I nodded. Smoothing my black dress, I was about to head for the box office when I noticed Dean monitoring the situation from a few feet away.

"Everything good?" he said.

I tried to process that question.

Piper was in my ear on the headset. Patrons filed through the doors, taking in the glamour of the remodel. There were a thousand little things happening all at once, but in the end, the man who had lost his daughter had cleaned up and showed up.

"Things aren't exactly good," I said. "But I'm starting to think that might be okay, sometimes."

Dean gave a slight nod. "Life got a little easier for me once I figured that out."

The houselights flashed.

"Five minutes," Piper called over the headset.

"I'm going to head back," I said.

"Break a leg," Dean said. Then, he made a face. "I don't even know what that means."

I smiled at him. "Thank you."

Backstage, the actors were dressed in their sparkling costumes, giddy with anticipation to start the show. Arlo stood beneath the black-painted eaves, deep in conversation with Benjamin Hamilton. The sight of Arlo filled me with confusion, so I turned my attention just past the red curtain to look out at the audience.

They chattered with excitement as the chandelier gleamed like a celebration above. Then, the stage lights went up, and the houselights, down. Silence filled the room.

I let out a breath and walked over to Benjamin Hamilton. "I'm going to say a few words, and then I'll introduce you," I told him.

Arlo tried to catch my eye, but I headed out to the stage.

The lights were hot, and my low heels drummed against the wooden floor. The hammering of my heart was loud in my chest, until I spotted my daughter, my father, and my grandmother right in the middle of the third row, smiling up at me. I gave them a little wave.

"Good evening, everyone," I said. "Thank you for joining us for a delightful night of theater here at the Starlight Cove Playhouse."

There was applause, and I took a moment, imagining what it would feel like if I could keep this theater going for years to come. It was a good feeling, one I definitely wanted to pursue.

"Before we get started, I need to remind you to take a look at the emergency exits and to silence your cell phones. Thank you so much for joining us tonight for our performance of *Chicago*, starring Arlo Majors."

The crowd applauded, and I noted the two security officers in the back. They planned to step out once the show began, to guard the auditorium doors. I glanced in the wings, where Benjamin Hamilton was waiting.

"First, I would like to take a moment to introduce someone very special. This man lost his incredibly talented daughter, Belinda Hamilton, to a fire here at the theater twenty years ago." There was a sympathetic murmur in the crowd. "Tonight, on opening night, we are grateful to honor her memory. Welcome, Benjamin Hamilton, back to the Starlight Cove Playhouse."

I saw Arlo pat him on the shoulder, but he stood completely still, as if frozen in time. So, Arlo took his arm and said something, and they walked onstage together. A picture illuminated on the backdrop, and there was another murmur through the crowd. Benjamin Hamilton stopped suddenly and looked up.

My eyes stung as he saw the picture of his daughter, and I realized what it must have cost him to be in this building, to be in this place. He stared up at her but maintained his composure. Arlo said something to him, and he nodded. Throwing his shoulders back, he walked over and stood next to me.

I shook his hand as the crowd applauded.

"The Starlight Cove Playhouse would like to share a slideshow in honor of Belinda," I said. "Mr. Hamilton, sir, this is for your daughter."

I exited the stage as Piper rolled the montage of photographs we had found of Belinda starring in the productions at the Starlight Cove Playhouse. There were beautiful photos of her in the greenroom, with the cast, and of course, on center stage.

Arlo approached. "Lily," he said quietly. "I heard that you and Piper put this together in the final hour. That you even printed up stickers to paste in the program. Thank you."

I gave a brief nod.

"Look, I . . ." He shoved his hands into the pockets of his suit. "I want to apologize. I could've handled everything better. Literally, everything."

His eyes had never been so blue, and I wanted to look away, to run from the heartache. But he had taught me the importance of facing my feelings, even if it hurt.

"I'm sorry too," I said quietly. The backstage was full of anticipation, and I didn't want the other actors to pick up on our conversation. "You were right to invite him here. You were right about a lot of things."

Being with Arlo had taught me so many things. He'd made it possible for me to believe I could move on from my marriage. To get past the hurt and the heartbreak and open myself up. To figure out what I wanted and to have the courage to accomplish big things.

"I've been going through it," I admitted. "It's not easy to set up a life and watch it all fall apart. You showed me how quickly things can change for the better. That it's okay to face the things that are hard, even if it hurts. I'm grateful for all of that."

"You forgot to mention my startling physique."

I laughed. "I didn't want to state the obvious. But I'm going to have to put it out of my mind because I think it's better for me if we're friends. Do you think that's possible?"

Disappointment crossed his face. "You sure?"

"Yeah." I reached up and gently touched his cheek. "Have a great show tonight, Arlo Majors."

The slideshow was wrapping up, and I walked to the edge of the stage to hear Benjamin Hamilton speak.

The screen faded to black, the lights came up, and he cleared his throat. That's when the applause began. It grew, getting louder every moment, and the audience got to their feet.

Not one to miss a cue, Piper projected the original picture of Belinda back up onto the backdrop. Benjamin Hamilton stood there in silence, looking out at the people of our town, and I realized his eyes were filled with tears.

There was a thundering sound as the audience sat back down, their foldable chairs shifting beneath them. Finally, he spoke in a loud, clear voice.

"I had a lot I wanted to say about my daughter," he said. "It seems like you just said it all for me, though. Belinda loved this stage, she loved this town, and I loved her. Thank you for keeping her memory alive, and thank you for giving me this moment to share it with you all."

He started to choke up. In the front row, a young girl got up and walked to the stage. She must have brought a bouquet for one of the performers, but now, she held out a single red rose.

Mr. Hamilton walked to the edge, took the flower, and pressed it against his heart. Shoulders shaking, he said, "Thank you," and left the stage.

I blinked back tears.

Piper called a cue. The houselights went down, and the music began with a resounding crash. The show—it always went on.

Chapter Thirty-Nine

The opening number took the mood in the theater and elevated it to something bright and full of life. The actors came out full force, singing and dancing with all their hearts. I sat watching in the back of the house, a smile stretched across my face, delighted that we'd somehow pulled it off. Then, Piper practically shouted into my ear.

"I need Cody Henderson now! He's not back here, and he's onstage soon. Lily, can you find him?"

"On it," I murmured into the headset and instantly texted Emma.

Where is Cody? The stage manager can't find him.

She responded right away:

Come out to the lobby.

I rushed out to see her hovering by the bathroom door. She looked pretty but panicked, dressed in a flowing pink dress with her butterscotch-colored hair held back in two intricate braids. She beckoned me over.

"What's going on?" I said. "Where is he?"

"In the bathroom. He's been throwing up for the past five minutes."

"He's sick?" Mentally, I riffled through the different people who could play his part while I simultaneously worried about him. "Is it something he ate?"

Emma shook her head. "Worse."

If Cody Henderson had the flu, it would sweep through the cast in no time. We'd have to shut down the production, and by the time everyone was better, we'd be on to the next play. It would be an absolute disaster.

"The flu?" I whispered.

Emma scoffed. "No! Cody Henderson is in there throwing his guts up because he's terrified. He has stage fright."

The relief that flooded me made me burst out laughing.

"It's not funny." Emma's eyes flashed. "He's really scared."

"I'm sorry," I said, but I still couldn't stop laughing. "I thought you meant—"

The expression on her face made me get serious. "Okay. Let's work together. We have exactly five minutes to figure out how to make that big strong man be brave."

∼

Two minutes later, Dean stood guard at the door to the men's bathroom while Emma and I went inside. The sound of retching greeted us.

"Cody," Emma called. "We're coming in."

Emma and I had run through a ton of options. Then, she remembered that some of the boys that Cody mentored through his youth outreach program had recorded him a good luck video. They'd sent it to Emma to surprise him, but she'd forgotten, since he'd been so stressed out.

"Cody, I'm going to pass a video under the stall door. I want you to do your best to look at it. Definitely listen to it."

The video started to play, and slowly, the sound of his gagging seemed to quiet. Emma and I watched in silence as his hand reached over and took the phone off the bathroom floor. The cheerful voices of the boys saying things like, "You inspire us, man" and "Can't wait to see you up there!" echoed in the bathroom.

"Are they here?" Cody's voice was weak and scratchy.

"Some," Emma said. "There's a whole group planning to surprise you."

Piper was on the headset, in an absolute fury. "I need Cody Henderson back here, *NOW*."

I looked at my watch. Five minutes.

The toilet flushed, and there was a small grunt.

Cody Henderson barreled out of the bathroom door. He splashed cold water on his face and in his mouth, then pounded his chest, eyes wild. He turned to us, eyes pleading.

"You're not going to tell anyone about this."

"You have my word," I told him. "You also have one minute."

Cody rushed down the hall toward backstage, and Emma grabbed my hand.

"Thank you so much," she said. "I thought he was going to run off into the trees and never return."

I giggled. "Go. You don't want to miss it!"

Dean, who had been positioned at the front door, raised his eyebrows once they'd both left. "Stage fright?"

Our eyes met. "I'm really not allowed to say."

He gave a conspiring nod, and I raced to my spot in the back of the house. I got there just in time to see Cody strut onstage like a strong, confident peacock. His small role as a police officer brought down the house because everyone knew him, and by the time the scene was over, the audience was laughing and cheering.

When it was time for my mother to enter, I held my breath, hoping she didn't suffer any of the same afflictions as Cody. Nope. She walked onstage with a big smile and played her part in the background without a hitch. I saw her look right at my father and wink. The moment her appearance was over, my father got to his feet, applauding and whistling.

My grandmother gently pulled him back down into his chair, but I could tell my mother loved the attention, and she blew him a kiss from the wings. Kaia, looking both embarrassed and proud, sank down low in her seat.

The first act was perfect, and after intermission, the second half had even more energy than the first. I was watching closely, tapping my toes to the music. My mind was also on the celebration scheduled after, the pizzas we'd ordered for the cast, and my curiosity at how long the patrons would linger after the show in the bar.

My grandmother had said that back in the day, they'd kept a piano there, and sometimes the cast would perform an impromptu cabaret. I vaguely remembered that, and it was something to consider for the second show.

The grand finale quickly approached. The cast had worked so hard on this last number, and I focused on the stage, ready to be dazzled. That's when I noticed unexpected movement along the aisle.

Someone who needed assistance had gotten up to use the bathroom and was keeping their balance against the shadows of the wall. The ushers were entranced with the show, so I moved forward to help. That's when I realized something was wrong.

The figure kept bending down, placing things along the edge of the wall. They looked like . . . rags. A smell wafted through the theater, and the patrons rustled, a few looking around in confusion. It took me a moment to place the smell, but when I did, my blood went cold.

It was gasoline.

Chapter Forty

Too many thoughts rushed through my head at once: *My family. The people. The theater.*

"Stop," I cried, but the sound garbled in my throat. Instead, I kicked off my heels, grabbed a fire extinguisher off the wall, and raced up the aisle, feet silent against the carpet. The figure wore a face mask and a dark sweatshirt with the hood pulled up, which made it impossible to see anything about him other than his green eyes.

They flickered to mine as he fumbled in his pocket. He took out a lighter. I slid the needle out of the fire extinguisher and pulled the release.

The heavy metal tank kicked back, and white foam shot out with a surprising force, covering the side of his head and body. There were shouts from security, and the people nearby began to rush down the aisle, but the loud music had the rest of the audience still focused on the stage. My headset had fallen around my shoulders, and I yelled into it for Piper to stop the show.

In the distance, I heard her bark out instructions. The performance came to a halt, and the actors ran off the stage, screaming. It was noise and chaos as I stood my ground, spraying the man and the rags that lined the floor.

He clawed at his face and eyes, slipping in the foam and onto the ground. His mask fell, and I froze as I recognized him—it was Ryder, Jade's son. The silver lighter gleamed in his hand.

Leaping forward, I tried to wrestle it away. One of the security guards had made it past the crowd and to us. He twisted back Ryder's arm, and I grabbed the lighter.

Ryder slipped out of his grip and scrambled to his feet. He disappeared into the surging crowd, toward backstage, the security guard trying to keep up. I stared after them, catching my breath, and was about to follow when I heard Dean shouting at me.

"Lily!" He was climbing over the backs of the seats and had almost made it to me. "Which way did they go?"

"Backstage."

Dean propelled forward off the chairs, jumped into an open part of the aisle, and raced toward the stage.

Over the headset, I shouted, "Get the cast outside," but no one answered, so I knew it had been done, following the plan the police had put into place.

Sirens blared. Two different kinds, so both police and fire were on the way. I held tight to the lighter, afraid to move. The firefighters rushed in, and once I explained, they took the lighter and sprayed additional foam over the rags before bagging them up. From the lobby, I heard someone on a bullhorn blaring instructions.

"Exit the theater in an orderly manner. Stay alert. There is still a threat."

Ryder was still out there, ready to burn the whole place down.

I felt someone watching me. Jade stood in the wings, her face as pale as a ghost. Our eyes met, hers wild with terror. She ducked behind the curtains, moving toward backstage.

"Where's Kaia?" I shouted into my cell phone.

"Right here with us," my mother said. "We're in the car. We have Kaia and your grandmother. Are you out?"

"Still inside," I said, peering into the wings and trying to spot him. "Get her home."

"We can't leave." My mother sounded like she was trying hard to stay calm. "Traffic is backed up down the bluff. We will keep her safe. Find us when you can."

I rushed down the hallway toward the stage door, determined to locate Ryder before he got away. A hand clamped down on my shoulder, gripping it hard.

It was Jade. Her green eyes were panicked, her face lined with fear.

"Lily." The word was breathless. "Please, you can't say it was him."

The image of her son placing rags up and down the aisle flashed through my mind, as well as the moment I had to wrestle the lighter from his hands. If it had sparked, what would have happened? Everything would have gone up in flames—I would have been in the middle of it.

The thought hit: Had he killed Belinda? Had he set the theater on fire back then too?

"You have no idea what he's been through," Jade pleaded. "My son has faced things that most people would never even consider, and he's survived. Please, I can help him. You can't tell."

There was so much pain in her face. My heart ached for her, but all I could think about was what could have happened. The people that could have been hurt.

"Listen to me," she cried, practically shaking my shoulder. "We're both mothers. I'll get the help he needs. I'll—"

I shoved her hand off me. "I have to go."

For a fraction of a second, danger sparked behind her eyes. Then, she turned and left out the side door, letting it bang shut behind her.

I took a few faltering steps, unsure whether to look for him backstage or in the offices. The smell of pizza hit me from the breakroom. There was a ridiculous amount of cardboard boxes stacked up on the tables. They would still be there in the morning, cold and left to waste.

Moving on autopilot, I rushed in, grabbed the drink cart, and piled it high with boxes. The rich scent of pepperoni and cheese filled the room, its smell as comforting as a warm blanket. Dean stormed past, down the hallway. He came to an abrupt halt, spotting me.

"What are you doing?" He rushed into the room. "You need to go outside where it's safe. This guy could be armed. We have no idea where he is."

"It was Ryder," I said, finding it hard to form my thoughts into words. "Jade Noor's son."

Dean radioed the information. "Do you know him?"

"I've seen his picture," I said. "I saw his face."

Shuddering, I remembered the moment his mask fell after he slipped in the foam, the scent of gasoline heavy in the air.

I didn't know how I'd spotted him there in the aisle. The fire extinguisher had been within reach. I was close enough to grab it and get there. The right place at the right time, the right moment. If I'd missed that moment, things would have gone such a different way. The thought made my knees weak, and I gripped the handles of the cart.

"We'll find him," Dean said. "I need to get you out of the theater."

"I'm getting the pizzas." My hands were shaking. "The cast is supposed to have a party. We were going to have a party."

Dean's face softened, and I realized that my cheeks were wet with tears. He pulled me in close, holding me tight.

"Hey." His voice was low. "Everything's going to be okay. Let me help you."

He handed me one of the rough brown napkins from the pizza company. I wiped off my face, blowing my nose as he led me out of the theater.

Outside, it was warm, and moths swarmed the outdoor lights. There was a huge crowd of people milling around behind the police barricades, most of them from the cast. The costumes were so beautiful under the stage lights, but in the dark, the sparkles were tattered and worn.

Over his radio, Dean said, "There are too many people still out here. We need to clear the outside."

The answer crackled back. "Traffic is the issue. It's a gridlock down the bluff."

"Be careful out here," Dean told me. For once, his voice was gentle. "I don't want anything to happen to you."

I walked out onto the grass, feeling numb inside. There were yellow sawhorses set up in a perimeter around the building. Such a far cry from that first day with the press conference, when there was such hope and possibility.

Over a bullhorn, a police officer kept repeating, "Everyone must remain behind the barricades. Please head toward your cars as quickly as possible. We need to clear the area."

I moved toward the crowd to get to the parking lot and my daughter when Arlo rushed up, his bodyguard close behind. He was dressed all in black, with a beanie low over his eyes. For once, no one was paying him a bit of attention.

"Hey." He took my hands and led me over to a side area, over by the trees. "Phillipe wants me to get out of here, but I wasn't going to leave without seeing you first. I've been calling you. I saw what happened from the stage."

"Yeah." Exhaustion hit, and I sank down onto the ground, sitting for a second underneath the nearest pine tree. The ground was cold and damp, and mosquitoes swarmed around me.

"It's Ryder," I told him. "Jade's son."

He let out a breath. "I hate that for Jade. She's got to be devastated. We've talked about him a hundred times, and she's always worried but never about anything like this."

"Hey, man," Phillipe said, scanning the area. "This isn't a cocktail party. We've got to get out of here."

"Two minutes." Arlo's bright-blue eyes searched mine. "Are you okay?"

"I'm worried," I said. "Scared. Jade's furious with me for identifying him."

"I get it—he's her son, but you had to. There's no choice there."

I stared down at the ground, remembering the rage on her face. "How did this even happen? We had security everywhere."

"No kidding. Phillipe came onstage and threw me over his shoulder like a sack of potatoes. I think I'm still motion sick." His face got serious again. "He said he was just watching the show when he saw you spraying down some guy who came out of nowhere."

I sat up straight, thinking about the way Ryder had just appeared by the wall. "It was him in the basement. The sleeping bag. Don't you think?"

Arlo gave a slow nod. "Yeah. I can see that."

"Because it's not like he walked in the front door of the theater with a can of gasoline," I said. "The only way he could have pulled this off is by hiding there the whole time. I mean, we have cameras everywhere now."

Arlo frowned. "Where could he hide, though?"

A chill ran through me. "There's a hidden room. When I was a kid, I used to play in it all the time. It's—"

"It's in the play," Arlo said, right as I realized it. "In that scene where they're hiding from the mayor."

"That's where he is," I said. "I have to call Dean."

"For real, Arlo," Phillipe said, stepping forward. "We've got to go."

Arlo squeezed my hands, then hopped to his feet. "Let me know if we're performing tomorrow," he called as Phillipe guided him through the crowd.

Picking up my phone, I blinked to see I had twenty-seven missed calls. I'd had the ringer on silent for the show and hadn't thought to change it. My mom had been calling repeatedly.

Heart sinking, I called her back right away. "What's wrong?"

"Kaia's in there!" My mother sounded close to hysteria. "They're searching for her, but they won't let me go in to get her."

There was a sudden shout, and I nearly jumped out of my skin. It was just someone calling to a friend, but the police had looked in that direction. I didn't stop to think—I ran straight to the side door where Dean had led me out, and I went right back in.

"I just got back in," I said, putting the phone back up to my ear. "Where is she? What happened?"

"Jin called," my mother told me. "They talked for a minute, and then she went ballistic. She went into a rage."

The pregnancy. I couldn't believe that he'd told her the news over the phone. He was such a coward.

"She ran into the theater to find you, even though I told her you were coming."

"It's okay," I said, feeling sick to my stomach. "I'll find her."

"Be careful," my mother said and hung up.

I called her right back. "Ask Grandma where the hidden room is. In the theater. I think that's where he is."

"She's in the car," my mother said. "I'll call you back."

Letting out a breath, I tried to think of where Kaia would have gone. There were two options: my office or the stage. I was closest to the office, so I ran there first, praying to avoid the police because I was not leaving until I found my daughter.

Relief flooded through me as I spotted a figure on the couch. Rushing in, I said, "Kaia, we need to—"

It was Jade. Her back was ramrod straight, and her face, streaked with tears. There was a cup of cold black coffee sitting in front of her, and she barely turned her head.

"Jade," I said, grabbing the doorjamb. "I'm looking for Kaia."

"Did you tell the police about my son?" she asked.

"I didn't have a choice," I said quietly. "You know that."

"Is that her sweatshirt?" she said, pointing toward the corner of the room.

I rushed over to check. In that time, Jade shut the door and stood in front of it.

"No." The word came out as a gasp. "What are you doing?"

"I'm a mother, too, Lily. That's the thing that you don't seem to understand."

I tried to get to the door, but Jade blocked my way. Her cat eyes flashed, and in the dim light, she looked dangerous.

"Give me five minutes," she said. "That's all I'm asking."

I swallowed hard, looking at the door.

Jade crossed her arms. "The guilt that has haunted me over the death of Belinda and the fire that hurt my son has been something I have never been able to shake. For the last twenty years, I've felt stuck in this place, in this theater."

"I know," I said, taking a step forward. "Jade, I'm sorry you went through that. That Ryder went through that."

"Oh, but you'll honor Belinda?" she demanded. "Invite her father to speak up there and forget all about my son?"

My heart sank. "I'm so sorry. It wasn't my idea."

"You know, I hoped that by reopening this theater, I could somehow find a way to come back and make things right, but it's not working out that way."

It took a moment for the words to register.

"You're the donor?" I said.

"Oh, yes." Jade closed her eyes. "When I first came to the Playhouse, all those years ago, I felt on top of the world. I'd raised Ryder on my own—his father was never present—and my career had taken off in a big way. It had been such a treat to come here for a break, really, and to spend time with my son."

I let out a breath. "Jade, I want to hear this. But I have to go find Kaia. Please. Get out of the way."

Kaia had to be hiding somewhere on the stage. I had to get out of this office, get to her, and leave. I could only imagine the panic my mother was feeling, wondering where we were.

"Just give me one minute," she demanded and started talking faster. "It didn't take long for my son to fall head over heels in love with Belinda. I treated her like a daughter, and when she asked me to read the play she'd written, I agreed without a second thought. I had set it by my bed, with no clue that the man I was dating had earned a starring role."

"Everett Ferris," I said.

"Yes." Jade tucked a strand of hair behind her ear. "He flipped through it while I was in the shower one night, thinking he would have a laugh. That didn't happen, did it?" Her green eyes met mine. "From that point forward, our world shifted. Belinda received an anonymous offer to buy the play. She refused, knowing it had to be someone who wanted to bury it. He kept asking me where it was, and I made the mistake of telling him it was most likely at the theater." Her eyes filled with tears. "I didn't know. I never once thought that he—"

"What?" I whispered.

Jade lifted her chin. "That he would set fire to the theater. I think he wanted to destroy that play and scare Belinda into silence. I don't think he had any idea that she and my son were in there and that they had fallen asleep. The years passed, and I've faced the truth—my involvement with him led to her death."

"It was him?" The deep voice behind me was raw with grief. "I have spent my entire life believing that it was me. That it was my fault. I was the one who lit the candle."

I turned to find Ryder standing next to an open door in the back corner of my office. The hidden room. It was right there.

My heart started to pound.

He took a step toward his mother. "Belinda and I met here that night. I lit a candle, and we fell asleep in each other's arms. Do you know how many times I have blown out that candle in my mind? A hundred thousand times. Again and again and again."

Jade's face was full of sympathy. "Ryder, we've talked about this so many times. The fire was set from outside. It was not your fault."

His eyes squeezed shut. He shook his head, faster and faster. "I lit the candle."

Jade took a step toward him. "You have been through so much. We will get help for you. We will move through this and away from the horror."

"I can't." Rage dripped from his voice. "I'm trapped here. No matter how many times I try to leave, I'm always here."

"Ryder," I said. He turned to me in surprise, like he'd forgotten I was there. "Belinda loved you with all of her heart. Her father told me that. He said she loved you more than anyone in this world."

Ryder stared, his breath coming in hurt gasps.

"You need to leave, Lily," Jade told me. "Please go."

I heard her words, but I saw his pain. "Ryder, did you know that her father told me that when Belinda talked about you, she used to smile in a way he'd never seen before? He said that you were the greatest thing that had ever happened to her. He was so thankful she got to spend her final days with you. I bet he'd love to share memories with you, to talk about all the wonderful things she told him about you." Out in the hall, there were sudden shouts and the sound of running feet. The footsteps thundered past, toward the front lobby. "He still loves her with all his heart, and I know he cares about you too."

"He won't feel that way now. I've made too many mistakes." Ryder's face crumpled, and his mother stepped forward to pull him close. "I'm sorry. There was only one way to get us out."

My throat, which had been itching slightly, started to burn. I coughed as a familiar smell hit me.

Smoke.

"Ryder." Jade's eyes widened. "What have you done?"

"This all ends," he said. "Now."

Chapter Forty-One

I pulled open the door of my office. Smoke poured into the room, burning my eyes and throat.

"Kaia," I screamed.

Dropping to the ground, I crawled into the lobby, desperately looking around. The smoke had created a thick haze that covered everything. My eyes watered and blurred, making it impossible to see.

Jade let out a cry, and looking back, I saw Ryder pulling her toward the door to the hidden room. She fought him, crawling toward the window in my office, and he tried to drag her back.

There were crashes and bangs, but I had to find my daughter. Desperately, I made my way across the red carpet, moving closer toward the thickest area of smoke, screaming Kaia's name. It hurt to take in a breath, but I pushed forward, my thoughts fading as I fought for air.

"Where is she?" said a raspy voice by my ear. "Where's Kaia?"

I turned to find a man close to the ground next to me. He had deep lines of anguish around his eyes, his skin was flushed, and he wore a haunted expression. It took a moment to process that it was Benjamin Hamilton.

"Tell me which way she went." Sweat dripped down his forehead, and he pulled his shirt up to cover his nose and mouth. "Lily, so help me, I will not let anything happen to her."

"The stage," I gasped, praying I was right.

Benjamin Hamilton moved fast, crawling toward the smoke like he'd been in the army, disappearing into the fog. I followed even as the room grew dim around me, my arms collapsing every few feet.

Get up, my brain screamed. *Get up!*

I pushed forward as firefighters ran in, pulling hoses and carrying axes. The big, heavy boots were next to my head, and then strong arms pulled me back, dragging me toward the exit. I kicked desperately, but my legs would barely move.

The night air hit my mouth like a cold drink of water. The plastic of an oxygen mask covered my face, but I ripped it off, struggling to fight my way back in.

"Kaia," I screamed, only half-aware of the stretcher beneath my body. I grabbed the arm of the man pushing it. "Let me go! My daughter's in there."

Smoke billowed from the front door. More firefighters raced toward the building when a man came stumbling out. It was Benjamin Hamilton—with Kaia in his arms. He carried her, with halting steps, to the front lawn. She lifted her head as he fell to his knees, gasping for breath.

Our eyes met as Kaia reached out her hand. Then, everything went black.

~

I panicked the moment I woke up. My heart slowed to a steady beat when I saw my daughter resting in the bed next to me. Her eyes were closed, but when I touched her hand, they opened.

"That's the last time I'm going to watch a musical," she said, her voice strong but scratchy. "Unless I get some serious extra credit."

I held her hand tight.

A nurse bustled into the room. She had a friendly smile, and her blonde hair was clipped back in a low ponytail.

"How are you feeling?" she said, checking my vitals.

"How's my daughter?" I asked. "Tell me that first."

It hurt to talk. My throat and lungs felt raw and painful, but I had to know the answer.

"Kaia is doing great," the nurse told me, and Kaia gave a vigorous nod. "Minor smoke inhalation. She was smart enough to get low to the ground, which helped minimize her exposure. She'll be absolutely fine. We'll keep the two of you here for observation overnight."

Once the nurse left the room, I gripped Kaia's hand tight. "I love you," I said, fighting to get the words out. "In case there is ever a moment where you think I haven't said it enough, I love you with all of my heart."

Kaia's expression went soft and serious, like when she was a child. "I know, Mom," she said. "I love you too."

≈

The next time I woke, it was morning, and my parents were in the room. I was thirsty, and as if reading my mind, my mother handed me a cup of water with a straw. I drank the whole thing and said, "Is it time to eat?"

Kaia was flipping through a graphic novel. "Breakfast was kind of disgusting, but I'm sure they'll be happy to scar you for life too."

"It's eight o'clock." My mother laid a cooling hand on my forehead. "I'll have them bring you some French toast."

The fact that I was hungry seemed like a good sign. It was also easier to talk, even though my throat still hurt. Outside the window, rain was coming down. I tried to sit up, and Kaia showed off the controller for her bed.

"You've got to push the buttons," she said. "It makes it go up and down."

It was such a relief to see her safe that I could have laid there for hours, watching her amuse herself with the acrobatics of the hospital bed. I wanted to know what had happened last night, though, the thing that had made her run into the theater, since it had led to all of this.

"Hey, guys." I beckoned to my parents. "Can I talk to Kaia for a sec?"

"Of course." My father gave me a gruff kiss on the forehead. Taking my mother's hand, he said, "Let's go hit the vending machines."

They shut the door on their way out, and Kaia looked at me.

"I can't even tell you how grateful I am that you're all right." My mind went back to the moment I smelled the smoke and she wasn't with me. "We can talk about the things that are on your mind, whatever it was that made you run into the theater in the first place. But the biggest thing I want to tell you is that there is not one thing about what happened last night that can be changed."

She wrinkled her forehead. "What do you mean?"

"It's easy to get stuck in the past," I told her. "I'm willing to bet that you've already thought about what happened last night a hundred times and wish you could go back and do it over."

Do you know how many times I have blown out that candle in my mind?

It broke my heart to hear that from Ryder. It made me think of how often I'd done the same thing, wishing I could change the decisions I'd made and all the missteps along the way.

"You can't change the past," I told Kaia. "We learn, and we move on. It's when you can't let go that it's hard to live in the here and now."

"Well, I'm definitely living in the here and now," Kaia said, her voice dry. "Wishing to speed up this chat and get to the future."

I smiled. Even though she was giving me a hard time, I did hope that, on some level, she understood.

"Can we talk about whatever it was that your father told you?" I asked. "The thing that made you run into the theater?"

Kaia stared down at her hands. "Norah's pregnant. Did you know?"

"Yes."

Her eyes flashed. "Why didn't you tell me?"

"Because you needed to hear it from him," I said.

We were silent for a moment. Then, she said, "He invited me to stay with him this summer. For a few weeks."

Fear rushed through me, but I knew it was important for her to carve a place in that family. I had to learn how to support her in that and not let my fear or resentment get in the way.

"How do you feel about that idea?" I asked, pulling the hospital blanket close.

"Not great. I don't want to watch him and Norah all excited about some other kid." She lifted her chin. "I want him to be excited about me."

"He is very excited about you," I said. "This could be a good opportunity to let him show you that."

We sat in silence for a moment, the hospital monitor keeping time in the background.

"You don't have to make the decision now, obviously," I said. "But if you need to talk, I'll be right here by your side. This is a lot for you to deal with."

"Mom, you're in the hospital," Kaia said with a groan. "Now is not the time for you to worry about me."

"I will always worry about you," I said. "That's what mothers do."

"Dads too," my father said, poking his head in the room. "You ready for us to come in?"

"Depends on the candy you got," Kaia said.

He held up a hearty display of chocolate bars and Cheetos, so Kaia waved him in. It filled me with relief to see her rip open the bag of Cheetos and start crunching away, considering how pale she'd looked the night before.

"Benjamin Hamilton," I said suddenly. "Is he okay?"

The memory of him bursting out of the theater door with Kaia in his arms came back in full force.

"Yes, he's good," my mother said. "They released him after only a few hours."

"Why was he in the theater?" I asked. "Weirdly, I didn't even feel surprised to see him, crawling on the floor next to me. That's how out of it I was."

"He saw me outside, and I told him Kaia was in there," my mother said, taking a seat on the edge of the hospital bed. "He rushed right past everyone, straight into the building. He didn't wait. He just went. We'll be grateful to him for the rest of our lives."

My father stopped eating his candy bar and took her hand.

"What about the theater?" I asked. "Is it destroyed?"

"It needs another remodel. Jade's son started the fire in the wings, and it spread up that big red curtain that covers the stage."

It made me shudder to think that Kaia had been so close to it.

"I know." My mother fussed with my blanket. "It's upsetting to think that any of this happened."

"I can't believe he went in there to save her," I said, my eyes filling with tears.

There was a knock at the door. Dean stood there, his black hair wet from the rain.

"Hey." His voice was gruff. "Big night, last night."

"Yeah, it was lit," I said.

"I'm just glad you're all right."

Holding his gaze, I nodded.

Kaia held up a chocolate bar. "Candy?"

Dean smiled at her. "There's the bravest of the bunch. Have an extra one for me."

"Dean, what happened with Jade's son?" my mother asked.

Dean shut the door and took a seat next to my parents, taking off his leather jacket. "We got a full confession." He looked at me. "Ryder's the one who was living in the theater, the one who sent the emails. It's a tough situation. The authorities will get him the mental health care he needs."

"He was living in the room off my office," I said.

Dean nodded. "We'd seen the space on the blueprints, but since there was no entryway, we made the mistake of believing it was no longer there."

Something occurred to me, and I sat up straight. "Dean, is it possible he set the fires? Not in the theater, but around town?"

My mother raised her eyebrows. "Good question."

"He said no, and I believe that," Dean said. "He's been pretty forthcoming, and the fire investigation reports never suspected arson to begin with. It was just too dry for a while. The fires stopped once it rained."

I nodded. "What about Jade?"

"She had nothing to do with it. She had no idea he was in town at all, thought he was back in LA." He glanced at the door. "Speaking of Jade, she's in the lobby now, waiting to see you. I told her I had to ask you first."

Even though I didn't want to get her in trouble, I was not about to hide a thing. "She trapped me in the office last night with her and Ryder," I said. "When I was looking for Kaia."

Dean's face darkened. "Do you want to press charges?"

"No." I shook my head. "But I don't want to talk to her alone."

"Then, I'll be there," Dean said. "You don't have to talk to her now. You can call me when you're ready. I'll be around."

I looked down at the outline of my feet beneath the thick white hospital blanket. Jade's son had been in this same hospital. It was hard to imagine the pain they had gone through.

Letting out a breath, I pushed back the blanket and swung my feet to the floor. "There's no time like the present."

Dean and I walked out into the lobby. I was surprised to feel pretty normal, just tired and a little chilly in the hospital gown. Dean noticed I was shivering and handed me his coat.

"You sure?" I said, surprised. "It makes you look so cool."

"It does?" He gave a half smile. "Good to know."

Jade got to her feet. She wore a plum-colored jumpsuit and looked like she hadn't slept in days. The waiting room was empty with the exception of a television in the corner.

"You good?" Dean asked me, and I nodded. He gave Jade a warning look. "I'll be right over there."

Jade walked over but stopped a few feet away from me, wringing her hands. Finally, she spoke.

"I'm sorry, Lily. My behavior last night—" She stopped talking and composed herself. "I am so sorry that everything happened the way that it did. That my son put your life in danger, that I kept you from getting to Kaia. If I would have known what he was going to do, I never would have stood in your way."

Looking into her eyes brought back all the feelings of the night before, and I pulled Dean's jacket close.

"I'm also sorry I wasn't up front about the fact that I owned the theater," Jade said. "I just wanted another chance to close out that memory in a positive way, and everything went wrong. In some ways, though, things went right. Ryder will finally get the help that he needs. I pray he'll be able to forgive himself and move on. I also plan to get help. I need to figure out how to support him appropriately, rather than the way I acted last night. Some painful truths have been spoken, and now, the healing can begin. I can only say I'm sorry and I thank you. I hope you can forgive me."

"Of course I forgive you," I said. "You just wanted to help your son. I'll always be grateful to you for bringing the Playhouse back. Did Arlo know it was you?"

She shook her head. "No one knew."

For some reason, I was relieved to hear that. Even though my relationship with Arlo had been short lived, I was glad to know that most of our conversations had been based in truth.

"There's something else," she said. "I spoke to the police the afternoon that you showed me the play. I told them everything I knew about Everett Ferris. They'll never be able to prove he set the fire, but they have quietly investigated him and his business practices ever since. It's not public knowledge, but this morning, Dean informed me that Everett has lost his license in this state, and the ski resort will be awarded to another company. Bigger than that, the mayor is under investigation."

I put my hand over my mouth. "You're kidding."

"No. The document that he forged is under review, and they've tracked down the engineer that took the fall. Things aren't looking good for Mr. Matty."

The news was huge. Mayor Matty and his colorful suits and questionable practices had been a staple in our town for years. The fact that he wouldn't be able to sweep this under the rug already felt like justice. I wondered if the reporter I'd met with would get to write an article about it.

"I would also like to discuss the Playhouse with you and what we can do next," she said. "I started this thing, and I intend to finish it. I'd like to finish out the season."

My breath caught. "How?"

"Well, I had a backup agreement in place with the high school for the use of their auditorium," Jade said. "I did that in the event that the Playhouse ended up delayed due to the remodel. I never dreamed it would be because of something like this. Either way, the show can and will go on."

My heart leapt. "That's great news!"

"Yes." She pressed her lips together, the worry lines deep around her mouth. "Lily, I realize what my son did last night was unforgivable. What I did. If you can find it in your heart—"

I held out my arms. "I promise you, Jade. We can move on."

Chapter Forty-Two

The Saturday-night performance of *Chicago* switched from the Starlight Cove Playhouse to the Starlight Cove High School auditorium without skipping a beat. Kaia and I were released from the hospital midmorning, and we went straight over to help. The cast and crew were already there, putting in place set pieces and backdrops.

Arlo Majors led the charge, moving heavy pieces of scenery and barking cheerful orders all around. When he spotted me, he excused himself and ran over.

He pulled me aside and gave me a long hug. Even though he was one of the biggest stars in the world with the softest clothing I'd ever felt, it was nice to finally think of him as just a friend.

"I'm beyond grateful you and Kaia were okay," he said. "How are you feeling now?"

"Thrilled," I said, looking around. "I can't believe we went from last night to this."

The stage was lovely, done in a deep walnut that matched the brown chairs that filled the auditorium. There was a huge backstage area with plenty of room for load-in, and the backdrop for the first scene had already been hung up.

"Teamwork makes the dream work," Arlo said. "It's kind of fun to be doing the shows here, right? It's a total vintage vibe."

"You're sure you're okay with it?" I asked. "Performing at a high school is somewhat of a step back for you, wouldn't you say?"

"It's either this or theater in the park, and Mayor Matty isn't going to be handing out permits to us anytime soon." Arlo lowered his voice. "Jade told me what's happening with him. Justice with a side of fries. Pretty incredible."

I looked out over the auditorium, thinking about how much had changed in just a few short weeks.

"I can see you're getting emotional," Arlo said. "It's kind of full circle for you, isn't it?"

I squinted at him. "What is?"

"Well, this is the same place where your career really soared, Seagull #2. Why don't you fly across the stage for old times' sake?"

I shuddered. "No, thank you."

"Look, though . . ." He pulled a piece of paper out of his pocket and handed it to me.

"What is this?" I said, unfolding it.

It read:

Cast List
Guy Who Saves the World—Yours Truly
Seagull #1—Lily Kimura
Seagull #2—Anybody but Lily Kimura

"Arlo Majors," I said, laughing. "I didn't think I'd laugh once today, and somehow, you made it happen."

He grinned. "Here's to a great show."

∿

That night, my father settled into a front-row seat. It was one of the few seats in the house that hadn't been taken. The auditorium was bigger, surprisingly enough, leaving a few spare spots that we could sell at the door. My father settled in happily, his camera in one hand and the program in the other.

"I'm impressed that you're going to sit through it again," I told him. "You said you were done letting the theater run your life."

"Nah. I'm coming to every performance." He smoothed his Lions T-shirt. "I've kind of taken a shine to one of the actresses. There's something about seeing her in sparkles that gets me right here," he said, tapping his heart.

"I sincerely hope you're talking about my mother."

"I certainly am." My father beamed with pride. "This whole thing has been quite a ride. How are you doing with it all?"

It was so strange to think that we were about to watch the exact same show in a completely different environment, without the threats we'd had the night before. The auditorium doors were propped open, the cool night breeze blew in, and the community had turned out in droves.

I spotted Kaia at one of the doors, chewing on a piece of bubble gum and handing out programs. Spotting me, she waved.

"I feel hopeful," I said, waving back. "Last night was a disaster. When we decided to move the show over here, I had no idea what to expect. But look at this. The place is packed, the people are excited, and life goes on."

"The magic of the theater," my father said. "Not to mention that here, there's the promise of better snacks at intermission."

The high school did have the option of popcorn, soft pretzels, and cookies instead of just coffee and cookies.

"It's the little things," I said.

Piper's voice came through on my headset. My dad gave me an expectant look, and I nodded.

"It's showtime."

~

The theater was dark on Monday, so my parents requested Kaia and I join them for dinner with a special guest. I assumed they meant my grandmother, and sure enough, the driver from Morning Lark dropped her off at five o'clock.

She eased out of the car dressed in a long satin gown and a pair of elbow-length black gloves. A ruby necklace sparkled at her throat.

Kaia clasped her hands together. "You look awesome, Gigi. I'm going to go put on something better," she said, before scrambling back up to her room.

"Mom, you do look wonderful," my father said, kissing her cheeks. He offered her an elbow to escort her up the front steps of the porch. "I didn't mean you had to get this dolled up, though. We're just having dinner."

My grandmother pulled out a compact and touched up her lipstick. "My darling, it is five o'clock in the middle of a sleepy town in the middle of nowhere. Let me flaunt it while I've still got it."

"Hear, hear," my mother said, handing her an old-fashioned.

Kaia banged out of the screen door in bare feet and a pink, ruffled princess gown, complete with a pair of satin gloves that matched the ones her great-grandmother wore. Her eyes were bright, and her smile, wide.

"Where did you get that outfit?" I said, feeling the soft satin ruffles of the sleeves. It definitely wasn't from her closet.

Kaia pulled out a lacy fan and fluttered it through the air. "Jade let me raid the costumes."

"I've taught her well," my grandmother said, taking a seat on the wicker bench. My father placed some cushions behind her back, and she smiled up at him.

The five of us sat on the porch enjoying the balmy evening and rehashing everything that had happened, when a sudden roar and rumble of an engine announced a new arrival.

"Who is that?" Kaia said, shielding her eyes from the sun.

We all stood as Benjamin Hamilton's white truck pulled in.

My parents waved, and I realized that when they had mentioned a special guest, they'd meant him. His sudden presence made my shoulders tense, not because I was afraid of him but because my emotions were almost too complicated to handle.

The other day, I had dropped him another letter in the mail, thanking him for saving my daughter's life. The letter could not capture the depth of my gratitude, and I knew that, but the idea of reaching out personally had not been a step I was ready to take. Now, I had mixed feelings that my parents had done it for me.

Mr. Hamilton got out of the truck. He was dressed in a button-up shirt and a pair of pressed khaki shorts, and he carried a bouquet of flowers.

I walked down the front steps, watching as he strode across the yard. When he got close, he stopped, and we looked at one another.

"Is it okay if I hug you?" I said.

Mr. Hamilton gave a flustered nod, and I pulled him in tight. His body felt rigid, nearly frozen. Then, he hugged me back. We both started to cry for half a breath but held it back.

"My girls would have been good friends with you," he said, wiping at his eyes. "I knew that from the beginning. The way you did those roundhouse kicks that night I showed up here? That was something."

We both laughed, and then he got serious. "I'm sorry that I scared you. I scared myself. Grief can make a person do funny things. Mine has gone on far too long."

I nodded, feeling the eyes of my family on me from the porch. Kaia was still blissfully unaware, on some level, of how significant it was that Belinda's father was the one who had pulled her out of the theater that night.

"I can never repay you for that moment," I told him. "I want you to know that I'm grateful with my whole heart."

We walked to the house together. Once we'd made our way up the steps, he handed the bouquet to my mother but not before plucking out a single daisy for my grandmother.

"What would you like to drink?" my mother asked him. "We'll have dinner here in about a half hour."

"Water." He cleared his throat, glancing around at us. "Sparkling, if you've got it. I've stopped drinking."

"Oh, yeah?" My dad clapped him on the back. "Good for you. Leaves more time for the other vices, like fishing. You want to join me out there sometime this week?"

The two launched into a lengthy debate about smallmouth bass.

I stood at the edge of the stairs, one hand on a wooden pillar of the porch, watching. Kaia put her arms around me.

"You okay?" she said.

"Yes." I was surprised but impressed that my daughter had thought to comfort me.

"Things come around," she said. "I'm starting to realize that everything has a way of working itself out."

"You're too young to be this smart," I told her.

"That's not true," she said. "I *am* your daughter."

~

Dinner was relaxed, with all of us telling tall tales about summertime, the theater, and our small town. It was only once my mother set out a homemade cherry pie and a pot of steaming coffee that Mr. Hamilton shared some unexpected news.

"I heard from Arlo Majors this morning." He added creamer to his cup and shook his head, as if he still couldn't believe what he was about to say. "He wants to buy the rights to the play that Belinda wrote. He wants to turn it into a movie."

I set down my fork, and Mr. Hamilton looked at me.

"He's not going to set it here," he said. "I told him that we don't want that kind of attention."

My grandmother nodded, taking a dainty bite of her cherry pie. "That's correct."

"He seemed to want the rights bad," Mr. Hamilton said. "I kept raising the price. In the end, I feel like I might've robbed him."

I hid a smile. There was no robbing Arlo. He had known exactly what he was doing the whole time, but I bet it was enough money to let Mr. Hamilton live in comfort for the rest of his days.

"Congratulations," I said. "I think that's wonderful."

My parents nodded in agreement.

"I'm trying to remember if there's a part in it for a dashing older woman," my grandmother said. "No bother. It can be written in."

Everyone laughed, and she added, "I do remember Belinda well, Benjamin. I do think she would be delighted to know that something she wrote brought in such a price. Not to mention the opportunity for her work to touch so many people. You should be very proud."

"Oh, I am," Mr. Hamilton said. "I was always so proud of her. I take comfort in the knowledge that I told her that, you know? Every day, I let her know that she was the greatest thing that had ever walked this earth. We've got to do that with our kids. They deserve that and so much more."

I looked at Kaia and opened my mouth to say it, but she held up her hand.

"I got it, Mom," she said. "I'm good."

Benjamin Hamilton smiled at me. "I know the insurance company will cover the cost of the damage that took place during the fire, but I've been hearing rumors from someone that admires you very much that you were thinking of taking over the theater. Would you be open to a donation that would keep it in business for at least the next two years?"

My mother gasped and clapped her hands.

"I would be delighted," I said. "On one condition."

Mr. Hamilton hesitated. "What is it?"

"I would need permission to install a plaque by the front door of the theater, honoring both Lucia and Belinda. Would that be all right?"

His eyes shone with tears. "It would be an honor."

Reaching out, I took his hand and held it tight.

My grandmother lifted her glass. "Brava."

ACKNOWLEDGMENTS

It was such an incredible joy to revisit Starlight Cove. Alicia Clancy, you made it possible, and I am beyond grateful. Thank you for your incredible support, humor, and brilliance. Starlight Cove shines brighter because of you.

Lake Union Publishing, it is such a treat to work with you and your team. Special shout-out to the Amazon Publishing Marketing Team for being the best in the world—you are amazing, and I am thankful for all that you do.

Brent Taylor, superagent, your magical ability to hear what I want and make it happen is a gift. I'm so lucky to have you guiding my career.

To my wonderful readers, thank you for falling in love with Starlight Cove. Your kind reviews, emails, and encouragement have meant so much to me.

To my writers' group—Jennifer Mattox, Stephanie Parkin, and Frankie Wolf—for your insight and feedback. There is chocolate in your future.

Kathy and Butch, thank you for the writing retreat. I loved sharing that time with you.

Mom, I've said it a million times already, but truly the greatest gift you and Dad gave me was the encouragement to go after my dreams. I love you.

Finally, to my precious family: Ryan, Hudson, and Hazel. You are my everything. You have my heart, forever.

ABOUT THE AUTHOR

Photo © 2010 Brian McConkey

Cynthia Ellingsen is an Amazon Charts and Apple Books bestselling author. She's written the Starlight Cove series, several women's fiction novels, and a middle-grade book, *The Girls of Firefly Cabin*. A Michigan native, Cynthia lives in Lexington, Kentucky, with her family. Connect with her at www.cynthiaellingsen.com.